DEADLINES

Chris Dunn

MINERVA PRESS
ATLANTA LONDON SYDNEY

DEADLINES
Copyright © Chris Dunn 1999

All Rights Reserved

No part of this book may be reproduced in any form
by photocopying or by any electronic or mechanical means,
including information storage or retrieval systems,
without permission in writing from both the copyright
owner and the publisher of this book.

ISBN 0 75410 841 4

First Published 1999 by
MINERVA PRESS
315–317 Regent Street
London W1R 7YB

Printed in Great Britain for Minerva Press

DEADLINES

1

Newspaper offices are clean and quiet and cool in the early morning.

No trails of agency tape litter the floor, and the shouting has faded away with the final edition. The telephones sit quietly in their cradles.

9.30 a.m.

Tom Stone drummed on his typewriter. The librarian was slow to appear with the file he'd requested, and time was short. In another hour his colleagues would arrive, then pry into what he was doing. He wanted to search the file, make the phone calls, and possibly tee up an interview, before they arrived.

He had a story. Maybe a big story. Certainly a scoop – if it was true. The page lead? Outside? The splash? It all looked possible.

Jesus, that would be something! he thought. Nobody ever wrote the splash from the City Desk.

Maybe I could screw them for more bucks, he thought. They couldn't say no.

He thought of the previous night, a drinking spree with Ursula in Hampstead. But then, the phone call.

As he walked through the door of her flat, towards midnight, he had heard the phone ringing. He had dashed to catch the call, abandoning Ursula halfway out of the lift.

It could be the newsdesk. Oh fuck them! Why do they always call at midnight? What do they think I am – a pumpkin?

He had picked up the receiver, braced for the bland, all powerful tone of the Night News Editor.

'Tom Stone?' a voice said.

'Speaking.'

'Wolf de Boys is going bust. Otter Securities is finished. Got that? – Wolf de Boys is *out*.'

Click. No more. The line was dead.

He had stood transfixed, the phone in his hand. Ursula, who was very drunk, started shouting.

'Well, who is it then? Is it that bloody newsdesk? Tell them to sod off. One of these days I'll tell them myself!'

'This is it,' he whispered to himself. 'This is the big one, this is how it's done.'

He felt Ursula's hand steal round his neck as he stood, still holding the phone. Excitement seeped through his stomach. The late-night tip-off, the big story... one of the fat cats beyond the deadline...

...And de Boys! He couldn't have asked for better. Even old hands at the game would drool at a story of this size.

Ursula twisted his head firmly, and as he turned he met her lips searching determinedly for his mouth, while her tongue probed for his. Her arm tightened round his neck, as, with her other hand, she took the phone and threw it to the floor.

9.50 a.m.

The librarian appeared with the file. Tom hauled it onto the desk, ripped it open and riffled through the cuttings, starting with the yellow ones at the beginning.

The de Boys story started with no photographs, just a few brief paragraphs. Then it built up to full page features with lots of pictures and even graphs and charts and, finally, began spilling over from the City pages into other areas, like the political sections, as de Boys grew richer.

As the tale progressed, the reporting became more frenzied and adulatory. But through it all scowled a young man, always composed, with hints of cruelty round his eyes, a heavy nose, a tight mouth, and a jowled, indulged look. A man used to power and pleasure from an early age, who could impress an older, more sceptical, generation – and who could pull off excellent deals.

No mention of bankruptcy in the file, no talk of failure – not a whiff. The company was as solid as a rock. And de Boys, like any other millionaire, was full of wise – and applauded – saws on the state of the nation.

Tom felt the story quiver in his brain.

10.00 a.m.

He read the first piece in the file, headed 'Cons Games Takeover'. It read: 'The affairs of Consolidated Games Ltd., the toys, property and investment company, have taken an interesting turn. Kestrel Developments Ltd has agreed to sell to Wolf de Boys its entire holding of 1,500,000 ordinary shares, which is 48 per cent of the total equity. The move will mean a change in Games' management as well as in its ownership. The present Board is to resign and will be replaced by de Boys and his associates. The property interests will be developed, but the toy interests are to be sold, while the other industrial interests will be extended.'

A little pompous? thought Tom.

'Old Etonian de Boys comes from a long line of English peers, and this is his first business venture after a spell in Hong Kong, getting experience as an analyst in a stockbroker's office, and running his own private investment concern.'

The next note revealed that the company's name was to be changed to Otter Securities Ltd. Reflexes guided Tom's hands for a few seconds. He leaned across to the TV, with its twenty-four channels of Stock Market prices, and pressed the banking channel.

The Otter Securities price burst out of the flickering screen – 300p a share. It was close to the year's high. So no jobbers' panic.

He went over to the City Editor's desk, where the Extel cards were kept, and searched for the Otter statistical card.

Profits had been moving up sharply ever since the mid-sixties. In 1966, de Boys made pre-tax profits of £200,000; profits, now in the mid-seventies, were £10 million. All very successful.

Tom dug into his briefcase for his contacts book. He never left it in his desk. Other journalists might prise open the drawer and photocopy his book when he was away.

Merchant banks, he thought, who do I know? What brokers cover them? They'll all be useless, anyway. The banks are like clams, and the analysts are too chicken to chisel anything hard out of them.

He left his desk and strolled across the news room.

To call up just anyone and ask the single question, point-blank, out of the blue, risked broadcasting the whole story to an avid City – or making himself look foolish. He hadn't been long enough in the Street to recover easily from such a gaffe.

As he stared from the window at a tug on the Thames rolling by beneath the office, his mind went back to his first encounter with de Boys.

Tom hated de Boys. It was a simple feeling. He yearned to take hold of the man and strike him to the ground, and leave him for dead. He dreamed of finding him alone in a deserted street or down a lonely lane, and beating him up, with no witnesses.

Tom had worked for a local Lancashire paper which ran into financial problems. De Boys had been a member of the

City consortium formed to bail the paper out. Everyone had breathed again on the paper when they heard the news, and de Boys became a popular name.

But, at the last moment, de Boys pulled out of the deal, saying he thought it wouldn't work and he didn't want his company to get mixed up in low-growth areas. Tom remembered that phrase well – the glib jargon obscenely dismissing the sights and sounds and smells of a newspaper office, with fifty or so people straining there to write their stories.

The inhumanity of the phrase had then been matched by the tragedy on the paper. Without backers – because the consortium fell apart after de Boys had pronounced – the paper folded. And Tom, with all his colleagues had been out of a job. The editor, sick with disappointment, had died.

Casually, de Boys had involved himself in a community, sniffed at its hind-parts, rejected it, and then created chaos – all in the name of what *he* called 'an appropriate return on capital'.

Tom felt a silent prayer form within him to the anonymous caller of the previous night who gave him the tip-off.

After the local paper had folded, de Boys had swooped to buy the presses at knock-down prices. Tom remembered de Boys' minions dining in the town as they dealt for the assets, waving their cheque books with offensive arrogance.

10.15 a.m.

His mind strayed back to the previous evening. He and Ursula had gone drinking in the Coach and Horses, just up the hill from Hampstead tube station. It was Tom's favourite pub. He loved the polished dark wood in the bar, and the brasses which hung beside the yellow lights among the spirit bottles. He liked, too, the calm mannered poise of the drinkers, who laughed and chattered among themselves in a perpetually carefree way, as if the whole of life consisted of such jollity. Most of all, he liked the view through the pub window, people toiling up the hill or descending smartly downwards and the tilted angle they assumed to the watchers within.

Ursula was meeting an old school friend, Patricia, who was busy with her husband Don converting a small terraced house in Kentish Town at great expense into a bijou residence.

Tom arrived late. He'd been drinking with the *Express* boys in the Poppinjay in Fleet Street, and betting on who was to be the new City Editor of the *Post*.

It hardly mattered. All were in mellow mood, sprawled in the back parlour of the pub, which was full of dark, wooden shades.

Ursula, in jeans and one of Tom's shirts slashed open nearly to the waist, lounged against the wall, looking tired and slightly bored, as Don described the changes he'd made in the house. Her job in PR was a source of parties, booze, and gossip about newspapers. She pulled Tom down to her when he arrived, and nibbled his lip, moving against him as he greeted her. He felt a slow rhythm begin to pound inside him.

'What kept you?' she drawled, a little reproachfully, breaking off from her talk with the others. 'We decided you weren't coming.'

'Gerald caught me over a detail in a story,' he lied. Gerald Acres was Tom's boss.

'You mean, *Gerald Acres*,' Don exclaimed lighting up. 'You mean you work with Gerald Acres!'

She rubbed her cheek against his. 'Tom, you are such a liar,' she chided. 'One day, it will catch up with you. What have yet really been up to?'

'I was down in the Poppinjay, playing on the fruit machine and getting all the gossip.'

'So childish. Really, journalists are the absolute end. If I didn't live with one, I wouldn't believe they could be so feckless,' Ursula said. 'But then,' she added sweetly, 'I suppose they're more entertaining than home decorating. Don, you haven't got Tom a drink yet.'

Don sprang to the bar. Tom gathered his breath, and Ursula gossiped with Patricia. Each time she moved, her breasts went peek-a-boo from behind the shirt, sliding in and out of sight. Tom thought of Ursula's long, broad bed, with its cool light sheets, and of a temporary truce to the hostilities which now broke out more and more between them.

10.20 a.m.

Suddenly, a wrinkle twitched at the back of Tom's mind. The tug still butted down the Thames, but last night's events cleared from his mind.

His hand was on the phone, dialling.

'Bring me the Bridge file,' he said.

He'd recalled a tiny detail from a filler paragraph he'd read weeks ago at the bottom of column eight. He remembered something about Bridge, some Congress somewhere, something about financing.

The file arrived. He grubbed through it. Nothing.

He snatched the telephone directory, looked up the 'B' section, and called the British Bridge Federation.

'Secretary, please.'

'Speaking.'

It was an old, scratchy voice, cold, cautious, and used to manoeuvring.

'*Daily Standard* here, Tom Stone.' He always quoted the paper's name first. It commanded more attention than his own.

The voice brightened up, scenting a free mention.

'Can I help?'

'Yes. Look, how do you finance your Congresses? I'm sorry to be so abrupt' – he broke off to laugh helpfully in mid-sentence – 'I mean, who puts up the cash? I'm trying to get a piece together on sponsorship. Bridge is booming, so you're my first port of call.'

'We take the money where we can get it. It's a lot easier now, after Mr de Boys' help. He put us on the map, really, by publicising his interest in the game.'

Tom could hear the Secretary listening to his own words as he dragged them slowly from the vaults of his mind.

'How much did de Boys put up? ...Or maybe I ought to call him and ask him... But, er... off the record, you know, was it a sizeable amount?'

'It was.'

Tom felt the phone grow tender in his hand. His pen started jumping wildly on the scribble pad, making insane whorls.

'Sorry, I didn't catch that.'

'I said he used to contribute a lot In fact, I don't mind telling you that he used to put up a very considerable amount – running, let's say, into thousands of pounds. No, I don't think there's any harm in your knowing that.'

I wonder what opening he's using, thought Tom. This is obviously some killer finesse he's developed.

The voice droned on. 'But then, this year, for some reason, Mr de Boys has unfortunately withdrawn his support.'

'Other people must have come up with the cash.'

'Oh, not on the same scale. Definitely not. Of course, I couldn't tell you precisely how much, but...'

Tom felt the trail going cold and ached to end the chat. He barked 'Just a moment,' down the phone, laid the receiver down, left his desk hastily, then returned.

'Oh, I'm sorry. I can see the News Editor waving at me. Can I come back to you on this one?'

'Yes, certainly. And if you do hear of people willing to put up some money, do give me a call. We're rather short now.'

A start. There was something hard there just a peek, just a crack, but definitely something.

10.30 a.m.

He began to clear the file from his desk. No hint of the story must reach his colleagues. He wondered whether to put in a call to de Boys, himself, under the guise of a piece on sponsorship.

Ursula floated back into his mind, as he stared at the new building on the other side of the river. De Boys, he remembered, had had a hand in financing that, too. He's too powerful, just too big, he thought gloomily – as the high bar stools and the bright lights on the pub broke in on his mind again.

*

After the pub, with all fairly drunk, they'd gone to a health food restaurant to eat. The hors d'oeuvres was a kind of scented lettuce leaf, which stuck in Tom's teeth. He complained bitterly as all the rest of them crunched away.

'It's not exactly macrobiotic, but it's very healthy,' said Patricia. She added that she always felt better after eating it. 'So purifying.'

Don fingered his beard, nervous about her views, and Tom felt Ursula's eyes light brightly on him, as he thought about his orgy of food that lunchtime. She grinned at him across the table.

It had been a routine company lunch, with a northern construction company down in London for their annual jolly. First, the hot thick soup, then a sliver of fish, then the steak with potatoes, the peas, the gravy and a heavy claret which hung, tingling at the back of his throat. He'd refused brandy and cigars.

Ursula asked him how he'd lunched.

'Oh, sparsely,' he lied. 'I was saving my appetite for this evening.' Then he remembered he'd been caught lying once already, and told the truth.

Don launched into his job, feeling he was now on safer ground. 'We're very busy in the office as always. We've had a lot to do with Peter Luckson, your property correspondent, you know, because of the Wessex Land saga.'

But Tom had been told about Don shouting at a secretary once, those thin features purple with rage as he abused her, like the courtier's face away from the sun.

More about Peter Luckson, the usual PR compliments laced with the usual sneers.

'He's terribly clever, of course, but so impetuous. I'm told he's tipped for very high things, though – a future star. We're doing all we can to help, naturally.'

The next course arrived. In a huge brown bowl lay a gleaming mountain of rice. The rice was brownish, speckled occasionally by peppers, red and green.

Tom refused the rice. Patricia shot Ursula a look of surprising sympathy, nodded, and asked Don if he'd like an extra large helping.

'Oh, rather,' said Don, happy to return for a moment to the obedience of childhood.

'Any chance of a drink?' Tom asked. It was a secret sign with Ursula.

'God, what time is it?' cried Ursula, glancing at her watch. 'It's nearly eleven! We'd better hurry.'

So the two of them shot off back to the pub, leaving Don and Patricia still ploughing through their health food. They shouted with laughter all the way back up the hill, a rare moment of unity.

10.40 a.m.

Tom thought back to his uncertain arrival on the *Daily Standard*. He had been surprised to find he had the job. His interview had been a disaster. He had written in, more out of bravado than conviction, from his provincial paper in Lancashire, and had been granted an interview, with travelling expenses. Worth coming up for a free day in London, he had thought when boarding the train, almost as one writes ritually to companies for a refund.

Williams, the managing editor, and a crafty Welshman, had interviewed him. Full of fake bonhomie and dated American slang. (Presumably his mother knew the GIs well, thought Tom.) Williams' eyes slid shiftily behind his thick glasses and he had shot question after question at Tom.

But each query had appeared to relate to another person, almost as if Williams had the wrong letter of application before him. Either he's looking for a different kind of person, or he's totally thick, thought Tom. The frequent polishing of the spectacles suggested inner mental turmoil.

'What college at Oxford?' he rapped at Tom.

'I didn't go to Oxford,' Tom said.

'Oh, that makes it more difficult,' said Williams, with a frown, squinting at Tom's curriculum vitae, which made no reference to any university.

'What university did you go to, then?' he continued.

'I left school at fifteen,' was Tom's stolid answer.

'Local boy made good, eh?' came the deprecating response. From the head of the valleys, thought Tom, and he's never worried about anything. That's why he's so thick and ugly.

'I left home before I joined newspapers.'

'Difficult home life?'

'I never knew my father – he was killed in the war. I was

brought up by my aunt.'

Williams leaned forward at that point, interested, in a little suffering by the lower orders, and keen to show sympathy.

'And your mother?'

But Tom was faster to the punch, sensing that Williams was indulging himself rather than conducting an interview.

'Hard to say.'

Williams leaned back, looked at the ceiling, and questioned Tom about his hobbies.

'Golf,' answered Tom.

'What's your handicap?' came straight back. Tom was unprepared.

'Twenty.'

Williams lost interest. It was the wrong number. A lower figure scored higher, Tom realised.

'Languages?'

'Pardon?'

'Foreign languages. Do you speak any foreign languages?'

Williams was capitalising by now on his small triumph to ram home his superiority. He began speaking slowly and emphatically. Tom replied curtly that he had only ever studied English.

'There could be a question mark over you if you join us, because of that,' said Williams pensively, assured now of his superiority.

'I used to have a German girlfriend. We only ever spoke in German,' said Tom, in a moment of inspiration. 'I couldn't pass an exam in German, of course, but I'm practically fluent.'

'I don't have German,' said Williams, stiffly.

'Ah,' said Tom, relaxing. He had never had a German girlfriend.

The interview dragged on. Tom realised that he was

possibly the last person Williams was keen to employ. But it was also clear that the paper had difficulties filling certain departments. Williams made his point by misspelling Tom's name when he offered him the job, on a meagre salary. Tom accepted because the bright lights attracted him, and it seemed as painless a way as any of breaking into Fleet Street. The subsequent humiliations had not endeared the paper to him, however.

But Williams had not calculated how easily Tom would take to the numbers work in City journalism. Like bookies from the slums, for whom juggling the odds spells wealth and freedom eventually, Tom fell in love with the dancing ciphers. He ignored the top hats of the Square Mile, and headed straight for those groups of shabby, worn-looking men who talk intently about deals at lunchtime around the bars which flank the Stock Exchange.

10.45 a.m.

Gerald Acres appeared in the office, weaving towards the City Editor's desk. Grey hair thinning at the back and his face already flushed, he took his seat firmly as the head of Tom's section.

He was a portly little man, with a young, pleasant face, which was by now twisted slightly at the sides. Tom had seen him throw telephones across the room during squalls.

Gerald was not yet City Editor, he was still the Dauphin (or M' Lady in Waiting, as the office called him). This was his last chance to make it in the style his rich northern background and expensive City friends demanded. But it was proving hard to land the big title. A trail of explosive clashes on other newspapers lay behind him, as did deputy titles and subordinate's rewards.

He spied Tom still drumming with his fingers on the typewriter in anxiety and wondering whom to call. He wandered across.

'Anything on the boil, Tom?'

Tom started, guilt shining in his eyes, as the cutting spread out, across his desk.

'Yes... I've been told de Boys is going to pull off a big one.'

'Nonsense. Don't believe it. Won't buy it.'

Acres was part of the de Boys coterie, one of the group of journalists who gathered each month to hear his thoughts and relay them further.

'Fascinating career he's had, though,' Tom said.

'What else are you doing today?'

'Hadn't thought yet.'

'Well, get all *that* cleared up, and report back to me in a few seconds, when I've had time to settle down.'

'Of course, Gerald.'

'Look sharp. Do it *now*, will you?'

Tom took his time tidying the papers back into the folder, with Gerald's round and slightly bloodshot eye rolling threateningly at him, as his fingers played with a collection of pens in his left hand.

The river drifted lazily under the bridge, and a gull swooped at the water.

The phone rang. The caller asked for Eileen Creed.

'Wait a moment,' Tom answered. Then, turning, he called out 'Gerald...'

'What is it?'

'Has the Royal Barge docked yet?'

'Has the what?'

'Sorry. Have we seen Eileen yet?'

'No, we haven't seen Miss Creed yet.'

'Haven't seen her yet,' said Tom to the caller, 'May I take a message? She's expected in today, I know.'

'I'll call back,' he said, and rang off.

Then Dunbar waddled into view.

Dunbar was short, broad and stocky with a gigantic paunch. People who forgot his name rang up and asked for 'that terribly fat man'. All of which Dunbar relished, true to his role of jolly fat man, the purveyor of a million stories in the bar after work. But he could also deliver the kindly word to the raw recruit, and had been gentle with Tom when he made silly mistakes.

'What have you got there, young Tom,' asked Dunbar, 'working so early?'

Acres interrupted, 'Tom thought he had something on de Boys. But I know for a fact that there's nothing on in that department.'

'You never know with that man. He's such a shit.' Dunbar was cautious about making definite judgements.

That's not the point, thought Tom, as he smiled formal agreement with Acres. It's not your story, it's mine. You lose nothing by killing it, but I lose my lever.

He picked up the phone and dialled Wedd, the jobbers.

Just then, Eileen Creed appeared round the corner, looking vengeful. Tom knew her story last night had been butchered and rewritten. Now for the storm.

'Oh, Gerald,' she started, as the pent-up fury began to explode, 'I'd like a quiet word with you. Now, if I may.'

Acres wore that desperate look of a boy searching for his nanny. Dunbar was busy at his desk, eavesdropping on the scene, as Eileen tore into Acres.

Wedd answered Tom's call.

'Your dealer in Otter Securities, please,' Tom said very quietly into the phone.

'Hold on.'

He waited.

Jobbers were the rough, tough, barrow-boys of the City, unlike the brokers who were the sleek front men. Jobbers drank beer at lunchtime and threw buns. Brokers quaffed wine and smoothed down their suits with their fingers.

'Who's there?' a voice shouted down the line. He was through to the Stock Exchange floor. He could hear the bustling and shouting of the market traders.

'It's Stone here, *Daily*...'

'Yes.'

'What are you calling Otter Securities?'

'99 to 1.'

'Big figure?'

'£3.'

'Any action?'

'Not really.' The merest hint of a lie crept into the jobber's voice.

'I'm told there's a seller around.'

The jobber paused. 'We don't know.' His voice sank a little almost inaudible now behind the market roar. 'We've seen a bit. Couple of big lines came out last week, at a big discount. Wasn't the shop, either.'

'Good. Thanks.'

'You writing on it?'

'Doing an Otter feature for next week. Tell you what, if I hear anything, I'll call you.'

'Thanks, boy. I'd like that. Bye.'

Another little brick, thought Tom. I know it doesn't mean anything, I know the story's gash and you can't stack it up. But that's two little points, isn't it? – even without Deep Throat last night.

10.55 a.m.

He heard Acres calling him. Obedient now, and prepared to cooperate, he trotted over.

Eileen sat like a warrior at her desk, the phone clasped in her hand like a spear, and she talked grimly. Acres was ready to go for him, after Eileen.

'What are you doing now? Have you put away that de

Boys story?'

'Yes.'

'Good. Now I want you to cover the Boream Securities lunch at the Great Eastern.'

'But that's so boring.'

'Don't argue. Now, where are all the others?'

'Still recovering from last night's giant Monopoly game, I would have thought,' said Tom.

'Great,' Dunbar replied. 'The last time I saw Pedro, he'd run out of money and Jock was squaring up to someone.'

'Details please, details,' cried Tom.

The Monopoly game was organised each year by a PR firm. During an evening, and surrounded by drink, food, and the faded beauties of the PR firm, a knock-out game of Monopoly was played. But all the journalists brought their own Monopoly money, so that much chaos and rising prices ensued.

'Pedro was very bad. You know how short of cash he is. Well, he kept on drinking, because it looked like the first time he'd been really able to go at it in an evening without running out of dough. Jock got very Scottish on the whisky, and they tried to smash the place between them. Jock had that hard look behind his spectacles. He'd started calling everyone Jimmy. That's when I left,' said Dunbar.

'Did Jock finish that stores piece yesterday?' asked Acres. 'I wanted to lead on that today.'

'Didn't I hear him shouting at Marks & Spencer?' asked Tom.

'No, that was last week,' said Eileen, with a sniff. She and Jock came from different parts and clans of Scotland. 'Yesterday, it was British Home Stores. By the way, have you seen a *Financial Times* today? I want to know what they had in on Lloyds; I couldn't get one at all this morning.'

She snatched a *Financial Times* from Dunbar, groped through the paper for their Lloyds story and began to read it aloud. Her own story had been butchered, because Gerald was timid on the legal side. But the *FT*, the Bible of the City and renowned for its caution, had run the story in full, on possible overseas losses, with a hint of embezzlement.

11.30 a.m.

Jock was pale beneath his tan when he reached the office. Gerald left him alone, presumably because he was anxious for the copy.

Jock was tall, slim, with jet black hair flecked with grey, and small, delicate hands. He wore black, and rolled his own cigarettes He was the master of the damning, menacing phrase. Always tipped for promotion, never quite making it, he wrote exquisitely.

'You won't be seeing Pedro today,' he said. 'He's a little unwell after last night.'

Gerald bustled about. 'Well, poor chap, no doubt virtue has its own reward – and that applies the other way round, too. Now, what about that stores piece, Jock. Is it ready?' Gerald's voice rose irritably at the end of the sentence.

'Yes, as ready as it ever will be, Mr Acres...' said Jock composedly, delicately rolling a cigarette.

'Can I see it, please!'

'...except for a few touches here and there, which I propose to complete now.' Jock finished his sentence and Gerald rode the sucker-punch conclusion awkwardly.

'As soon as it's ready, then, and not too late. It's not deathless prose we want, just the facts.'

Jock heaved a deep sigh and his hands shook as he completed rolling his cigarette.

'*Just* the facts?' he muttered with heavy sarcasm.

11.45 a.m.

Ursula rang. Tom thought she sounded strained and a little frightened.

'Tom, is that you?'

'Speaking,' he drawled at her in friendly provocation.

'I've just had rather a strange phone call. A man with a terribly deep voice rang and asked for you. Naturally,' and a flash of Ursula's usual arrogance returned, 'I told him he had the wrong number, the fool. Nobody called Tom Stone works in my office, I said. But he insisted. And then he said that if you weren't there could I give you a message? I said yes, and the man, said, "Tell him to be sure to ring Burger, the brokers in Fife." He made me repeat the name. Then he rang off, saying it was bound to be a good story. He said Burger are good on banks. What does that mean, Tom? And why should he ring *me* at my office, if he knew you're a journalist in the City? It's crazy.'

PR firms work off very close relationships with journalists, because it is their role to influence the writer, and get the client's name into the paper. They surround the hack, like fleas on a dog, aiming to know his most intimate thoughts. But what had just happened to Ursula was a reversal of the normal role. And quite clearly she didn't like what had happened. She sounded as if she'd had a glimpse of the real business world, instead of the image of it she was always peddling.

Tom was flipping through his contacts book, as he placated her down the phone.

'No, it's quite simple really. I asked this chap to do some research for me yesterday, and then to call me back last night at home. That's who I thought it might be when we'd just got back from the pub and the phone went. And that's why I rushed out of the lift...'

He could feel the Brownie points mounting up.

'I wasn't sure if I'd be in the office today when he called,' he continued, 'so I gave him your work number, just in case. I knew you'd pass on my message. I should have told you, pet, but it slipped my mind.'

As he spoke, he recalled what had happened after she'd taken the phone from him the night before. He had moved inside the shirt, searching for the breast he'd been ogling all evening, as her mouth reached for his. He felt her nipple rise to his touch as the curve of her breast filled the palm of his hand. She moved her leg against his calf, her fingers snaked up and down his back.

She had pulled his shirt out from the band of his trousers, then fumbled with his fly. He felt her hand reach urgently into his groin.

They had sunk down slowly to the floor, and he kissed her hair and her forehead as she struggled out of her jeans, moaning slightly. Then she pushed his trousers down and he moved on top of her. Her eyes were closed and her mouth half-open as she pulled him inside her. Her legs locked themselves round him, and she moved exquisitely from the loins, only shifting a fraction, just enough to absorb Tom's movement. Then, she stiffened, and licked his face frantically as the moment of orgasm approached. Tom felt the room growing dark around him.

Tom returned to the present. Ursula was still at the other end of the phone, and snapping at him, confident now she'd been reassured. 'It could have been someone important,' she chided.

But Tom could feel an explosion taking place inside him, as he rambled on to her. He had the number now. It was true. There was a firm of brokers in Fife called Burger. The story must be good.

His mind moved away from Ursula, and hesitated briefly at the thought of her parents. Ursula's mother, Mrs Parker, was a tough powerful woman, and she had reservations about Tom. Tom thought with dread about their next meeting, which was now imminent.

11.55 a.m.

'What time's the Boream lunch, Gerald?' Tom cried. He wanted a quiet run with no interruptions when he spoke to Burger.

'Twelve thirty. You'd better cut along there.'

Nice, thought Tom, the verb 'cut'. Now Jock would say 'scoot' and Eileen would say 'hurry'. What would I say? – 'walk'?

'Can I just make a phone call? I've got a couple of minutes still. Oh, any story in Boream?'

'I doubt it but you never know. Take a notebook, anyway.'

Tom called the library and requested the Boream file. And, while he waited, he dialled the Fife number.

Noon

'Burger, good morning,' said a sweet Scottish voice.

'Your banking analyst, my dear. I'm afraid I've forgotten his name.' Tom could feel the Scottish syntax taking over.

'That must be our Mr Hawthorn. Shall I put you through?'

'Now just hold on one moment,' said Tom. 'Just let me gather my papers together.' He felt his hands going moist. 'Right, now put me through.'

The phone clicked.

'Hello.' It wasn't a Scottish voice, rough and pleasing, but the toneless, tasteless, crisp sound of a City man.

'Mr Hawthorn?'

'Speaking.'

'I'm told you're the world's greatest living expert on

banks.'

Laughter from the end of the line.

'I used to be that. But now that I've moved here, I'm not the world's greatest living expert on anything. But is that what Brasenose said about me?'

Brasenose are the bluest-blooded and best respected firm in the City.

'That's right, I called them, asked for you, and they said you'd gone native.'

'Not quite right. I came up here because of North Sea oil, to try to get the facts right. And then, I just stayed on here. Anyway, what can I do for you?'

'I'm told de Boys is planning a really big deal. I wondered if you knew what it was.'

Tom felt a presence beside him. He looked up.

It was Acres, hands playing with pens, twitching and red in the face.

'I thought I told you to abandon the de Boys story!'

'Oh, just a moment, Mr Hawthorn... don't go away. I'll put you on hold,' Tom barked into the phone.

'But he called me,' he said plaintively.

'That is a complete lie,' said Acres. 'I saw you dial the number myself. Now put that phone down and get off to the Boream meeting. That's far more important.'

And Acres reached out and pushed down the buttons in the cradle of Tom's phone, killing the call.

12.15 p.m.

Dunbar was at Tom's side shouting at him. The river ran through the light.

'Tom, what the hell are you still doing here?' You promised to buy me a drink before that Boream lunch.'

He hustled Tom to his feet, as Acres stood frozen by Tom's desk. It took a second.

'I heard that Roy was incredible last night,' Dunbar went on, 'I just spoke to him before I came in here. Let's go and see him.'

'I can't see Roy,' said Tom, his mind slowly untangling itself from the horror and the indignity. 'I hurt him last week over that Pilks story. He's really cool now.'

'For God's sake!' Dunbar's voice went up. 'He's not a baby, you know. He's been in journalism for some years now. He doesn't throw fits over stories.'

Tom felt there was a rebuke implied there, and would have protested. But already Dunbar was easing him from his desk, dragging his jacket off the back of the chair, smoothing him down out of the desk and into the walkway and closer to the door.

Waterloo Bridge gleamed white in the sun. Fleet Street was filling up. The cars stretched out in long lanes in both directions, moving with difficulty and revving their engines. The girls were walking from their bosses' offices with their arms folded beneath their bosoms, a sure sign of rain to come.

They went up the steps into the Old Bell, at the back of the parlour bar with its uneven floor; through the window, behind the lilac sprays, you could see St Bride's Church, with its wedding cake structure.

'You had a row with Ursula last night,' said Dunbar.

'Not true,' Tom replied. 'But it is breaking up, I think.'

'Always the same story,' said Dunbar sympathetically. 'Has she got someone else yet?'

'Certainly not,' said Tom with horror, recoiling for all his bravado at the idea of Ursula taking a rival. But then he added, recalling her waywardness and ability to do exactly what she wanted, when she wanted and with whom she wanted, 'At least, I don't think so.'

'I'd take it easy. She may have someone else, she may just be looking round. But you'll find out soon enough.

Women attached to journalists have a way of leaving them alone with canned beans and dirty washing in a very dramatic way. That's possibly the only thing they learn from their cohabitation with hacks – how to make a stunning exit.'

Tom stared mutinously through the window at St Bride's.

'You're crazy if you think you can take Acres on and beat him,' Dunbar went on remorselessly. 'He is after all Deputy City Editor. He knows a lot of people, he's been here a long time, he's well backed by the management. Just take it easy. You nearly hit him back there.'

'I know I've got a lot to learn, but I'm in a hurry,' snapped Tom. 'I've got a good story, and I'm not going to let that red-faced clown stand in my way. He wouldn't know a story if it jumped up and bit him on the nose.'

'Yes, but the trouble is that your story, whichever way you look at it, could jump up and bite your nose right off,' said Dunbar laughing. Then he reverted to Ursula.

'Why are you falling out?'

'Can't say. I want to move on, taking her with me. But I don't think she's serious about that kind of progress. I think she's just having a good time. Away from home.'

'Sounds a complicated relationship,' said Dunbar cautiously. 'May I ask what the great story's about?'

'No comment,' said Tom, then tapped Dunbar on the paunch, trying to signify that the interview was over.

'Where's Roy?'

'Too drunk to care, probably.'

'Didn't Roy invent that phrase about inflation? What was it again?'

'Against a background of raging inflation and a tottering pound.'

'And what was the story behind it?'

'The story, as you put it, was that when the UK was

going up the pictures and the pound was sliding out of sight, every financial story started with that phrase. Coined, as you so rightly say, by Roy. Eventually the subs got so mad at the phrase, they began striking it out of the copy.'

'What happened then?'

'We used to get the chairmen of companies to quote it, so that by putting it in direct speech, the subs couldn't touch it. The only thing that killed the phrase was a recovery in the economy. Had to look around for a new cliché then.'

They left the pub together and headed towards the City.

2

1.10 p.m.

Tom went into the Great Eastern Hotel by the side entrance. Just behind the door stood two phone booths. Both phones always worked and the money never jammed.

He dialled Mr Hawthorn, the mysterious banking man in Scotland. The same sweet obliging Scottish voice answered the phone.

'Is Mr Hawthorn there?'

'Oh, no,' came the reply. 'He's gone to lunch. He'll be back soon, and I'll tell him you called. He shouldn't be long.'

'Ask him to call me at the *Daily Standard*,' said Tom. 'Around three o'clock.'

He went into the press conference. By the door stood the PR girl, behind a small table. She wore green. Her smile switched on and off like a lighthouse.

She smiled as she gave Tom the handout, even though he was more than half an hour late.

He glanced down the press list. They were all there. The *Daily Mail*, the *Express*, the *FT*, the *Telegraph*, the *Guardian*, *The Times*, Reuters, Extel, and the BBC's 'Financial World Tonight' man.

He looked at the handout. There was a story there. A small one – say, six paragraphs for the early page. He relaxed a little. He wouldn't be distracted from chasing de Boys.

As he went into the press conference room, he looked at the chairs. They still stood neatly in rows. That was good.

When they all lay higgledy-piggledy, some with legs in the air, some kicked on their sides, some turned backwards, that indicated a story.

Boream were paying a cash dividend for the first time. That was possibly bad for high taxpayers. For years, Boream had paid them bonuses through scrip issues. The cash which Boream saved, they hoarded and put into mineral exploration, where they'd been fairly successful. It was a cosy company, with long-established shareholders and a good hunch.

Now Boream were breaking with their tradition. Would their move hit the share-price?

Tom went up to Extel, the City wire service. 'What's the story?' he asked. 'I'm a bit late.' Extel obligingly held open his notebook and started reading through it.

'Nothing much. Time has come to change... blah, blah... committed shareholders... blah, blah... record payout this year. Not doing too well in Australia, shutting down a factory but the Far East is good. Order books are full and the UK plant's going very well indeed. That's about all.

'Thanks.'

The wire boys were always helpful. They sold their stories to the newspapers anyway, so they had no incentive to hoard their information.

Tom moved towards the bar. The question and answer session was over, and people were still milling around in groups before going into lunch. He spotted the Chairman, Lord Matcham, and buttonholed him.

Lord Matcham, a slim, tall man of about sixty, with high cheekbones and waved hair, rocked back and forth on his heels like a waltz king. He was elusive, brought in to give the company respectability – a figurehead, and part of that sprawling network of contacts called the Establishment. He was easy, relaxed, genial.

'Stone here, sir, *Daily Standard*. Couple of points I'd like to check with you if I may, on the dividend.'

'Yes, go ahead, dear boy.' He rocked back on his heels, waiting for the music to start.

'No boardroom split on the dividend decision?'

'No, it was all perfectly amicable.'

'Any thoughts on next year's payments?'

'Not so far. Too early to say.'

'Any idea what profits will be next year?'

'Up to our usual standard, I expect.'

Lord Matcham rocked forward, fixing Tom between the eyes. Tom felt poised to glide away to the big band sound.

'What about the balance sheet?'

Lord Matcham's foot stretched out a little. Tom felt him wince a fraction.

'In good shape.'

'Any thoughts of a rights issue?'

'We don't need one.'

'Not right now?'

'Not right now.'

'How much would you raise if you did one? Now you're paying a cash dividend, you could get one away.'

'Yes, we could. I think that with this kind of question you should talk to Peter Hayden, our MD. Peter, here a moment.'

He caught Mr Hayden by the sleeve, a little imperiously, Tom thought.

'Mr Stone want to know about a rights issue.'

'We might do one, we might not. It's up to us. We'll choose our time.'

The tone had changed from the careless drawl of the politician and front-man to the tough gravel of the professional industrialist.

'Is that on the record, Mr Hayden?'

'Yes, you can quote me on that.'

'Anyone else raised the point?'
'Not so far.'
'So it's to us?'
'So far.'
'Fine. How much would you raise if you did a rights issue?'
'Say, £50 million.'
'That's a lot.'
'Once and for all money, though. And we'd get the institutions in. We want to change the balance of the shareholding.'

Lord Matcham was rocking gently backwards and forwards, like a vigilant buzzard.

'I'm going to intro on the rights issue. Is that okay?'
'Perfectly by me,' said Hayden. Lord Matcham nodded. They moved away.

Suddenly, Pedro appeared. He looked pale.

'What the hell are *you* doing here?' Tom asked him. 'I'm covering this. You're supposed to be back at the office.'

'Don't worry, Tom,' said Pedro. 'I came by error, I'm still completely pissed after last night.'

'Oh yes – Jock came in and said you were dead or something.'

'Nearly. Not quite, though. Guess what happened last night!'

'Tell!'

'I finished up with Ed and Dave from Company PR, and we went down Soho!'

'How much?'
'Guess.'
'I dunno...'
'Go on, guess!'

Pedro's voice had risen and the other journalists began to crowd round.

'What happened?'

'Pedro went down Soho last night after the Monopoly game.'

'What did it come to?'

'He won't tell.'

'Go on, Pedro, tell us.'

By now, Boream and its affairs had been forgotten.

'I'll guess,' said Extel. 'This is one night with two PRs down Soho, right?'

'Right.'

'£200.'

'No.'

'I think we should all be going in to lunch now,' said Lord Matcham, like a school prefect.

'£500?'

'Guess again.'

'It can't be more.'

'We give up.'

'I'll tell you then. The bill was £732.'

'Seven hundred and thirty-two pounds? Christ, that's a lot.'

'Ed ran out of money. He nearly had a punch-up over the bill.'

'But £732! That must be a record. All-time.'

'What did you have?'

'That's the point. It didn't seem all that much. Just a few bottles of champagne and a couple of dances.'

'Chicks?'

'Dave had one.'

'But they're cheap, aren't they?'

'Not Dave's. She wanted £100 before she'd even sit on his knee.'

'Did she get it?'

'Dave beat her down. You know what he's like. Charm, he calls it. Charm!'

They started to move towards the dining room. Tom

was thinking of the introduction to his story.

How do you describe Boream? he thought. Construction giant, construction major, building concern with mineral interests? I know. I've got it. Construction giant Boream, who sell factories and office blocks to Britain's industrialists... Or – Boream, the company which is blowing a north wind of change through conventional attitudes to construction... that's it!

The waiters hovered round the table, where the white napkins stood in pyramids among the goblets.

Tom found his place. He was next to Gerald Stanford, the planning director, on his left. They made their halting introductions.

On Stanford's left sat Priscilla Burne, the journalist's journalist, scantily clad as ever.

The soup was served. Tom looked at the menu. After the cauliflower soup came grilled turbot. Then steak, with new potatoes and fresh peas, with side salads. Then there were strawberries and cream. There was claret and Muscadet.

'Makes a change from the prawn cocktail,' Tom remarked.

'Er – yes,' said Stanford, turning from Priscilla with a start. 'You're from where?'

'*Daily Standard.*'

'Oh yes? Have you been there long?'

'No, not long.'

The conversation died away. Stanford turned back to Priscilla. Tom could hear the inevitable flow of talk filtering through, as Stanford plunged into his autobiography.

Stanford, Tom learned, was a Chartered Accountant, married, two children, used to work for Ford, hadn't come down often enough to London. This was his first big job, and he was based in London. He was trying hard to get used to it. His wife and family were still in the north right now, and he was sorting out the place he'd bought for them all in Kent. He liked the cinema.

Tom glanced at Priscilla. Her eyes sparkled as she talked.

I wonder what she really thinks of British industry, thought Tom. She must get a very one-sided exposure to it.

He asked Stanford how he saw Boream's capital requirements.

'Oh, I don't deal with that side of it,' replied Stanford, testily. He was preparing to launch himself into the saddle and wanted no rivals.

Stanford turned away from Tom, seizing his glass as he did so, and jolting the plates.

Lord Matcham's eye travelled down the table.

Tom turned to the guest on his right. It was the PR girl in green. She smiled at him; he smiled back. He asked her how long she'd been in PR.

'A year or so.'

'Straight from Oxford?'

'Oh, I didn't go to Oxford. I did social studies at Essex.'

'I thought they were all Trots there.'

She veered off the subject, and talked about her boss. She liked him a lot.

Tom glanced across the table. Pedro was opposite, telling the story about that expensive Soho jaunt to Boream's finance director, who was bemused. A worried frown blanketed his features at the thought of so much money spent on one night.

Tom asked the PR girl's name.

'Sandra.'

He started to chat her up, knowing that her reaction would be one of frigid withdrawal. She knew she was there to be part of the expensive wallpaper. In PR they told you that the very worst thing you could ever do was to fall in love with – or do anything with – a journalist. Sleep with the client, yes, good for the account. But not with a journalist. They had nothing to offer.

Tom bore on. He could hear himself making the ritual complaints about a journalist's life while he listened to Stanford on his left ploughing on through the recitation of his life story. Stanford's cheeks grew redder and his hand kept reaching behind to smooth down his hair.

It was Gerald and Priscilla now, as they talked about Priscilla's ex-husband.

She laughed her toothy, jolly laugh.

Stanford's hobby was country walking. Priscilla had no hobbies.

Stanford was explaining in detail his latest ramble in the Lake District, sticking mainly to the first person singular but slipping occasionally into the 'we' of married habit. Priscilla replied appropriately, asking about the mountains, ropes, rocks and crevasses.

Stanford talked about the difficulties he'd found in clambering to the top of Helvellyn, feeling his way through the undergrowth, then reaching out and hanging on to whatever bits of rock came to hand, and finding no obstacles.

Priscilla said she was aware of the dangers. People might fall. It would be terrible to be so alone.

Stanford said she need have no fear. 'I'd be there.'

They both laughed.

The brandy was served. Lord Matcham stood up.

He spoke quietly and clearly, with the fluent precision of a man used to slow shorthand-takers.

It was an important day for Boream; they had thought long and hard about the decision on the dividend. He knew they were right. They had to change – not all change was bad. That was something the Government should realise.

The notebooks closed shut round the table. The pens went back to the pockets.

Lord Matcham continued. This was a government

which did everything in its power to hinder businessmen. Had it not realised that only the businessmen actually created wealth? He didn't want to turn his speech into an election manifesto, but the point had to be made. It was his duty to say it. Equally, it was the press's duty to report it. Thank God, we still had a free press which could still report it. And thank you all for coming.

He sat down, and the journalists from the quality papers went over to thank him for the lunch. On the *Daily Standard*, they never bothered.

Tom left the room, the taste of Muscadet still in his throat.

He found a quiet corner in the hotel and began fitting the story together, working from the press handout and his notebook. He'd decided to pre-empt any moves by Acres to burden him with extra duties that afternoon by phoning the story through. Any more of this, and I'll get a reputation for early copy, thought Tom. It'd make a change from being 'Señor Spike'...

Soon his notebook was like a map of devastation, with lines of writing interrupted by erasures, arrows and brackets, as he crammed the sense of what had been said into the house style.

We'll choose our own time is a good quote, he thought. Wonder if I could juice it up a bit? No one's going to tell us when to do it. We'll seize the opportunity when the time is ripe. That sounds better. Would they complain? Doubt it. They were keen enough to be quoted.

He got the story down to eight paragraphs – about 250 words. It'll make a good little tale for the early page. Nice if nobody else gets that rights issue angle – they'll all get thumped tomorrow.

He found another phone, called the operator, and reversed the charges. As usual, the switchboard had never heard of him and wouldn't accept the charges until he talked to them.

'You are so dumb,' he said to them.

'Oh, it's you, is it? We thought the operator said Bone. There's no Tom Bone working here.'

'That's what you said last time.'

'Oh? Must be getting careless. Well, come on, who do you want? Not the Editor again?'

'Yes, to tell him to replace you. Give me copy, please.'

There was a click and he was through. He heard the light tap of the key on the paper, as the copy-taker tested his equipment. He'd just looked up from the girlie mag he'd been reading, touched his headphones, turned on his tape recorder, and was now ready to go.

'Who's it for?'

'Attention Acres, City Desk, from Tom Stone.'

'Right. Ready when you are.'

'Fine. Construction giant Boream…'

Tap, tap, tap. 'Yes.'

'…surprised the City yesterday…'

Tap, tap, tap.

'…by paying a 2p cash dividend…'

'Yes.'

'…after announcing a big jump in profits…'

Tap, tap, tap.

He droned through the story. Sending copy over like this was like a trapeze act. You had to throw and he had to catch it in time. Otherwise it all spluttered to a halt.

He liked the copy-takers on the *Standard* because they had quiet machines and didn't crack the grammar in the story. The machines in the provinces were so old that they clattered like a battalion on the march.

At the end, the copy-taker sounded quite disappointed.

'You like that?' said Tom.

'Well, I was just wondering whether to buy some of the shares myself. I've got a bit to spend just now.'

'How much?' asked Tom.

With that openness people display to professional advisers they trust, the copy-taker said, 'About two thousand pounds.'

'Come over to the desk this afternoon,' said Tom. 'We'll have a word.'

That'll upset Acres, Tom thought. He doesn't like the proles, particularly the ones with spare dough.

'See you later then,' said the copy-taker.

2.25 p.m.

As Tom left the hotel, his stomach started to churn, because the de Boys story was coming back.

3

The tide had gone out, leaving the banks of the Thames exposed, littered with rocks and debris, and the river ran sullenly. It was still sunny, though a breeze was whipping up.

Only the sub was in when Tom returned. He was a burly, jolly man, with a beard and a passion for fishing. He nurtured no rancour about failed writing ambitions, as did many subs. He preferred the open air.

'Hello, you bugger,' he cried to Tom.

The sub had already started on the business of carving and filleting up the day's news into digestible shape for the next day's readers. On his left lay a huge steel basket, and on his right a pile of annual reports and a heap of agency tape. He whipped through the reports, 'tasting' them for news, then dropped them, rejected, into the basket as a butcher would offal. In front of him he had the page dummy.

'How many columns today?' asked Tom.

'Too many for you,' said the sub, not pausing in his butchery.

'Why did you cut my story right back last night, Pete?' asked Tom.

'Look, wonder boy,' he said. 'You were asked to write two hundred words and you did three hundred. I saved a lot, but in the end it was snip, snip. You were lucky to have it in at all.'

'It was a good story.'

'Dear boy, it could be the world's end, but it'd still have

to fit into the space.'

Other subs were appearing now across the room. Voices filled the air and tape began to strew the floor. Phones rang.

Tom's phone rang. It was Hawthorn.

'We were cut off,' said Tom.

'Yes. You asked about de Boys and a big deal.'

'That's right. Heard anything?'

'Yes. First, he's been trying for too long now to do such a deal. He just can't find the right partner. Second, his balance sheet looks awful. It's only a matter of time before it cracks.'

'I'm very surprised to hear that.'

'The key to it is the change in accounting technique. Look at the way he's shifting investments into associate status. That boosts the profit and loss account but does nothing for cash flow. In fact, his cash flow hardly exists. Now look at the other side of the balance sheet. All his debt – and there's a lot of it – gets shorter and shorter in term. Now, I happen to know he's trying hard either to change the coupon on his Convertible and scale it down, or to force the holders to convert into ordinary – without much compensation, either. That means he's absolutely strapped for cash. The only thing keeping business afloat is the dealing profits. But he made all those last year. This year, he'll be lucky to do that again. So what does he do? I don't know. But the whole thing looks terribly rocky. No, I don't think he's doing a big deal. I think he's going bust.'

The last words came down the line with a sharpness out of context with the rest of the conversation.

'Oh, and another thing if you're looking closely at the report, take a glance at the notes to the accounts. One of them, I think it's note twenty-two, shows large losses for capital gains tax purposes which are available to carry forward to offset against future profits. See how much those losses are up on last year's figure. So, as well as the dealing profits, there must have been plenty of losses. I don't think anyone's picked that up yet.'

'Can I quote you?'

'Rather not.'

'But can we come back to you.'

'Sure. What time?'

'What time will you be there till?'

'About five.'

'That's plenty of time. What's your home number, just in case?'

The magic home number came gliding down the line, and Tom felt happy for the first time that day. Hawthorn rang off.

Tom looked around. He'd been so absorbed he hadn't realised they were all back from lunch.

'Gather round,' cried Acres. 'Let's see what we've got.'

They crowded round his desk. Acres looked like the boy who tramped through the house beating his drum-set on Boxing Day, when nobody, not even the nanny, dared to say 'stop'.

'I've got rather a jolly tale,' said Acres. 'We all know Hoares and Child...'

'No,' said Tom, hoping to score slightly on deference grounds. It might be useful later in the afternoon.

'Hoares and Child are both independently owned banks, and both are in Fleet Street. You should know that!'

Tom mumbled something.

'We'll come back to that. Anyway,' said Acres, turning with his dinner-party smile to the rest of them. 'They've fallen out over their butler. Hoares have a great head butler, Child have just lost theirs, and so they've tried to lure Hoares' Jeeves away. There's an absolutely first-class row broken out between them.'

They all applauded the story, Tom included. Acres was pleased. 'I wouldn't mind the job myself, one day,' he said.

'Do we have a lead?' broke in Jock.

'Yes, I think so. I'll write on the banking figures, the money supply and so on. I'll do about seventy lines. I know it's boring, but our readers have to know these things. Jock, what have you got?'

'I had lunch with Quinn, who, as you know, is an exchange rate freak. He wants the abolition of Exchange Controls now. He says our invisibles will dry up in ten years' time, if not before.'

'Good story. Twenty lines,' said Acres.

'It's worth more. Maybe even a lead,' said Jock, carefully.

'We've got a lead already. Eileen, anything interesting?'

'Yes, Gerald. What I've got is the stores credit card big rip-off. They're all making so much money out of it that even the customers are beginning to react.'

'Talk to Marks, talk to British Home Stores, talk to Currys. We'll have thirty lines, if you can write it up. Pedro?'

'Nothing much so far.'

'And Tom? I see you've filed already on Boream. Isn't that a bit ambitious. Don't you want to talk to more people?'

'Well...'

'What's the share-price done?'

'I don't know.'

'Well, you should, instead of chasing after those gigantic stories. You're flying too high, and you'll regret it. Be warned.'

'Of course. Thank you very much.'

'Now go back to the Boream story. Check it all out and then come back and talk to me. We'll see if we can get something in.

The sub winked at Tom as he returned to his seat.

'You're gated, you naughty little boy, that's what you are,' he whispered.

3.30 p.m.

Tom opened his contacts book and looked up the number of Clive Logue. Clive ran a small investment company, specialising in share ramps. He knew there was more mileage in staying straight, but he couldn't resist a deal with an angle. Nothing ever jail-worthy, but too wide for the big financial institutions ever to take Clive seriously. He was a new contact of Tom's.

'It's Tom Stone here.'
'How much?'
'What do you mean, how much?'
'How much of a favour are you going to ask? How much will you pay? How much do I get in exposure?'
'Clive, I thought you were a businessman.'
'With you, I develop teeth and fins.'
'Tell me something. It's worth a lunch.'
'I'm too busy.'
'Okay. What's the latest on de Boys?'
The line went quiet.
'Come on, Clive. You're close; what is it?'
'There's talk.' Clive sounded worried.
'A deal?'
'I'm not talking about it. Look, Wolf's a great chap, and a good friend of mine. But he's got some very funny people on his books. You know what I mean?'
'I do.'
'But I'll tell you this. When Wolf started off, it was a straight little business, and he hired boys like you, who almost knew what they were doing.'
'Yes.'
'But now it's different. Too many debby birds there, and too much celebrating.'
'What do you mean?'
He rang off. Tom sat back stunned.

3.45 p.m.

Acres appeared. 'Who was that?' he asked gently.

The talk started to slow down around him. His colleagues assumed that intent appearance people wear before a fight. Acres' eye was rolling, and his hands twitched at the pens.

'How's the Boream story coming along?'

'Still polishing.'

'May I see?'

Acres reached over and snatched the copy from Tom's desk. He read through it slowly, and his eyes seemed to converge as his face twisted in on itself.

'You've done absolutely no more than when we spoke an hour ago. Why is that? Will you tell me? Now please! *Now!*' He was working himself up into a fury, and his voice had a scream within it. He had the authority, and the job, and therefore the right to behave like that.

'A chap rang up about Boream just now. He told me that line about a rights issue was dead right. In fact, he said it could come sooner than we think.'

Tom thought it was a good lie which should hold the pass long enough for the fury to abate. But he was wrong.

'I don't believe you! I just don't believe you! What you've been doing is working on that de Boys story, when I expressly told you to leave it alone. And you've disobeyed me!'

The office was quiet now. As the abuse built up, the pretence of concentrating on other things had been abandoned. They all stared at Tom and Acres.

'In fact, this is just the latest in a long line of incidents. You come in here; you expect to be treated like a king; you're late with your copy, you're boorish, you're insolent and, most of all, you're useless! What do you know about de Boys? What do you know about anything, you little guttersnipe?'

'As a matter of fact, I've learned a lot about de Boys today, and the only reason why you don't know more now is that you're too fucking busy finding out stories about fucking butlers! Butlers! And you got it wrong too. Child isn't an independent bank. Get your fucking facts right if you're going to write about fucking butlers! But why don't you concentrate on getting some real stories for a change?'

Tom was on his feet now, and they were close to each other.

Tom felt a hand pluck at him. It was the copy-taker.

'I'm sorry to disturb you. I wondered if we could have a word about Boream. You remember, we chatted about it over the phone.'

'Who are *you*?' Acres screamed at him.

'I'm Hollis, from copy.'

'Well, why aren't you in copy right now, Hollis, taking it?'

'I'm sorry sir. It's Mr Acres, isn't it? I'm sorry, I should have picked a better time. I'll go now.'

Head bowed, he shuffled off, and Acres drew strength from his victory.

'So unless you buckle down immediately, Tom, and I see evidence of this...' he began.

Eileen Creed broke in. 'I agree with you absolutely, Gerald. It's just like having the casuals in. You're so disruptive, Tom. You have to realise that working on a national newspaper is not like the provinces. And working on the City desk of a national newspaper is even more difficult. Some people never make the jump from the provinces, and maybe you're one of them.'

Acres shot her a took of rapturous gratitude. Tom could envisage the cosy little drink they'd have together that evening, and he gathered his forces once more.

'Can I make this quite clear. You're telling me these

wonderful things about yourselves, and how great you are, and you're all backing each other up; but you've forgotten one thing – you haven't asked me once just what I've got as a story on de Boys. So, maybe you're not that keen on stories. All you want to do – and that's you in particular, Acres – is you want to go and kiss de Boys' big fat arse!'

A gleam of pleasure began to creep into Acres' eye. Tom didn't have the right to insult Acres like that, even if Acres was wrong.

The tide was beginning to turn as the sun started to set through the window.

Jock interrupted. 'Tom, if you're so sure it's a good story, take it to the Editor. Don't hesitate. It's too big for Acres.' And he rose slowly to his feet, drew long on his cigarette, puffed out the smoke, and disappeared across to the newsdesk.

4

4.30 p.m.

Tom quailed at the idea of the Editor. He had only spoken to him once. That was nine months ago, when the *Daily Standard* had hired him. He had managed exactly ten words at that interview.

Acres looked a little shaken, too, at the prospect of the Editor taking an interest in his department. He motioned with his hands, almost beseechingly, but said nothing.

They had both forgotten now what the original cause of the quarrel had been.

Outside, the sun was setting magnificently. Giant fiery fingers curled across the sky – a delicate azure washed at the edge by paleness. It was apocalyptic.

4.40 p.m.

Tom walked along the narrow corridor which led to the Editor's office. He was still angry, but now he was also afraid. He thought of the sneer which might accompany the crushing exercise of the Editor's power.

The mid-afternoon conference was just ending. The senior journalists emerged, like eighteenth-century grandees, from the Editor's office. They all wore a fine air of confidence as they moved down the corridor, and Tom hugged the walls as they passed.

He knocked on the Editor's door and went in. The office was very sparse, with deep leather chairs round the walls and one standing in the middle of the office in front of the Editor's desk. The Editor, feet on the table, cigar in mouth, tie loosened, motioned him to sit in the single chair before him. Tom sat down, feeling trapped as the waves of leather rose around him.

The Editor did not seem too surprised to see him. The atmosphere was charged with a dangerous calm.

There was an external smoothness and politeness, rather as if Tom was trying to negotiate a colossal loan with very little security from an experienced and world-weary banker.

'I have this story, sir, about...' Tom began.

The Editor lean forward, crisply putting the tips of his fingers together, as if he'd suddenly made a long-mooted decision. Tom petered out.

'The first thing I want to say is that when you go to a company lunch, you don't interrupt the proceedings by talking about your excesses of the night before. I've just had a call from Lord Matcham, who complained that you monopolised the proceedings, talking about how much you managed to drink your way through yesterday. And you terrified his finance director.'

Tom gasped for air like a drowning man. The pace and turn of events were beyond him. The game was too fast.

'I have this story on de Boys,' he stuttered.

'What does Mr Acres think of it?'

'That's exactly what I've come to see you about.'

'Tell me the story.'

'I'm told de Boys is going bust. His balance sheets look terrible, his cash flow's non-existent. He's even making losses on dealing now. He's cancelled his Bridge subscription. The shares are being sold.'

'Interesting. Mr Acres must be jumping up and down with excitement at this.'

Tom had the impression he'd heard the story already. And the routine seemed familiar, as Tom was relentlessly wrong-footed.

'No, the problem has been...' It was impossible to crack the code in time. Tom was already many points behind.

'You should realise Mr Acres is a very busy man. If you haven't told him about the story it's your fault. You should have been more persuasive.'

Tom gasped, thinking of the insults they'd both just been trading.

'What I propose,' the Editor carried on, 'is that you go back and put the story to Mr Acres just as briefly as you have done to me.'

The Editor smiled seraphically at Tom and drew deeply on his cigar.

Tom hauled himself out of his chair in silence and made for the door.

'On second thoughts, why don't you ask Mr Acres to step in and see me. I have a couple of points to go over with him. Tell Jock to get on with the page.'

4.55 p.m.

After Tom had returned to his desk, Acres bustled with great despatch towards the Editor's office. Jock moved into Acres' chair and called Tom over.

'That Boream story. Get the share-price right, rejig the quote a bit, and we'll lead the page on it. Okay?'

'Yes.'

'And quickly. I'm going out tonight and I want all the copy down as soon as possible.'

A new regime seemed to have arrived in the last five minutes, but the sub was still chopping his way through the day's news with great cheerfulness and zest. Nevertheless something seemed to have loosened up, so that the natural rhythm of the work ran more easily.

Acres reappeared, took his bowler from his desk, and

crammed it on his head.

'I'll be out of the office for about an hour, Jock. You can take over – I'm going to see de Boys immediately. I've just been talking to him on the Editor's phone. He says the story's rubbish. But I'm going over to his office now.'

He disappeared, with his nose tilted up. Then the sub whacked Tom on the back. 'Have you finished that Boream story yet?' he growled.

'I'm getting through it now.'

'Well, bustle, bustle!'

Jock was staring out of the window at the river, smoking with great deliberation, in Acres' chair.

Tom's phone rang. It was the Editor.

'Oh, Mr Stone, could you step into my office again for a moment?'

Tom thought he recognised the voice. Was it the same deep, calm, controlled voice he'd heard last night at midnight? He felt the sweat breaking out on his temples. He felt the same numbness as he went again to the Editor's office that people do faced by a firing squad. The mind stops in front of the imminent pain and destruction. The bullets tearing into the flesh are incomprehensible.

He walked into the Editor's office. Since they last met, he'd travelled a few paces more round the Editor's own Monopoly board. Had he reached Vine Street? – or was he going to jail?

This time, the atmosphere was brisker.

'You will be working on general news from next week. Your salary will be increased by four hundred pounds.'

And the Editor dismissed him by reaching for his telephone and dialling.

5.55 p.m.

Acres was jubilant when he returned from seeing de Boys.

'Nothing in it,' he asserted. 'We had some tea and some cakes, and he showed me the books. They're all on target this year. There are no problems and he can't understand where the stories are coming from. So, that's nailed that!' And turning to Jock, still sitting in his chair, he asked testily about the page, preparing to resume control.

'The Editor's been looking for you,' said Jock. 'I think he'd forgotten about your jaunt. You'd better go and see him.'

Acres went off again, this time with that secretive, authoritative air he wore when close to the great – an air of untouchability wrapping round him like a cloak.

Tom's phone rang again. It was Ursula, who knew more than even the most diligent PR might about recent events. Who had been tipping her off?

'Congratulations, Tom. I'm told you had some great news today.'

'How the hell did you know?'

'We have our spies, you know. Even close to you. What time are we meeting?'

'About six forty-five, I think. Where?'

'I want to walk along beside the river. It's such a beautiful night. I'll see you in the Blackfriars.'

'Right, I'll look forward to it.'

'You do sound pleased.'

'I'd be more pleased if I understood what's been going on today.'

'See you later.'

6.15 p.m.

When Acres came back from the Editor's office he looked shattered, and he drooped like an old daffodil.

'I've been moved,' he said, 'I'm to be Banking Correspondent. Jock takes over here.'

That look of sharing in the secrets of the great and refusing to pass them on to the underlings below had gone. He was deflated.

Jock did not budge from his new chair at the head of the section. He seemed unsurprised by the turn of events.

'Why don't you go home and get over it there? We've got a page to get out and we're late,' he said flatly.

Jock gee'd up the rest of the section firmly to make sure he didn't miss the deadline.

6.45 p.m.

Tom met Ursula, who was brimming over with excitement at his news.

They walked beside the river, which streamed by, black, misty, and gleaming beneath the soft dusk. The lights along the embankment danced in the water's reflection and the old boats rocked at their moorings. The bridge stood firm against the tide. Gulls swooped down screaming to the water, and a motor launch putter-puttered down the middle of the streaming flood. The factories, the office blocks, and the houses stared impassively at the volume of water flowing by eternally, and inevitably, before them.

7.30 p.m.

Papers lined the floor in the news room as the Editor, seated in the middle of the room, surrounded by his cohorts, flanked by the subs – who moved swiftly from phone to copy, from page layout to composing room – searched through the stories of the day for the next day's lead.

7.45 p.m.

Tom told Ursula what had happened during the day. He

was jubilant about his rise.

'What about the story?' she asked. 'I was told there was a story, that you were about to write the most important story of the year, that you'd get an award.'

'Who told you that?'

'Whoever it was that rang me. It was a deep voice, I didn't know it. But... the story?'

'Acres killed it. There was no story.'

'You worked on it, though. I heard you last night, in your sleep, muttering.'

'It's nothing.'

She turned to him, and the light from the lamps along the embankment played on her taut features, catching her bright blue eyes.

'You stupid, stupid, stupid little man,' she said. 'Can't you see you've been set up? Maybe de Boys is bust, maybe he isn't, but you've been used. Whoever called you last night knew exactly what was going to happen today. But it was *you* who rowed with Acres, it was *you* who did the work, it was *you* who went to the Editor, and it was Acres who got the push. But it was *Jock*,' – her voice rose – 'it was bloody Jock who got the big job. You fool. You great, stupid provincial clod! Can't you see that you've been fooled? And who was behind Jock? That's what I'd pay dearly to know.'

And she swung off into the darkness, leaving Tom speechless and alone.

5

8.15 p.m.

Tom slid into the semi-darkness of the Judge and Wig, the *Standard*'s local. He had a few minutes to himself before he was due down on the stone. He'd promised to stand in for the sub, who wanted to collect some fishing gear.

The elders of the *Standard* assembled here to discuss the day, after their deadline. Tom had learned to be wary of approaching them at their ease. They stood in what looked like casual groups scattered here and there throughout the pub, exuding cheer as rounds were bought and consumed. But every group looked in on itself and stood at a fixed distance from each of the other, competing, groups, like a tribal gathering. Defections from one group to another were rare; newcomers were rejected.

Here stood the Industrial Editor, with his cronies. There was the Features Editor, with his acolytes. And, close to the bar, the Foreign Desk boys who, Oxbridge to a man, were less obviously clique-ish, because their attitudes had been formed too long ago.

Tom crossed to the bar and ordered a beer. He found himself next to Maynard, the Religious Correspondent.

Like all special correspondents, Maynard had gradually taken on the look and behaviour of the area he covered, hence his tendency to grasp journalists ecclesiastically by the elbow as he made a point. But Maynard was also a heavy drinker, and could only finance both his large family and his drinks by running the 'secondary bill market' in the paper.

Maynard collected bills from every possible source and then sold them on to the journalists for a fixed, pro-rata sum. This brought him in cash, and it also solved the journalists' problem of finding enough bills to maintain their expenses at an appropriate level.

'Any problems?' he asked Tom, with a twinkle in his slightly bloodshot eye. That was the prelude to negotiations.

'Not this week,' replied Tom, realising angrily that he'd failed to agree a new expenses level with the Editor that afternoon.

Just then, one of the newsdesk tyros loomed out of the darkness.

'Tom Stone?'

'That's me.'

'I hear you're joining us.'

'That's right. Next week, I believe.'

'Where did you get your news-writing experience?'

That was a big, big, question. Dukes and earls may measure their breeding by harking back through the centuries. But in a newspaper, the cracks are the news writers, and each one comes from a recognisable provincial stable.

'Preston and thereabouts in Lancashire,' said Tom. It was a so-so stud, like one of the lesser-known Oxford colleges, but still Oxford at least.

'You must have worked under Wally Stott.' The question came flickering through the half-light.

'Yes, I worked with Wally just before he retired.'

'Nice man, Wally. I was with him at Oxford. Beautiful operator. What's your shorthand like?'

'Rusty,' said Tom.

That was the correct answer. What the newsdesk always hoped for, when a specialist journalist joined them, was a complete inability to take shorthand. Because they hated specialists, they could break the new recruit by putting him on covering stories like court cases or Parliamentary affairs, which needed shorthand. That way, they kept out newcomers and preserved the purity of their race.

'See you in a few days' time. About eleven.' And he loped back into the darkness, bearing the report back to the stockade for analysis by the other head men of the tribe.

8.30 p.m.

Should he ring Ursula, he wondered. No, let her bake.

8.31 p.m.

He started collecting the long strips of galley proofs and, like an East End bride festooned with bunting, made his way towards stone number eighteen, where the City page was being assembled.

The rules were strict. He could watch what was being done, he could indicate what changes should be made to the page, but he couldn't touch the metal. If he did, the paper wouldn't come out that night. The printers, the oldest of all the craft unions, were tough, and preserved their negotiating power with the newspaper management by refusing to allow anyone to touch their equipment. Their sense of demarcation lines made the Berlin Wall look like a bridge. Graham, the stonehand, was a fresh-faced dreamy-looking man, with long delicate hands and, as Tom knew from previous conversations, a passionate love for football and his wife.

Graham's fingers travelled stealthily round the steel frame of the chase, fitting the metal type in columns, separating the columns with tiny metal strips and then opening up the spaces between the lines of type with even thinner strips. He shortened the strips to measure, using a blunt-nosed chopping instrument, and then fitted the metal and the strips into place with a pair of tweezers.

The air was full of bustle, cheerful shouting, and abuse, as the metal emerged from the Linotype machines – huge black clanking monsters in the corner – and was carted over in trays by grinning geriatrics.

De Boys, Tom thought, and, recalling a phrase Ursula had used in one of her attempts to educate him, *'Mais où sont les neiges d'antan...'*

'Any cuts?' he asked.

'Yes. I want ten lines out of column one, and a couple of lines from column two,' answered Graham. 'And if you can lose a line down *there*,' he said, 'we can cut out the widow.'

Leaning on the stone beside the chase, Tom began to make the cuts, as the metal was smoothed into place.

'See you wrote the lead,' said Graham. 'That's good.'

'Easy story, though.'

'Yes, I can tell. Look, what's happened on the City desk? The layout's very different tonight. I'm going to miss my train, I've had to spend so much time on it. It's very ambitious, with all those pics.'

'There's been a palace revolution. Acres is shifted sideways and Jock comes in as the new boss.'

'Jock's the big man, right? I've met him... Oh look! That head's busting – it's too long in thirty-six point.'

'What if I cut it down to thirty point?'

'Won't look as good. Can't you rewrite it?'

Tom began to re-phrase the headline, to ensure that the number of characters didn't exceed the space available.

Sometimes, busting heads was an agreed fraud between the journalist and the stone-hand, because a new head had then to be set up by the case, who were paid for piecework.

As Tom made his corrections to the copy, the stone-hand tucked the corrected galleys into his apron. Much financial haggling was involved in working out who made the mistake in the first place.

Beside him, on the next chase, Tom could hear the clear fluted tones of Alastair – the Arts page sub who wore a spotted bow-tie – contrasting with the grim rage of Petal Smith, the best stone-hand on the paper, with the long, narrow, intense face of a nineteenth-century radical. Petal was so called because he worked himself up into the most un-flowerlike rages over amateur style-sheets, and the 'rash pansies' as he called those who ventured down from the Editorial floor to the composing room.

Petal was the more enraged because he'd spent the day playing golf. Playing golf convinced him that he was getting on in society, and winning a place there equal to his enormous weekly wage – that is, unless he talked to Alastair, who exuded effortless superiority through his bow-tie.

'Here,' Graham said to Tom. 'What does this mean?'

He pointed to a caption beneath a picture in the middle of the page, forgetting that Tom was unable to read back to front.

'Oh, wait a minute...' he went on, 'I've got it here.'

He pulled out a black of the caption. It was Acres' butler piece, boiled down to a paragraph but attached to a picture of the butler – part of Jock's tact.

'What does he mean here, when he says that the butler likes Proust but is no Baron de Charlus? I don't know what he means by Proust. But this "Charlus" – surely that should be spelled "Charles"?'

'I dunno,' said Tom. 'I've never heard of Proust. I've heard Gerald on the phone about him, but I thought he was a stockbroker or a fund manager.'

'You'd better find out, before I set it,' said Graham. 'Give him a ring at home.'

Tom went to the phone in the middle of the composing room. It wasn't like any of the phones on the editorial floor with the little white oval in the middle of the dialling disc and the numbers picked out tastefully. No disc, no black plastic with the numbers printed on it. The numbers were handwritten against the side of the battered dialling circle. But the tone, when he picked up the receiver, was wonderfully clear.

9.10 p.m.

He rang Gerald's home number in Hampstead. He knew it was a Hampstead number from the dialling code: 435. But in any case, Gerald always answered by using the old Hampstead prefix instead of the number code. 'These things shouldn't die,' he always said.

Someone picked up the phone. A girlish voice. Tom could hear laughter in the background.

'Who's calling him?' she said, gaily.

'It's the *Daily Standard*,' said Tom. 'Tom Stone.'

'*Oh!*' she squealed. 'Gerald, it's your newspaper calling you from Fleet Street. How terribly exciting.'

A pause, as Tom could hear Gerald giving his guests – it sounded like a dinner-party – instructions not to start the claret yet.

'Bring up some more from the cellar, Jocelyn,' he commanded, and then picked up the telephone.

'Gerald Acres,' he said, with the usual emphasis on his Christian name.

'Tom Stone here. Sorry to disturb you at home. There's a slight query on the copy.'

'It's Tom Stone on the stone. How funny.'

Tom could hear the rage of the day beginning to stoke itself up again, and interrupted hastily. 'It's about your caption on the butler. We couldn't decide if it should be "Charlus" or "Charles".'

He said it humbly, knowing how disadvantaged his ignorance had left him.

'There's a man here who doesn't even know about the

Baron de Charlus!' Tom heard Gerald bellow out to his friends. 'God! They do send us some stupid fools these days. He's *Charlus*, you clown, with a "u". He was queer, and so are you, but in different ways.'

And the phone went down.

Tom told the stone-hand the copy was correct, collected the proof copy of the page, checked the tapes for a late story, said goodnight to the Night News Editor.

9.45 p.m.

The first edition dropped, a little late.

10. 30 p.m.

Tom let himself into the flat. Ursula was still there but asleep. Tom mused that their disagreement that evening would hardly help his forthcoming meal with her parents.

10.45 p.m.

The second edition dropped, on time.

12.30 a.m.

The third edition dropped.

2.30 a.m.

The final edition dropped.

6

Tom stirred as he felt the grey morning stealing up against the windows in the flat. He breathed from beneath the counterpane and saw the exhalation form into a grey pillar above his face. Dull shafts of light speared across the floor, but it was chilly and deep in November – the cold plucked at his mouth. Tom shifted his knees further towards his chin, rolled his arm over his stomach, and shifted himself into a warmer position in the bed. He felt the heat swelling up from the pit of the coverings as he moved.

Today was his first day in the news room. It marked the start of a new career for him in journalism.

From where Tom lay, he could feel the objects in the room forming themselves in the light out of the darkness. Directly in his line of vision lay what Ursula called the Hanging Gardens of Babylon – her flower-pot full of fuchsias suspended from the ceiling. The chain which held the pot never budged, not even in the strongest wind when the windows were open.

Behind the Gardens, and between the two long elegant windows now masked by curtains, stood an eight-foot high mirror. As soon as Tom rose from the pillows he could see his blurred shape struggling into life and focus, tousled hair, stubble, blotchy face and grimy teeth.

He hated the mirror, complaining to Ursula that it started the day with too much realism. But she insisted that it remained, maintaining that she could never see anything wrong in the mirror when she got up. Perhaps it was the debauchery in his life rebuking him, like Dorian Gray. If so, he could always opt for a more sensible existence.

On his right lay the clothes cupboards, with latticed doors, running the length of the wall. On his left stood her night table, crowded with a telephone, letters and postcards from friends, a sprig of heather and a round bottle of rose water shaped like an Aladdin's lamp.

The light stole reluctantly across the floor towards the bed. He knew what lay outside the room. In the quiet street, guarded by shops at both ends, the newspaper boy and the milkmen were already at their chores. Occasionally Ursula, or her sister when she came to stay, would get up early to catch the papers as they fell through the letter box, summon the newspaper boy from his round, and make much of the bewildered youngster over a cup of tea.

In the house opposite lived Theo, renegade American, holder of wild parties, itinerant journalist, pot smoker, voracious reader, boundless enthusiast, and a puzzle to Tom.

Tom liked the flashing lights in Theo's flat and the uncouth beautiful women who attended his parties. But he was slow beside Theo's eloquence.

Further down the street lived Charlotte, Ursula's closest friend. Ursula and Charlotte had met at university, and had stayed together ever since. Charlotte was rich, with the careful but capricious taste of a junior Gertrude Stein. At the front of her flat stood an elegant curved piece of stone sculpture, while paintings by her friends ('my lotteries', she called them) hung on the walls inside. She adored the media. But she distrusted Tom, whom she felt, so Ursula said, was likely to bring the whole of Fleet Street crashing down rather than enhance it.

Through the lightening gloom, Tom searched for his favourite spot in the bedroom – the painting on the wall. It was a reproduction of Hockney's 1971 portrait of Ossie

Clark, Celia Birtwhistle, and cat, with Celia standing to the left of louvre windows and Ossie sprawled on a chair. The cat, looking very white and pompous, perched on Ossie's knee. Tom loved the opulent purple worn by Celia, the sense of early morning flooding in through the high French windows, and the impression of self-confidence created by all three.

He felt little for Ursula's bedroom. It was warm, it was neat, it was opulent. But it was not home.

As if stung by the guilt of such a reflection – after all, she did pay the rent – he rolled over again, searching for her with his arm. All he found was a deep hollow left by the impress of her body, glowing with a silent, slightly musty, heat.

Then he remembered. She had risen early to make breakfast for him, on his first day in the news room.

'I don't mind making the supreme sacrifice, once in a while,' she had announced last night to the assembled throng at Charlotte's. 'It'll come as quite a shock to do the traditional thing, and make breakfast for my man. Bacon and eggs in the morning before he goes out, it's quite Lawrentian.'

More light was streaking across the floor as Tom rose shivering from the bedclothes and groped for his dressing gown. He swung his feet down on to the floor, avoided looking at the mirror, and padded across the room to the door.

He slipped through the narrow vestibule beside the front door to the flat and into the living room. Through the window here, he could see the fields which led to Hampstead Heath spread out before him. Mist was rising slowly, as walkers here and there across the fields swung into view and then disappeared; the sky was leaden grey.

Silently, he approached the kitchen. He could hear Ursula at the stove, tending the bacon in the pan as it hissed and sizzled. Occasionally, a cup or plate clattered.

He went into the kitchen, creeping up behind her quietly. She wore a pure white silk poncho slung over her night-dress. Her hair was uncombed, and lay blonde and wild across her shoulders and beside her cheek.

This was the moment when he loved her best, when the defences she put up through convention and breeding were down, and she was once again a bright, wild thing.

Through her poncho and night-dress, he could half see her breasts standing up sheer against her body, and her flowing slender haunches. Her feet were bare on the kitchen floor.

He slid his hands under her poncho. Her head went back against his shoulder and she sighed quietly. 'Oh Tom,' she whispered involuntarily, and he felt her body moving limply into his.

But then she stiffened, the pan rattled against the stove as the bacon crackled, and the moment was over. Like an Amazon of old, she slipped on her shards and breastplate and cuirasses, ready for the fray.

'Another time, love,' she said. 'I'm not really ready for you this morning.'

And she moved away to the kitchen table, shaking the plump pink bacon on to the plate, and then pouring out the tea.

They sat opposite each other as Tom ate his breakfast, with his back to the window. Ursula could look out to the fields and groves of the Heath behind his head.

'How do you feel?' she asked.

He answered noncommittally. For Tom, news stories were something associated with the provinces, a necessary piece of purgatory in order to reach the bright lights of Fleet Street.

'There's nothing to them. It's pure formula writing. You put all the story in the first paragraph, body it out with a quote in the second, shove in the background, and then ask the stupid newsdesk whether they want any more after eight paras. I've done it all before,' he replied.

'But surely there must be a difference between writing for the *Scunthorpe Strumpet*, or whatever that filthy little rag was called that you worked on, and contributing to the *Daily Standard*,' Ursula persisted. 'It's like the difference in everything between the capital and the country – they're practically two different nations. You'll need to discover a whole new language.'

Tom disagreed with her violently and then went on to expand his ideas about the de Boys story, and to outline how he proposed to follow up the scoop. But he felt Ursula's attention fading with her scepticism.

Then she interrupted him again, this time half-smiling, as if to make up for her previous coldness.

'But how far will it take you off the roundabout?' she asked.

They both laughed together, and Tom watched her face dissolve into a quiet puckish smile.

It was their private joke, which dated back to the very first moment of their relationship. They had met at a party in Goldhurst Terrace, one of the most unpleasant bed-sitter regions in North London.

Tom, standing by the door at the party, had watched Ursula saunter in, then ignored her when somehow she finished up leaning beside him.

'That man has Jesse James eyebrows,' he muttered to her after some time, indicating a drunk on the other side of the room, who had brows which met together in twin parabolas.

'But he'll never get off the roundabout,' she replied, and they started talking. 'The roundabout' was her phrase for the poor hopefuls who trekked down to London to find streets paved with gold, higher wages, more beautiful people, and a better life.

But instead they encountered rapacious landlords; dank flats with rotting joists; unbalanced tenants, who schemed to rob them; a working life of constant hand-to-mouth living and worry, backed by credit cards. Only in the summer did prospects brighten for the hopefuls. In Ursula's phrase, they could afford to carry their drinks out of the pub, where they normally squatted, and bask in the sunshine. And outside one of her locals, where she had lived briefly, there had been a real roundabout, covered over with grass, where they all disported in June and July, as if in Biarritz or the Costa Brava. Roundabout people are always doomed to disappointment or asthma, she had said, after Tom moved in with her.

In the early months of their relationship they had fashioned a whole mythology for the roundabout people, and it symbolised their meeting, and a truce.

'I think it takes me a step further from that dread place,' grinned Tom. 'Wouldn't like to be there, now that winter's deep upon us.'

'Dogs in the bathroom.'

'Snakes in the loo.'

'Spiders in your cheese.'

'Failed Open University First Part.'

'Damn! Forgot to read *War and Peace* again.'

'Cancelled order for the *Financial Times*.'

'It's back to Mum and Dad in Huddersfield.'

'All of which reminds me,' said Ursula, breaking off the fantasy, 'what time will you finish this evening? Seven? Eight? You know my parents are coming up and we're all meeting in Covent Garden with Theo and Charlotte for dinner. What time can you make it?'

'I'll ring you when I know. I should be free by seven, if not earlier.'

Tom could tell that Ursula was preparing to deliver one

of her devastating parting shots. She had a way of pursing her lips and fluttering her eyelids as the thought worked its way into words.

The line came from the side of her mouth, almost as a whispered afterthought, and was flung over her shoulder as she reached the door.

'And if you order steak tartare, try and get the pepper mill the right way up.'

She was out of the kitchen, making her way towards the bedroom, as Tom relaxed next to the teapot.

The crack referred to a pair of his social blunders committed in his early days in London. Once he had taken a pretty girl out to an expensive restaurant, ordered expansively and lavishly for them both, and then tried to use the pepper mill by turning it upside down and shaking it, rather than using the grinder at the top. The look of stupefaction on the girl's face, as she realised she was dealing with a well-meaning rustic, was unforgettable.

The other reference wrapped up in the insult was to one of Tom's first business lunches in the City. Tiring of the eternal but safe rump steak on the menu, he had decided to opt for something a little more adventurous. When the steak tartare arrived, freshly ground, at his table, Tom snarled unpleasantly at the waiter – 'Aren't you going to cook it, then?' – and then tried unsuccessfully to pass the whole solecism off as a joke, which aggravated the situation still more.

Ursula was sure to bring up either gaffe as a safety valve before important occasions. It was a sign that she was worried about something. To bring up both augured badly.

7

Tom was due in the news room at eleven. Fortified by Ursula's breakfast, he set out for the paper in good time. But it was already about ten past the hour when he arrived at the main building.

First the tube had been slow, and then he had lingered chatting in the weak sunshine to the newspaper seller on the corner of Ludgate Circus. He then lost a little more time after he entered the building, because instead of heading direct for the news room, he had taken the route, through sheer force of habit, towards his old spot on the City desk.

By the time he actually passed through the door and into the news room, it was a fraction after eleven-twenty. It won't matter on my first day, he thought. Anyway, these boys never start writing anything until after lunch.

The door swung to behind him. Tom found himself facing an extraordinary figure.

A burly, thickset young man sat on a desk dead in front of the door. He wore thick blue corduroy trousers and a pair of brown shoes with thick soles.

The young man was tapping one foot slowly against the desk as he peered with exaggerated attention at his nails. Tom saw that his fingers were thick and stubby and strong, but that the nails were surprisingly neat and delicate.

The young man's head came up, and he stared at Tom with an unblinking steady glare of dislike mingled with contempt.

'So you're Stone, are you?' he said slowly, calmly, levelly. 'You would be late on your first day, wouldn't you, you little bastard.'

Tom felt the fluid start to drain out of his knees, as the young man went back deliberately to his nails, dropping his head in the process.

He had long, unkempt hair, which tumbled well over his shoulders. But it was black and thick.

He looked up again, and reopened the conversation, still on the same deathly calm note.

'My name's Vaughan. I'm your boss. I am never anything else. You never call me by my first name. Only friends of mine and people I respect can do that. I am Vaughan to you, Vaughan the boss. Got it?'

Tom stuttered agreement. By now he had started to take in the young man's face. It was chilling. He had a strong, broad forehead, a nose which sprang out from his face like the prow on a Viking longboat, and strong clear white teeth like tombstones. The eyes were grey and cold.

'You will be here every day on the stroke of eleven. You will answer to me for whatever you do during the day, and you will leave at the end of the day at seven, unless I tell you to work later.'

He turned from Tom, and in an expansive gesture, from which Tom initially shrank as if about to be struck, he indicated a desk in the dark corner of the room, far away from the windows.

'That is where you sit. It is the worst spot in the room. I have selected it for you. I don't want you here. I have been told I have to take you, because for some reason or another they have decided we need news writers who know a little about finance. But I plan to make you leave. They know that; now you know it. I have warned you.'

Vaughan prepared to leave the office. He stood up and marched towards Tom, who shifted out of his way quickly.

As Vaughan reached the door, he turned, and snapped to Tom, 'I have also been told I must have lunch with you today, in order for us to get to know each other better. I can't think of anything I would like less. But we will lunch together – for three quarters of an hour, and then you will be back here again working for me. Be ready at one – on the dot.'

The door crashed to behind him.

Tom heard footsteps behind him, and turned. He saw a slight, coltish-looking girl with close-cropped hair and slim hips, sauntering towards him. She had a slight upturn to her nose, which gave a kind of supercilious overhang to her manner. But her eyes, with full lids and large oval brown pupils, suggested humour and distant sympathy – the reward, so to speak, for the most perfect and gentlest knights, after the absurdities of their pilgrimages, their jousting, and their pangs of love in all-night vigils.

A crinkle of pleasure crept into her eyes and across her mouth as she spoke. Tom noticed she wore a man's shirt, as if it had been the first thing she'd found that morning when she awoke. It occurred to him that perhaps some stout merchant banker had wandered bereft of shirt and half naked into the local Burtons in search of a suitable replacement.

He discovered that she was telling him not to take too much notice of Vaughan – well not too much at first, anyway.

'He's new to the job. Only appointed two weeks ago, and he's frightfully keen to make changes. I'm told he has a thing about English, but nobody here is awfully sure. He just bounds in; delivers his orders; bounds out again. You're unlucky. You're his first real possible victim – all the rest of them are too tough. I think you'd better be careful.'

She delivered her opinions with a carefully modulated precision, as if auditioning for a small but significant part in an English classic. Tom found himself inventing a background for her.

'Do I have to sit there?' he asked. 'It's a long way from the window, and it seems very dark.'

He found himself unconsciously failing into her trick of speaking.

'There's nowhere else. Besides, you won't be staying long, will you? You're only on probation.'

Tom felt a kind of mental hamstring snap inside his head. The gay waltz they had been dancing together ended.

'What d'you mean, probation? I've written news stories before, I know all about it. And I came here as a promotion. You're crazy.'

He was conscious as he spat out all his sentences that perhaps he might have put his thoughts less violently.

'Well, Vaughan insisted that anyone straight from the City desk had to be put on probation. And we understand that he won his point. Out of the two of you, only one will stay. At least, that's what we understand.'

'Two of us?'

'Oh, they didn't tell you that either? That's very unkind of them, really. It seems that they've already decided who's drawn the short straw in this deal. No, there are two of you from City – you and Pedro. But he won't be in today. He's been sent on assignment to the North. They've asked him to file about five hundred words, so I heard this morning.'

She took him by the elbow and, as he thrilled to her touch, she guided him gingerly, as if he might snap violently at her, over to the desk in the corner.

'You'd better make the most of it all, because I don't think there's much else you can do about the situation,' she stated. Tom had the distinct impression that everything she said could be a careful translation from another language.

'We always know about these situations,' she added, as the sleeves on her shirt billowed suddenly. 'They like to keep at least one desk free in the news room. But with you and Pedro in here now, every desk is taken. So it's only a matter of time before somebody drops out.'

Then she added as an afterthought that it was always possible that someone else might have to leave. He oughtn't to ignore that. Then she loped off to answer the phone.

He watched her as she talked confidingly into he receiver. A smile crept over her face, as if she and the caller were old friends. Then Tom began to register what she was saying.

'Yes, Sir Charles, I quite understand, the Minister won't be able to make his briefing with Damian today, arranged for two thirty, but he can be there tomorrow at ten in the morning. Could you wait one second, while I check Damian's diary? I'm certain he's free, but I will look to be absolutely certain.

'Yes, he is free. I'll write it in now, and I'll make certain he's there. Thank you for calling. Goodbye.'

She replaced the receiver and carefully scored out the original appointment in the large book beside her on the desk, then turned the page to make the new entry.

Tom watched the sleeves on the shirt slide across the diary as she scribbled. She turned towards him again.

'Look,' she said, indicating the diary. 'Everyone's out this morning. You won't meet anyone until this afternoon. I expect by that time you'll be past caring, after Vaughan's finished with you over lunch. They say he's very difficult at midday, when he's still waiting for stories.'

She pronounced her sentence of doom with a strange combination of offhandedness and precision, as if death, in some shape or form, had become an everyday event.

'Which Minister was that you were talking about?' queried Tom, conscious again as he spoke that his sentence could have been better constructed.

'Only Regional Development. A tiddler really. I think

he's keener to meet Damian than Damian is to see him. Damian normally refuses to see anyone outside the Cabinet. He says they always believe what they read in the newspapers until they get into the Cabinet. Damian's the Industrial Editor,' she added helpfully, conscious that Tom was gaping at her in his ignorance.

The news room door opened suddenly, and a short, red-faced man with black spectacles and a barrel chest strode puffing into the office.

'This is Mick, the copy boy,' she said. 'Let me introduce the two of you. Mick, this is our latest – and greatest' – (turning with a smile to Tom) 'recruit to Hades. They say he won't last. Tom, this is Mick. When you've finished writing, shout, and Mick will ferry your copy to Vaughan.'

'Thank you for the kind words,' Tom said to her. 'But what is your name?'

'I don't like my name much. I'm called Gloria. I think it's such a common name. But then, I'm stuck with it. And everyone seems to think I make such a perfect Gloria that I'm very loath to change it now. What do you think of "Gloria"?'

For the first time, Tom detected a slight defensive note in her voice. But he was too worried by the events of the morning to exploit the point.

'I agree with them,' he said gruffly.

Then Mick thrust a sheaf of papers into his hand, saying that if he was Tom Stone, he'd been told to hand him these. Tom looked at the bundle. Each one was headed by the words 'Tom Stone', and then underneath was scored a number, in some cases two hundred and fifty, in others five hundred.

'Vaughan's starting you off quickly,' said Gloria. 'He'll want these stories by lunchtime. I think you should start writing immediately.'

'But I haven't got a typewriter,' moaned Tom.

She paused for a second, and then looked over at Tom's desk in the corner.

'You've got a phone, I know, because the engineers installed it on Friday. But I still haven't cleared out your desk. I was hoping to complete that this morning.'

'Clearing out, clearing out, what does this mean? Is it full of junk?' asked Tom wildly.

'Not necessarily,' relied Gloria. 'But it's still got a lot of Jake's things in it. He only died a fortnight ago, and we just didn't get around to it. It could be quite gory, because he used to keep all sorts of spares in his desk, like false teeth and glasses. You don't want to get mixed up with all that, do you?'

Tom said nothing. She put her hand to her chin, and then smoothed down her hair, reflectively. Then she said peremptorily, 'Sit down at my desk. You can probably use an electric typewriter, at a pinch. Do your best with it, but try not to destroy it, it's awfully hard to find a replacement. Use my phone. In the meantime, I'll go and find a typewriter for you.'

She moved to the door, followed by Mick who scowled back at Tom, as they both left the room.

Tom sat down at her desk, noticing, as he did so, the neat way the biros stood in the pot beside the typewriter; the pad carefully laid out on the desk; and the pleasing sense of objects and space linked by a gentle personality.

He looked at his sheaf of papers, all handouts of some description. He selected one at random, about National Savings returns for the previous month. He felt confidence return as he manoeuvred some paper into the machine, which hummed quietly to his touch.

They're making it all up, he thought to himself. Vaughan can't be that much of an ogre. And anyway, it's only a sodding news story. I've written hundreds of them in the past.

He worked away at the story, slotting the main point of the handout – a fall in government receipts – into a jokey little opening about the Government approaching Christmas empty-handed.

As he warmed to the theme, he felt exhilaration creeping into the prose style. Although Vaughan had specified two hundred and fifty words, Tom eventually got the story up to three hundred and fifty, which he felt was fully justified.

I'll show these buggers, he thought, as he clattered away. What do they know about news writing that you can't learn outside London?

He finished the story and, as an afterthought, typed his by-line on the folio at the top, then shouted 'Copy', and sat back waiting for Mick to reappear.

The door flew open. Mick rushed in, seized the script and vanished.

A second later, Gloria returned, staggering under the weight of a typewriter. Resisting his efforts to relieve her of the burden, she tottered to his new desk and slammed it down. Gasping, she explained that she had managed to wheedle it out of the stores people, but it was really promised to someone else. It was only a temporary loan, until they could find a permanent machine.

He sat on the desk and laughed as she recovered her breath. Then the door opened again, and Vaughan strode in. Tom looked at his watch and realised that it was close to one o'clock.

Vaughan stood in front of Tom. Without a word, he produced paper from his pocket, paper which Tom recognised as his story. Slowly, carefully and deliberately, Vaughan tore the piece of paper into shreds before Tom's eyes, and then sprinkled the bits on the floor at his feet. When he had finished, he looked at Tom again, and said, 'It's time for our lunch.'

8

Vaughan and Tom slipped swiftly down the stairs from the third to the ground floor and then out into the street. The sunshine was still weak, but the day had that air of ease and feel for talk which Fleet Street assumes after noon.

They walked down Fleet Street towards Ludgate Circus in silence, with Vaughan ploughing a deliberate path through the lunchtime throng at a fairly rapid pace, and Tom dancing and bobbing in his wake, trying to keep up.

They came to the traffic lights together and halted. Tom asked where they were going, more to break the silence than as a genuine request for information. He was used to lunching at smart restaurants, from his stint on the City Desk. Vaughan's blue corduroys looked shabby and stained in the sunlight.

'We're going to a small place just beside the Old Bailey,' Vaughan replied. 'It's quiet and quick and cheap.'

They walked on, past the Ludgate and up to Sea Coal Lane. Tom, still smarting from the destruction of his story and what he saw as its melodramatic end in front of Gloria, asked Vaughan where he had gone wrong.

Vaughan grunted in reply to the question, a kind of sharp intake of breath followed by an 'aargh', and continued walking. Tom persisted, saying that he had written thousands of news stories in the provinces and that they had never had that kind of treatment meted out to them.

Vaughan stopped and turned to Tom in the sunlight, with the railway bridge behind his left shoulder.

'I'll tell you what was wrong with it. I think I'd rather do it now than over lunch because explaining it then could spoil my digestion. I don't take long for lunch, and I like my food.

'You didn't call for the files. I know that because I checked with the library. You made no telephone calls, because I asked the switchboard to give me details of any calls made from the news room between twelve and one. The introduction was wrong because you editorialised the story in the first line rather than giving it straight and factual. The grammar was wrong because your tenses were completely awry – you left one sentence, which should have been in reported speech, which takes the past tense, in the present tense. The style was wrong, because you had three words in the story that had more than three syllables.

'I don't know if you know the old *Express* rule,' Vaughan continued, 'but just in case you don't, I'll spell it out for you. It might be useful to you in your next job. No word may have more than three syllables. No sentence can contain more than seven words. No paragraph longer than three sentences. That makes a total, in Beaverbrook terms, of twenty-one words, maximum per paragraph. We are slightly less severe.

'But you had forty-three words in your first paragraph. Now do you grasp why the story was spiked – or, rather, destroyed?'

There was a savage look in his eye as he went through the shortcomings of the story, like a visionary explaining heresy to a delinquent acolyte.

'The story bored me. It was worthless,' he finished up, crushingly.

But as they entered the restaurant, he added, as an afterthought, 'Don't assume that I'm spying on you. I don't watch people out of choice, only to find out how good they are. So far as I'm concerned, they can do as they like, provided they get the stories.'

They pushed into the gloom of the restaurant. Tom took in a bar on his right, running nearly the length of the room, as the door banged behind them. On the left were tables crammed with a jolly laughing throng, but it was a crowd which looked as if it had an office to return to, rather than those City hordes which always seem set for the duration. Pictures lined the white walls. A thin lean-to of a table ran down the centre of the restaurant.

It was clear from Vaughan's reception that he was known and respected in the establishment. Instead of the proprietor rushing up with a laugh in his eye and a bottle in his hand, full of the latest gossip – the kind of treatment Tom was used to with Ursula – the two of them were waved immediately to a table.

Menus were placed before them at once. They ordered, with Tom by now following Vaughan's lead, two beef salads, and two glasses of house white wine.

Vaughan smoothed his hands on the table and looked away from Tom, through the window into the street. Just then, the door to the restaurant opened, and two bewigged barristers from the Old Bailey entered, deep in talk. Vaughan cleared his throat, still with that level presence which Tom was beginning to dread.

'Let me explain to you a little about myself. I was appointed to the job of News Editor a week or so ago, as you possibly know. I love the job. I have always wanted to be the News Editor of a national paper. Now, I have my chance. I will succeed at it. But I too, like you, am on probation, and I do not see how I can succeed with you as one of my staff.'

The food arrived, and Vaughan began to pick at it as he spoke, with the fastidiousness which Tom imagined Jesuits employed at lunch, temporarily released from their divinity studies.

'I think I could succeed with almost anyone but you.

You think I'm harsh? Let me explain. I started, like you, in the country, working for a newspaper. Originally, I wanted to write. But then I found that I couldn't write. I couldn't string the sentences together, I couldn't put in the quotes, I couldn't manufacture a story out of mid-air... not as the greats can.

'I was taken aside and I was told to quit the business or go into production. I went into production. I learned subbing: page make-up; headlines. And all the rest of the idiot, ball-breaking production side which writers never see.

'In the process, I watched how the writers carried themselves, and I decided that this game is about quality. Some writers are brilliant, but they never make it from the country for one reason or another. Some writers are foisted on us, because somebody takes a fancy to them, or has a lunch, or wants to repay a favour. These people, your sort, are hopeless. They do not care about the business, about the techniques, about the boredom of papers. They are in love with its fiction. They chase the fast buck, and they ruin the front pages with the stories they write and the time they absorb. And all the time they are doing this, as people fetch and carry for their mistakes, another man, out there, striving away, is denied his opportunity. That is one reason why I don't want you in my department. I had a man ready to move in, and now he can't.'

The girl arrived with the wine, as Tom listened hard.

'My other reason for rejecting you is more straightforward. Oh, incidentally, don't assume that I'm in love with the provinces, and nurture some mystical nostalgia for the "good old days" in Weston-Super-Mare. Far from it. I hate the provinces. I would as soon go back there as I would emigrate. But I prefer taking provincial journalists, because they're easier to mould.

'I plan to build up a team of writers who can write good, fast, news stories, because that is where this paper is weak.

The Editor has given me a break. He knows my plans. He doesn't entirely agree with them. But those are my plans. You don't fit into them.

'Coming back to my second reason – you had a story on de Boys. You turned the paper upside down, but no copy resulted from the disruption. I hate that waste. And you never followed the story up. I hate that still more.'

Tom had to agree with Vaughan. He had done no more work on his Wolf de Boys scoop. All his notes now lingered in a drawer in Ursula's flat.

Vaughan stopped, and Tom could see him frowning. A winsome look passed across his face.

'I don't think I'm entirely qualified to judge your de Boys story. I know nothing about the City. It is a gap. Tell me, what is it like in a stockbroker's office? I've never been in one.'

He was leaning forward intently. Tom felt that here, suddenly, was an opportunity to make an impression. He thought very quickly.

'Similar in some ways to a news room. Lots of bustle, people running about, shouting and all that lark. But there's more machinery around. All stockbrokers have banks of telephones; they have TVs with twenty or so channels for the market prices. Normally, too, they have a huge board at one end of the main dealing room with more prices marked up there from minute to minute, because the screen and the tape can get behind. And, of course, they have dealers on the floor with the walkie-talkies.'

He eased up a little, then, seeing that Vaughan wanted more, added, 'The people are very different. They're chasing business, so behind all the elegant Lord Fauntleroy bit, they're pretty hard. A minute away from the phone could mean they miss a big order.'

'And what happens when they get an order? What happens then?'

Tom was beginning to realise that it was at this point that Vaughan's logical mind failed him.

'They execute it. What that means is they call the dealer and tell him to buy or sell whatever shares or stock they've been told to deal in. It's very simple.'

'You mean they actually buy or sell, just like that, in millions?'

Tom piled on the agony, hoping to make such an impression that it might cancel out some of the mistakes of the morning.

'Sometimes they deal on their own account. If the desk salesmen (those are the people who speak to the big investing institutions to try and sell them ideas) think that a stock is going to go up or down, more so than the general market, or that it'll move against the market trend, they'll take out a position, just for an hour or so. And then they get out of it, at a profit if they're clever.'

Vaughan fiddled with his coffee. Plainly he was dismayed by the idea of such manoeuvres. He looked like a man who kept his savings in a building society account, and worried, without knowing too much about it, over inflation. His eyes cleared. They returned to news.

'Thank you for the snapshot. It sounds very dangerous. I prefer to stick to news. But I will tell you something, in return. I advise you to buy three reference books; a reasonably-sized dictionary; a book of quotations; and Fowler's *Modern English Usage*. All three will help, either over spelling, grammar or just to refresh the vocabulary.'

Suddenly, he smiled. It was a shy, boyish smile, almost virginal in its fragility, as it flashed from his eyes, across the tombstone teeth, and round the prow of his nose. It was like glimpsing a different person.

'You see, I don't know anything about writing. But I have observed. Now, I'll tell you a story about a man who was posted to the Middle East, for Reuters.

'When he arrived at his posting, he met a very rich woman with whom he fell madly in love, and his love was returned, as it is in stories. And of course he never filed any copy.

'After a fortnight, Reuters in London grew worried, and sent out a cable which read, "Why no news?" Blissfully happy, the journalist replied, "No news, good news." To this, Reuters answered, "No news, no job." And received the crushing reply: "Up job, stick arsewards."'

Tom laughed. They both laughed. It was like two people waving across a canyon. Vaughan didn't seem the kind of man who changed his mind easily, though, despite the jollity. But Tom couldn't say he'd been badly treated over lunch.

The bill arrived, and Vaughan carefully calculated the total and paid. As they prepared to go, he fingered a 50p piece nervously, which he eventually slid under the coffee cup. 'Working out the tip gives me agonies,' he said.

As they walked back to the office Vaughan added, 'Your probation lasts until the spring. This afternoon, you will meet Jimmy, my number two. You will find Jimmy hard. He is from the Gorbals, and practically illiterate. But he's like a fox with the hounds over news. He's brilliant.'

9

When Tom returned to the news room after lunch, he found that Gloria had constructed beside his desk a three-tier edifice of wire baskets, marked 'In', 'Out' and 'Library'. He was grateful to her for such help, but he also cursed her a little, because it made the job of getting into his desk even harder. His desk was in the corner, and beside the nearside angle closest to the door stood a filing cabinet. With the baskets as well, he had to perform a sort of belly shuffle to reach his chair.

The chair was uncomfortable, too. Instead of the executive chair with arms he had enjoyed on the City desk, he now had a simple chair with a low curved back and a nail sticking up in the right arm.

Stuck in his typewriter, he found a simple message from Gloria: 'Ring Ursula. She called at 1.15 p.m.'

He rang Ursula's number, got through to the switchboard, but was told her line was engaged. He asked the operator whether she could ask Ursula to ring him back. To his surprise, she giggled a little, and then said solemnly, 'I think you'd better call again, Mr Stone. We're not allowed to take messages on the board.' He was about to protest that he had always left messages with the operators in the past, when she suddenly cut him off. He was left with a dead line.

He turned to the in-tray and lifted a sheaf of documents out and on to his desk. There were about seven pieces of paper in all marked for him, but now he noticed a new refinement. As well as the lineage required, a time had also been written into the top right-hand margin.

Looking more closely, Tom noticed other changes. The handwriting was different; he judged that it must be from the number two, Jimmy. And instead of 'Tom Stone', the papers were simply addressed to 'Stone'.

He looked at the times and reckoned he had a quarter of an hour to write each story. He looked at the clock, it was two forty-five.

He looked at the clock again and slowly, with an almost discernible sense of terror, felt complete panic beginning to sweep over him. He looked at the first story he had to write. It concerned the Liberal Party, a manifesto calling for a wide range of political reforms. It meant nothing to him. He felt his mind beginning to blank out. He looked at the sheet of agency tape, with a clear summary of the Liberals' political points. But his mind refused to take them on board, refused to react to the sharp edges of the data and fit them into words.

He looked at the clock again. Five minutes had gone by. He should have written at least half of the first story. Again he looked at the tape. It stared back at him, lifeless. Almost lovingly, he gazed at the sweep second hand on the clock spinning round the dial. There, he thought, was peace, there was tranquillity. What calms there must be in the life of a clock – no Vaughans, no Jimmies, no deadlines, no stories to chase. Just the calm measurement of existence, the relentless, implacable, definition of time.

He felt sweat beginning to form at the tips of his fingers, his stomach starting to contract, and his knees going rubbery. He picked up two sheets of paper, fitted a sheet of carbon between them, wound all three into the typewriter, typed his name in the top left-hand corner, the tag 'Liberal' in the top right-hand corner, and then stared at it. Nothing happened. He didn't know where to start. He could still see

Vaughan standing in front of him and ripping, ever so slowly and deliberately, his first news story of the day into shreds, could still hear his calm voice saying how unwanted he was.

He looked at the clock again. Another five minutes had gone by. It was now almost time for him to hand the story in. In desperation, hoping that the mere act of writing would summon the habits of construction, composition and identification back again, he typed a few words, but then tore them out of the machine in disgust. They were useless, sordid, stupid, trivial, meaningless, insane.

He could feel panic rising through his chest to his throat, and yet a curious dream-like sensation too, as if the whole experience was divorced from reality, and that it just didn't matter any more. Let them sack me, he thought. Let them shout at me, let them say how much they hate me. Why? Why, why, why, why, why? Why me? Why should they pick on me? It's not fair, they never gave me a chance. And he thought of the dislike in Vaughan's eyes over lunch.

He fancied now he could hear the shouting which would undoubtedly hit him in a few seconds' time, and he found he was clenching his fists in readiness. 'Just let them shout at me, the bastards,' he muttered defensively to himself. 'I'll smash them, particularly that illiterate Scotch bastard, just let him come near me.'

He found himself breathing more quickly and he looked at the clock again. Time was up. This was it. Now for it. The big showdown. He would leave the building in disgrace. But he could show them a thing or two. He looked across at Gloria, who was staring calmly out of the window in the empty office, and reflected that it would be a pity not to see her again, but that his next existence would be a happier, less charged and traumatic one than this had been. Where are they, then, what are they waiting for? Come on, let them come, he thought.

He looked again at the copy. It was still meaningless, and he glanced away again at the clock. He thought of the people leading happy, contented lives with no stress, no upsets, no disappointments; in banks, and shops, and insurance companies, and the idea of walking out before they even came to shout at him sprang up in his mind. He toyed with the thought of just putting on his coat, striding out of the door, to be heard of no more.

Something different happened instead. From some mysterious caverns of Tom's mind, from the very depths of his terrified, tortured and demoralised consciousness, now so racked by pain, frustration and disappointment that it even hated itself, a small gush of wind blew; a cooling breeze which fanned the clouds away, gently rocked him, and charmed his wounded brain.

Feeling slowly drifted back to his fingertips, as an unconscious, unknown force began to drive him back to reality. He looked again at the clock, but now it was different. The hand no longer swept the dial, it swept for him. It was meant for him, he knew it; it meant life and money and laughter and drinks and fine clothes and perfume; it was for going on, for bracing, not yielding. It was his time he was wasting.

He looked at the agency tape again. It still meant nothing. But he had a plan. He would copy it straight out, as it stood. They could shout. But it meant he had written, or at least submitted, one story. That gave them less to complain about. There was still hope, there was still life, he could glimpse survival somewhere, even though a long way distant.

He rolled more paper into the typewriter, and felt calmness descending on him. It was rubbish that he was about to write, but he knew it was rubbish. He could live with the idea that he, Tom Stone, the fancied financial journalist, was about to write rubbish. It was something to him, it was a small beginning. It was creative even if it was meagre, a small reflection of what he could achieve. But the difference now was that he could wait for the achievement to come.

He would take his time, and let something else, the mysterious forces which now pushed him back from the brink and into the instinctive configurations of a journalist, fashion him as they would.

The door crashed open. A small slight figure, with tousled hair streaked with grey and blue piercing eyes, rushed into the room. Behind him a huge man with black hair and a black, bushy, moustache entered quietly.

The small man raced over to Tom's desk. But Tom, with the spirit of survival beginning to burn within him, slid the piece of agency tape off his desk and down to the floor through the crack between his desk and the wall. The man reached over to Tom and plucked the paper from his typewriter, tearing it in his haste.

'Is this all you've done, you little fucker?' he shrieked at Tom. Tom winced, whereas two moments before, he would have collapsed sobbing on the ground.

'You little bastard! Is this what they've given me as a belt man? Christ, *I* wouldn't have given you a chance, you little bastard. I'd have fired you on the spot and got a real journalist instead.'

Tom's brain was beginning to move again.

'The ribbon on my typewriter broke. That's why it's taken so long, Jimmy.'

'Don't you Jimmy me, my little man, don't you call me anything yet. I pay your wages, and you wait until I say you can speak to me with a civil tongue. Gloria,' he screamed, turning to the secretary, 'did this bastard's ribbon break?'

Gloria looked at Tom, and then she looked at Jimmy. There was a pause. Tom held his breath, ready now with another lie, if she told the truth.

'I've been in the loo for the last half hour,' she said

calmly, so calmly in fact that Tom himself began to believe her.

Jimmy began to read the story, tapping his foot as he did, and swaying slightly from side to side. He let out a long whistle as he reached the end of the first page, all that Tom had written.

'So what d'you add now, little man?' he asked.

'Not sure yet, Jimmy,' answered Tom.

Jimmy bent down and thrust his face close to Tom, so close that he could see the puckers within the folds of the skin that lay beneath the jutting cheekbones. The eyes burned into him with a kind of manic hatred.

'I've told you once and I'll tell you just once more. Don't you "Jimmy" me or I'll skin you alive, so help me, you little bastard.'

He withdrew his face, and as he did so Tom caught sight of Gloria, whose face was suffused with suppressed laughter, so much so that her eyes were rolling within their sockets. Tom looked away, and by chance glanced over Jimmy's head, where he encountered the face of the black-moustachioed individual who had entered so silently in Jimmy's wake.

He had sucked in his cheeks too, and was mouthing obscenities behind Jimmy's back, dancing from foot to foot and waving his hands.

Tom was so surprised at this demonstration of spontaneous wit that he grimaced. Jimmy whirled round, but the man with the moustache was quicker. By the time Jimmy had turned, his face had resumed its normal bland shape.

'I'm watching you too, Sidney,' snarled Jimmy. Then he turned to Tom again. 'Get on with the story, Stone, or so help me, I'll crucify you,' he shouted, striding from the room.

'You must be Tom,' said Sidney, walking up to him and holding out his hand. Before Tom could reply, Sidney took off again.

'Yes Jimmy, no Jimmy,' he shouted, whirling on one foot. 'God, how I hate that streak of Gorbals piss. Yes sir, no sir, three bags full sir – well possibly four, but certainly not less than two.'

He bounded over to Gloria, whose eyes lit up as he approached. Her face split in a huge smile. He knelt before her, his arms extended wide in a gesture of beseeching adoration.

'Oh, Lady Gloria! Madonna of the news room – answer me this question. Is it better to be persecuted by a thousand aunts and uncles, or to be hounded by that lump of Scottish excrement? What indulgences do I gain for suffering the greater persecution?'

Gloria said nothing, but leaned over and patted him on the head. Then, glancing over to Tom, who was staring pop-eyed at the performance, she said: 'Sidney comes from East London. Hackney, I believe. He has tried to improve himself, so he says. But every time he writes a big story, all his relatives – of which he has thousands scattered throughout London – ring up to discuss the story, and to congratulate him at great length. He has a hard time, poor lamb.'

'It's true!' shouted Sidney, leaping to his feet. 'But all is not lost. The unconquerable will and spirit of revenge, immortal hate and what not else, is not to be overthrown – Milton, you know; I was weaned on it. Had a literary father,' he added in a normal voice, coming over to Tom.

'You're the new boy, are you? Looks as if you're in for a rough time. But we can soon test how tough, can't we Gloria my sweetest child,' he laughed, whirling round kissing her suddenly on the forehead. '*Un moment!*' And he paused for thought.

'Call copy,' he said to Tom. Tom did so obediently. Nothing happened. Sidney then shouted the same. Mick appeared instantly. Sidney motioned him away.

'Mick has heard that you are a bad thing, as we call it in the trade. He will be laggard. You must fend for yourself, which means, basically, taking your copy over to the news room yourself. Otherwise it'll get lost, or mislaid, or finish up at the bottom of the lift-shaft, or worse. Be warned.'

Tom explained that Mick had been attentive that morning, but Sidney dismissed his objections. 'It is the Sidney test of status. It never fails,' he said grandly. 'This morning he had not heard the news. Now he has.'

Tom returned to his desk and completed copying out the story. He walked out of the office, hearing as he did so Sidney whirr once again up to Gloria shouting 'What's the gossip, what's the gossip? I can't live without the tittle-tattle of the Street,' and her laughter. Suddenly, he felt better.

He walked on to the editorial floor, by now humming with activity as the subs arrived for the early shift, and plonked his copy down on the newsdesk in front of Jimmy, who fortunately was preoccupied on the phone. Vaughan nodded at him.

He returned to his desk. He found Sidney bent over his in-tray. Sidney straightened up as he returned.

'You are in a lot of trouble, my son,' said Sidney. 'I've never seen date-stamping like this before. Either it's new, or you've committed a special crime, the kind for which you need a special dispensation from the Vatican for forgiveness.'

Tom explained his situation, and Sidney listened. When Tom had finished, he reached down into the tray without a word, plucked out four of the pieces of paper which had to be turned into stories, and carried them over to his own desk.

'Let's rattle a few of these off, if only to frustrate that Scottish pig,' he remarked. Tom blushed, and felt tears welling up in his eyes. Sidney brushed aside his thanks.

'Pure self-interest,' he said. 'If we give that Gorbals moron an iota of a chance he'll be at all our throats. A solid front to give you a breather and we'll keep him where he belongs – at our knees. You see, I don't like the race myself. Been savaged too many times by them in the past. But to work.'

His fingers flew over the keys, as his eyes moved swiftly from the paper beside the typewriter to the platen and back again, translating the one-dimensional news data into a two-dimensional news story. After about a quarter of an hour he stopped, handed three stories to Tom and said, 'There. You're up to date in time terms. Hand them in, and the best of luck. I must leave you now. I've got my own to write.'

Tom thanked him, picked up the folios, and trudged over to the newsdesk. He handed them in, and saw Vaughan's eyebrows raise a flicker.

When he returned to his desk, another sheaf of documents lay waiting for him. He picked up the first one, tabbed two hundred and fifty words – it was four-fifteen – and had a bright idea. If I call down the file, he thought, I can check this time last year, and see what crap he wrote on the subject, then copy from that.

He called up the library and instructed them to bring down the file on Ink.

Recalling Vaughan's advice, he then shouted over to Gloria and asked her to order for him the books of reference which Vaughan had recommended – a dictionary, the book of quotations, and *Modern English Usage*. This time, Gloria's eyebrows shot up. Tom decided he was involved in a very complex situation indeed.

Just as the file was being placed on his desk, the door opened again, and another stranger entered the office. Tom realised at once that it was Damian. Tall, lean, slender, with a deep tan, he paced across the room to Tom's desk, and shook him by the hand whilst introducing himself with a smile. He had a deep, rich voice, and graceful manners. He said how glad he was to see Tom in the office, and that he hoped they'd get along well; he normally did the heavy industrial stuff, but occasionally strayed on to the parliamentary beat; if he could be of any help, he'd be only too pleased to give his assistance; he hoped that Tom would enjoy his new job.

But Tom wondered if he really cared about what he said. There was something not so much theatrical but weary in his manner, as if he'd said the same thing many, many, times before, in just the same graciously aloof way. Plainly Damian was well connected, trained to command, rich, socially skilful, poised and kind. But he was also possibly unable to drop that poise and grapple with the painful side of life. Had it all come too easily, the effortless path to greatness which stems from the smooth conformity to the principle of privilege, leading from prep school, through public school, on to Oxford, with the same boon companions from school to school, and then the tip-top velvet escalator with the other top chaps to the acme of British society? He'd let his hand linger in Tom's as a kind of keepsake of feudality, a restitution of allegiance, a demonstration of superiority.

Damian launched into an anecdote about his experiences on provincial papers, just after leaving Oxford.

'I remember,' he said, glancing towards the windows, 'we had a chief sub there of the most almighty power. Once a chum of mine, straight down from Oxford, failed to indent a paragraph just the fraction of an em required. D'you know, that sub – I can't remember his name, it was Bloggs or something – he stopped the whole edition to correct that mistake. Sacked my chum as well. I could never forgive him for that.'

Jimmy entered at that moment. His eyes had that bright light of the starving hound scenting prey, as he advanced into the room shouting 'Where's that Sidney? I'd recognise his style anywhere. You'll swing for this, Stone.'

Then he caught sight of Damian. His features softened. His eyes took on that quiet, pleased subservience which hits people who love rank, and he whispered – 'Afternoon, Damian. Nice to see you. Got anything for us today? We're a mite short on the front page so far.'

Damian smiled at him with his eyes, like a man who realises that somewhere lurks at least one man, albeit a peasant, who has the nous to doff his cap to the old order. They went off together to Damian's desk, deep in talk, Jimmy nodding his head frequently in agreement.

Tom looked at the Ink file and felt saved yet again. There just a year ago, was an identical story on the rate of consumption of printers' ink. He compared the present figures with the historical ones and knocked out the story quickly. Something nagged at his mind, despite his feeling of well-being at completing yet another story.

But he was beginning to feel tired. It had been a hard day. His fingers ached from typing.

The phone rang. It was Ursula. 'Darling,' she said, 'Tonight, seven thirty at The Grange. You will be there, won't you? It's such a big night, with my parents arriving. Can you make it?'

He said he thought so. She asked him whether he'd written any good stories. He answered thousands. She told him to tell all later, and then added, almost as an afterthought, that he'd have to behave himself in the first part of the evening at least, because one of her clients was joining them very briefly for a drink. She rang off.

He looked up and found Vaughan standing at his elbow. 'In at eleven sharp,' he said, then added that he wanted Tom to cover a CBI lunch. 'Scrub everything from your diary from now on, in fact,' he said. Vaughan then called out to Damian to follow him to the newsdesk.

A look of pain spread across Damian's face as he followed Vaughan out.

Then Tom's phone rang again. It was a voice he had heard long ago and had almost but not quite, forgotten.

'Remember de Boys. There's something big in the post for you about him tomorrow. Look out for it.'

The line went dead.

10

Tom sat at the bar of a pub halfway to Covent Garden, along Fleet Street, alone, and thought about the day. He knew that the dinner with Ursula, her parents and their friends would be a heavy affair. But he wanted to reflect a little on the day's events, before plunging into those of the night.

His hand grasped a pint of Guinness, but he felt his body sag against the bar in fatigue. He knew he was lucky to be still alive. Memories of that incandescent panic spreading through his body and numbing all in its path were still fresh in his mind. How many stories had he written? He didn't know; couldn't remember, didn't want to know; no longer cared. He felt a warm heat of oblivion seeping mercifully through his limbs, choking off the precise recall.

Around him roared and chatted and gossiped and caroused a crowd of lawyers, fresh from the Middle Temple. But he paid no attention to them. He was, even then, nearly out.

Tom stared at himself in the mirror and recoiled at the pale, drawn face, with staring, frightened eyes which confronted him. Christ, what has that bastard Vaughan done to me? he thought. Is he tough, though, is he tough! He whistled softly to himself, remembering again the lunch. He mused about Vaughan, wondering where he came from, where he'd acquired that inflexibility and steely fixity of purpose. He thought about him with a mixture of fear, wonderment, resentment and awe that the utterly determined and ruthless often stimulate.

I think he could do me in, if he wanted to. Or even if he didn't want to, and I just interfered with his plans, thought Tom. Then he recalled that he had done just that, and a shiver ran down his spine. *Is he, then, going to break me and leave me for dead?*

Tom did not complete the thought. He found the barman staring at him. 'You all right, son?' he asked. 'You keep mumbling to yourself. You look as if you've had a very hard day, you do. Now do you want that Guinness glass of yours refilled?'

Tom drank into the second pint and felt that slight wooziness which a combination of great fatigue and a small intake of alcohol stimulate. He looked at his hands. They lay pink and inert on the bar, ready to do his bidding. It seemed inconceivable that a few hours previously they might have suddenly gone out of control, along with his mind, his legs, his eyes, his torso and the rest of him. That was how close he'd come to breaking down completely. He marvelled again at how near he'd been to the flames, and how the odds had broken lucky for him on the edge of the margin.

At the back of his mind, he kept recalling examples of other narrow escapes, like Ulysses, or secret agents left alone deep in enemy territory, and he realised that the game during the next few months was going to be very hard. Nor did he know, or even dare speculate, whether he could survive, or even wanted to.

They were dining at The Grange, because whenever Ursula ate in town, they ate at The Grange. According to her, it was the best restaurant in Covent Garden. She also liked Covent Garden.

Tom found the party waiting for him in the short, tiled, spot-lit passage which leads from the entrance into the main bay of the restaurant, with its open middle space and small alcoves, all discreetly lit.

Ursula looked stunning. Her hair, piled up above her head, shone in the arc lights. She wore a black, backless dress with a plunging front, which partly revealed the soft downy contours of her breasts. Around her neck was a gold chain. She wore black stockings and extravagantly high heels which showed off her long slender legs. There was energy, rage, poise and desire in her eyes, as she swung to her feet at Tom's entry.

She introduced Gunther, her client, who had been deep in conversation with her. Gunther was thickset, tanned, mid-European, with that expensive, well-manicured look of the high German bourgeoisie. He bowed to Tom.

'I am sorry to interfere with your dinner party,' he said. 'But I have had some important business with Miss Parker relating to my company's imminent opening up in the UK, which unfortunately could not wait until tomorrow. I shall not detain you long. Can I order you a drink?'

As he signalled imperiously to the waiter, Tom caught the flash of a heavy gold identity bracelet on his wrist, and an excited, almost girlish, look on Ursula's face.

Ursula turned from Gunther to introduce Tom to her parents, Mr and Mrs Parker, and suggested they all wait for a second before going over to the table. Tom sat down beside Theo and Charlotte.

Theo, US journalist and playboy, with whom Tom enjoyed relatively cordial relations, was wearing a white polo-neck sweater and a blue tartan jacket, a hopeless combination for anyone except an American that evening. He was heavy and bald, with a thick moustache and long, greying sideburns. He looked well trained, as if he knew his weight to the nearest pound, and Tom knew that he worked out twice a week in the gym. But there were the beginnings of a paunchy look, after too much Scotch, pot, travelling and deliberate disorientation. He had that amused, offhand, deprecatingly knowing manner which Americans adopt far from home, when few people are around to check their extravagances. He created a heavy physical, almost sterile impression, but backed by sufficient wit from a tuned, flip mind to buck the tortuous complexities of London – and for a time, succeed.

Charlotte was different. Dressed in skin-tight jeans and long gleaming boots, an open silk shirt she nevertheless was built to last. She had a tough, meaty look, and definite views.

Charlotte taught in a school for deprived kids in North London. She had a way of taking over a conversation and imposing her personality on it, which Tom hated. He called her the Rosa Klebb of education. But Ursula protested that Tom didn't look beneath the surface.

They all rose to take up the table, and Tom muttered spitefully to Charlotte, 'Still tending the delinquents, eh Charlotte?'

Her head came up sharply, as if she'd been slugged by a bottle, but she reacted fast. 'Still living, I see, off your crutch,' she sneered, yet another reference to Tom's continued rent-free habitation at Ursula's.

As they all sat down at the table, which was over to the left of the main bay, half in a musky shadow, half in light from the lamps on the table, Tom thought how beautiful they all looked.

Ursula, in black, still deep in conversation with Gunther, on his right; Ursula's father on his left, next to Theo, with Charlotte sitting opposite. Then directly in front of Tom sat Mrs Parker. She was dressed in some kind of rustic Lincoln green outfit. A society photographer, thought Tom, would snap them all as the perfect London party out for the evening.

Charlotte was talking to Theo as they ordered, asking him about his TV appearance. Mrs Parker showed immediate interest.

'Yes,' Theo said, 'it was my first appearance on British TV. I enjoyed it.'

'What were you on the box for?' queried Mrs Parker immediately.

'The Presidential elections. Over here, you get some crazy ideas about the US. Every now and then, they need straightening out.'

Mrs Parker ignored the jest, and asked how difficult it was to get on TV. It was clear where the question was leading. She wanted her Ursula to do well, and in her book that meant getting on to the box, and making the neighbours squirm.

Theo, as if forewarned, made a non-committal remark, and then the hors d'oeuvres arrived to break up the sequence.

Tom glanced to his right, watching Ursula's mass of hair nodding as Gunther, with great precision, went through a series of points. He then smiled, flashing white teeth at her, shook her hand and stood up. The talk stopped immediately. Ursula stared rapt at him.

'I am sorry to have intruded on your gathering, but, as I explained, it was necessary if the business was to be completed,' he said. 'It shows how keen we are to do business, too, with your country,' he concluded rather lamely. He then shook hands solemnly with everyone, including Tom, on whom he bestowed a special flash of the teeth and glint in the eye. Tom saw Mrs Parker watching Ursula closely, as if measuring her reactions to the situation.

It returned to him with a shock, as Gunther departed. Christ, maybe *I* don't even have a job. It's true. I'm on probation; I've got six months to prove myself. What the hell am I doing here, then? I should be working away or something, learning something...

Mrs Parker leaned across the table to Ursula and took

her hand with that special familiarity, a mixture of complicity and intimacy, which mothers have with their daughters. Ursula smiled back and then, as if dismissing her thoughts, addressed the table with her eyes.

Mr Parker was by now discussing Wall Street with Theo. It was the usual mealy-mouthed provincial claptrap about the Stock Exchange. He had a few thousands to invest; equities in London didn't look too promising, what about the US?

Theo gave a series of smooth replies, losing Mr Parker gradually in a stream of complex jargon. Terms like reverse yield gaps; liquidity traps; random walks; concept stocks; high multiple performers, and smokestack America syndrome – all darted in and out of his sentences, with Mr Parker tapping his finger quietly on the table.

Charlotte was questioning Ursula about Gunther. Ursula was explaining that Gunther's account was a breakthrough for her in the firm. It was the first time she'd been allowed to handle such an important account entirely on her own, right from the start. Her boss had promised that if she made a success of that one, other larger accounts would be steered her way.

Turning away slightly from her excitement, Tom found himself talking to Mr Parker, who immediately told him a dirty joke. Tom laughed automatically and then wondered if he'd been fooled again. Old Parker's a dentist, he reminded himself. So he's probably only telling the joke to get a look at my teeth...

Tom found himself thinking about Vaughan, and Gloria, and the new colleagues he'd met that afternoon. There was a certain integrity about what they were doing, even if they were so brutal about it. But *this* – what did it mean? Had Charlotte slept with Theo? Had Charlotte slept with Ursula? Would Ursula sleep with Gunther? Who would sleep with whom? He didn't know. He doubted if any of them could remember many details about any of their fornications. But he knew it was going to crop up in the conversation during the evening.

Theo was taking the strain of the conversation now, as they reached the end of the second course. The plates strewn with the remains of the meat, and the odd potato still uneaten, gave a dishevelled look to the table.

Tom half listened to Theo. He'd heard it before and found it witty enough to lend half an ear again. Theo, who genuinely liked London, had discovered Latin, so that a fair chunk of his conversation was now sprinkled with references to the Caesars, Virgil and Horace. But he could only read the literature in translation. His joy, therefore, had been considerable when he discovered that some bright Californian student had fed Virgil through a computer, with startling results.

'It's quite remarkable what he found,' Theo explained. 'Virgil is organised into numerical sequences, like a giant crossword puzzle. I guess he must have belonged to some ancient Pythagorean cult – you know Pythagoras was the mathematician of the ancient world, but he also founded this cult, which didn't believe in eating meat…'

He carried on, but it was clear that Mrs Parker was only paying a modicum of attention too. Tom could imagine what was going through her mind. 'Here is my Ursula, living with this awful hobo journalist when she could have someone like Gunther, just for the asking! But what can you do? You have to give them have their freedom, and just hope for the best if you've brought them up properly, sooner or later they'll realise what's right for them… And doesn't she look pretty this evening. I remember when she was just a little girl going to school. She was such a tomboy, but now…'

Tom studied her across the table. The nose was straight and firm, like the mouth, and the brow was broad. A woman used to successful command. Tom remembered one of Theo's quips – 'I've seen them like that in the old Indian country. They turned their families into businesses' – and looked sideways at Ursula. She looked much the same, with the same firm nose. There was more softness round the mouth, and her eyes had something of her father's dreamy look, but that, no doubt, would fade with the years.

It was uncanny, too, how both mother and daughter had the same way of twiddling a glass, turning it round and round by the stem with the thumb and forefinger.

So far, thought Tom, the talk has all moved away from the questions she wants to ask. But sooner or later she'll get there, either brutally or by stealth. It's like a Baskerville hound prowling round the stockade, snuffling, sniffing, racing from scent to scent, always looking for the opening.

She found the opening through Theo, over the coffee. Dissatisfied with the reception to his Virgil researches, Theo interrupted the general chat about the cost of living and mortgage rates, to return to the plight of the writer without a patron, in modern days. Some, like Bob Dylan, struck it rich. Others languished.

Mrs Parker leapt on to the subject, like a dog finding a bone.

'Tom's a writer, aren't you?' she exclaimed, flashing her eyes across the table and through the lamplight at Tom.

'That's right,' he said, realising that for the second time that day an assault on his humble, innocent pretensions was in progress.

'It's the *Standard*, isn't it?' she asked archly, as if some secret existed between them. Then she started to probe.

'Tell me, Tom,' she said this with the practised grace of the killer interrogator who holds all the cards, 'just how do you write? I mean, without wishing to sound rude, the *Standard* is not a very respectable paper. But, well, with the best will in the world, I wouldn't have thought, how shall I say, they would normally look beyond Oxbridge for their material?'

'It's mainly formula writing. Pure technique,' replied Tom dully, realising that after the events of the day, he wasn't qualified to make any assertions at all. Then he lapsed into Fleet Street jargon. 'Some of the Oxbridge boys find it very hard to adjust to the Street...'

It was a mistake. She wasn't interested in such fine points. Interrupting him curtly, she swept on, with a light smile.

'No, you're misunderstanding us. We are not newspaper people. We don't know anything about your world, except what we see at the flicks. And that paints a very brutal picture of very nasty people, always drunk, smoking too much, no home life, divorces, and everything else. All that, I'm prepared to accept. But the *writing* part I find very mysterious. Who tells you what to write? How do you decide what to write? Can you give us a typical day in your life?'

Tom started off wondering whether to give her details of his great scoop and the agony that had caused, or a sneak preview of what tomorrow might bring, with Jimmy on the rampage.

'We get in, and we slope around, looking for stories, and then...'

'That's just what I mean. What is a story? How can you tell what is a story and what isn't?'

'That's the sixty-four thousand dollar question, Mrs Parker. That's what news editors get paid twenty thousand pounds plus a year to do.

'I'll tell you a funny story about that, and money,' he added despairingly, trying to change the subject. 'There was a terrific furore years ago, when the *Sun* started up, so they say, because they had to hire a caption writer for the bird on page three...'

Tom could see Mrs Parker leaning away from the filth he was about to spread across the table, glancing protectively at her daughter, and even slightly reproachfully.

'...The only man they could find who was remotely good enough was the man on the *Mirror*, who said he wouldn't budge for less than £15,000, which at the time was more than the *Sun*'s Editor was getting. In the end, they had to pay him the money, because they knew it was one of the surest ways of selling the paper.'

'You mean those nasty little sayings beside those disgusting photographs? That's appalling,' said Mrs Parker. Then she went on to say that she still didn't understand what a scoop was; how journalists did their research; how they worked; what the qualifications for the job were; what the average salary was; how it compared with the outside world; what the prospects were. In short, what it all meant.

'It's a job, though, isn't it?' answered Tom, defensively, and sought refuge in another story. He could feel Ursula's eye on him, as if she realised by his defence of the profession that something had happened. Tom went on with his story.

'Talking about the social problems in newspapers, it's true that you do get strange situations. I remember working for two people in one office. One – the boss – was a man who'd come from the bottom; actually from King's Cross. His number two had been educated at Harrow, so they made a perfect duo. I was a pretty lowly member of staff. I was summoned once to their office – I used to call it the "smoke-filled room" – and they both started shouting at me simultaneously. And I found myself saying, "Ah! Attacked at both ends of the social spectrum." The reaction was terrible. It took me three weeks after that of solid grovelling to get my expenses signed.'

The story produced its usual explosive reaction among

the assembled guests, but by now Ursula was roused too. She knew that Tom only told that story under extreme pressure.

'What happened? I thought today went fine. That's the impression you gave on the phone,' she said suspiciously, and excusing herself for her neglect of him throughout the evening. Tom could feel the nausea building up inside him and decided to terminate the suspense.

'It went very well, except that I don't think I've got a job after the spring. They're all very tough, with no love lost for me.'

He didn't feel any better for the disclosures, just more tired at the reproaches, which started immediately.

Mrs Parker shot a triumphant glance at her husband, who looked sad. Theo was bewildered, Charlotte delighted, and Ursula furious. Tom realised he had lost face in the party, eroded his position with Ursula, and given Mrs Parker enough material for the bridge table tittle-tattle to last her a couple of winters, as well as justifying all her scepticism about Tom.

The dinner started to break up. Theo shuffled off, saying he had some work to finish. Charlotte stayed to hear more. Mrs Parker wanted to hear more, too, but her husband insisted it was time to go; more explanations would follow later. As he got up, he turned to Tom apologetically and whispered, 'Any time you want some crowns done, old boy just come to me. I can do them on the NHS for you, but with the top treatment, you understand. Just costs a little more between dentist and patient.' And then, as if recalling, Tom's changed status, 'It has to be cash, of course. The Revenue, you know.'

Tom was left with Ursula and Charlotte, and the empty coffee cups. A small stain was spreading across the table-cloth on his left. Charlotte was looking at Ursula, who was smoking a cigarette nervously. The hair was still piled high on her head, and the bare arms and back still gleamed in the lamplight. But she had returned to her normal pattern of behaviour.

'You bastard,' she said, staring at the coffee cup. 'What did you have to say that for, and ruin the evening and upset my parents as well. God, you've got no bloody tact at all, have you? You're not fit to be in society at all, you're so fucking selfish. And you're such a loser, too.'

She stubbed the cigarette out savagely, leaving it to fume slightly in the saucer.

11

Ursula gave Tom a hard time that night.

'Now that you've upset her, she won't leave me alone. She'll keep popping round, just to see that I'm all right, and I'll have about as much freedom as I did when I lived at home,' she shouted when they got back to Ursula's flat. 'God, she can be a pest when she tries. But then so can you. Fancy coming out with all that claptrap about probation tonight of all nights, with my parents there, and Gunther arranging his deal.'

'That's another thing I want to talk about,' said Tom rebukingly, but received a crushing reply. 'Well, if you want to, I don't, and you can jolly well sod off.'

She tossed a great mane of blonde hair in his face, turned on her side, and was silent.

*

When Tom reached the office next morning, he found Gloria sitting tranquilly at her desk looking slightly glazed. She wished him good morning, with a kind of shudder.

'I know it's wrong to say this, and I realise that we are a family newspaper, read by millions and all that, but really some of Sidney's relatives give me the pip.'

Sidney had written the splash story on the front page that day. His aunts and uncles and been phoning in their congratulations.

'They always say the same thing, in this deep nasal

Cockney whine, "I'm terribly sorry to bother you, but could you just tell Sidney we liked his story, and we think he's doing awfully well, and isn't it about time he came round to see us." Then, if they're male, they try to chat me up, and say what a nice girl I sound. The women just sound like cows. Ugh!'

Tom walked over to his desk. A long flat envelope had been stuffed into his typewriter, clearly addressed to him and marked 'Personal, Private and Confidential'. He took it out of the typewriter and pushed it into his pocket. Later, he thought, when I've had a bit more time in the office.

Gloria came over to him, carrying three large volumes. 'These are the books you ordered,' she said, 'and much good may they do you. Here's the receipt, if you want to claim them on your expenses. I would if I were you. Vaughan doesn't give that kind of tip and expect you to pay for it. He sees it as part of the team effort.'

She handed over the slip and asked him if he'd found his letter, adding that one note the day after joining was promising.

'I can't stand those people who sign up on hundreds of mailing lists, so they can get a huge post bag and impress the office. When you have to open all the garbage, you soon lose any respect you had for someone.'

Tom sensed some kind of warning in what she said and nodded. She continued:

'I've had Vaughan on the phone for you. He says to be sure to remind you about the CBI lunch, which I now have done. I think you're going to have a better day today. Jimmy's cried off with toothache, which he says he gets quite frequently. I don't believe him. I think the only thing the Scots really suffer from, apart from pride and hypochondria, is a raging hangover at Hogmanay. D'you know, he just takes a week off for Hogmanay and disappears into some kind of Scotch mist. I think he must be drunk the whole time – either that, or beating people up.'

Tom detected some sympathy behind these comments, and gazed with gratitude at this slender poised apparition beside him.

He drew further hope from the fact his in-tray contained only two stories to process, and it was already eleven-fifteen. Since he had to leave for the lunch at about twelve forty-five, it was possibly he might have an easy morning. Neither of the two pieces of tape were time-stamped. Was this an encouraging sign?

Sidney came in and made straight for Tom's desk. Brushing aside Gloria's complaints about the number of his relatives she'd been forced to fob off on his behalf, he addressed himself directly to Tom.

The gist of his conversation was that, first, he had no desire to teach Tom to suck eggs; presumably his grand-mother had taught him to do that years ago. Nor did he want it to be seen, or even to appear, that he was going out of his way to help him. It was a competitive business, they all had to live, and someone had to draw the short straw. If it was Tom, well, too bad.

But, he went on, here were a few words of advice. He regretted giving them, because they might rebound to his own detriment, but he had to give them. He couldn't bear to see anyone mauled by that swine from the sewers of Caledonia.

Gloria interrupted at this point to say that Jimmy had toothache and wouldn't be in that day, whereupon Sidney burst into great peals of laughter.

'Pray God it's an abscess,' he shouted, 'and they have to cut his head off.'

He then told Tom how he should approach his new job. 'You are the feed man,' he said. 'They want edition stories from you, fillers. They don't expect front page news, or scoops, or anything fancy or dramatic, just a stream of short pieces, which they can slot into the paper anywhere.

'You must provide them with what they want, in one of three ways. Look at the feedstock they give you in the shape of those bits of paper. Either that is the story, or there's another angle. If there's no other angle, just write the story straight, giving it a little bit of embellishment, but don't spend time on it.

'But if you can see something more, call for the file, write the other crap while you're waiting, and then make one phone call – well, never more than two – to check the angle. If the angle works, write it. If it doesn't, go back to the original story. The trick, and the skill, lies in recognising what is a story and what isn't, so that you don't waste your time. Presumably that's what you're here for. Your job may be an inglorious one so far as the outside world is concerned, but in trade terms, it's one of the most crucial ones on a paper. Once you've acquired the skill, you'll never lose it. So it's worth persevering.'

Tom thanked him, but as he did so, it was clear that the interview was over. Sidney flung his arms round Gloria, who smiled her cheeky, voluptuous smile, and began waltzing round the room singing, 'Who's got an abscess, who's got an abscess,' like a soccer hooligan.

Suddenly, he returned. 'How many stories did you get in yesterday anyway?' Tom said he hadn't looked. Sidney looked stern.

'Look, this is no joke, you know. If you haven't looked, you don't know what you've got wrong. So you're vulnerable to the big attack from the desk when you first get in, the early cruel dawn of the news writer, when he confronts his news editor, with them both rubbing sleep, snot and drink from their eyes. Naturally news editors, being bastards, will want to maim quickly at the first strike. That is why they become news editors. Did you read the other papers?'

Tom said he hadn't.

'That means you don't know what beats the opposition got on us, which makes you twice as vulnerable.' He shook his head, sadly. 'What lambs they send us here to the slaughter. *Agnus Dei, qui tollis peccata mundi, dona nobis pacem,*' he intoned, adding that his prayer was for Tom's soul, and that he hoped he would survive the holocaust.

Gloria chipped in suddenly about Pedro. 'He's a friend of yours, isn't he?'

Tom agreed, although by this time he was doubtful whether he could distinguish friend from foe.

'Well, you'd better make shakes, because Vaughan was awfully impressed by his story yesterday. He wanted to put it on the front page. The only reason he didn't was that the US story was so big. But he ran it in full inside. So Pedro looks as if he's going to do rather well, which leaves you with the short straw still. He's going to be in this afternoon. Vaughan's sent him down to the House this morning to interview some MP.'

Tom looked at the two stories in his in-tray, decided that neither had much to offer, and copied them out more or less from the handouts. But then he had a stroke of luck.

He had been taught how to read the *Financial Times* by an old-timer years ago. 'If you are looking for stories always read the appointments page,' his mate had advised. 'You'd be amazed how many little nuggets are tucked away there.'

Tom, more by chance than anything else, now turned to the page, and his eyes lit upon what looked like an interesting new job. Henry Foster from one of the City's leading merchant banks was joining the BBC board of governors.

Tom called for the file, asking in the process for the one on Wolf de Boys. I'll open the letter on the way to the CBI, he promised himself. I have to concentrate on the job in hand. No straying.

Down came the BBC file. No other paper had covered

that appointment. Tom called the BBC; was given an interesting line about the Corporation's financial difficulties; checked the angle with Henry Foster's bank, and wrote a neat six paragraph story.

Tom trudged over to the newsdesk, popped the stories in Vaughan's tray and wandered back to his desk. The phone rang just as he was sitting down. It was Vaughan. 'Nice story on Foster,' he said crisply. 'I like that mix of news and figures. We can always use them. Have a good time at the CBI.'

Just as Tom was preparing to depart, the door opened again and a stranger entered. He had a grizzled grey beard; a stick; and a limp. And he was clearly in a ferocious mood. Even Tom, who was by now adjusting to the caprices and vagaries of the office, could guess that he was a man who was genuinely and unrepentantly bad tempered that morning.

He negotiated the swinging door with difficulty and, limping a little, arrived at Gloria's desk.

'Are there any spare desks in this office?' he barked. 'I've been turned out of my own office by the decorators, and I have nowhere to go.'

Tom noted that he spoke as if composing sentences for a feature, with every phrase clearly enunciated and balanced within the sentence. He concluded this man must be very important, and busied himself with extracting various parts of the de Boys file, to read in the taxi.

Gloria, a little hesitantly, as if she too were overawed by this stranger, answered that he could have Pedro's desk until the afternoon, whereupon the man snorted, then thanked her with a smile and left the office, to return a few seconds later with a sheaf of papers, which he scattered across his desk.

'I expect I'll be spending the odd day from time to time here as the painters come and go in my office,' he said. 'I ought to introduce myself,' he continued, turning to Tom. 'I'm Black, senior leader writer.'

Tom shook him by the hand, blinking a little at the enormity of his contact with such a grandee of the paper. To see a leader writer with a waistcoat button undone was an event; to work cheek by jowl with one, even if he did seem very ill-tempered, was something to dine out on.

Tom left the office with Black telephoning the Prime Minister to confirm their lunch together and hailed a taxi. He climbed in, told the driver to head for Victoria, and then feeling in his pocket, drew out the envelope.

He slit it open with his thumb and pulled out the single sheet of photostatted paper inside. He stared at it. It looked like dynamite.

It was the copy of a contract note from stockbrokers Brasenose & Co., which showed that their client had just sold 50,000 shares at 300p a share, netting after commission and stamp duty £147,998.50p. The company in which the shares had been sold was Otter Securities, and the seller was Wolf de Boys, Chairman, Managing Director, founder and guiding spirit of the whole operation.

'He's selling his own shares. Things must be bad. And I must be right – he must be going up the pictures. What a hell of a story,' breathed Tom to himself, as alarm bells clanged through his head. His mind leaped back to the moment when he'd tried to break the story of de Boys' impending doom.

Jesus, he thought, it's all starting up again. But who is sending me the notes, and giving me all the dope on de Boys? It must be someone terribly in the know, otherwise how could he get hold of a contract note like this, and photostat it? That kind of thing is strictly confidential.

He opened the file on de Boys. It had an immediate warning mark from one of the subs on the inside cover, which read: 'De Boys is an Old Etonian (underlined four times) and not, repeat not, an Old Harrovian. He is sensitive about this and complains.'

As if to ram the message home, one helpful soul had pasted next to the message a copy of the de Boys family tree.

> Lineage – Galfridus, Lord of de Boys, in the time of William I, male and had issue –
>
> Ranulf de Boys. Gave the church of Delmar, Notts, to Lexton Priory, Notts, around 1100, and married Matilda Malesendre and had issue –
>
> Ralf Barrie de Boys, perhaps identical with Ralf Barre de Boys, mentioned, around 1130, and had issue –
>
> Richard Barri, confirmed his grandfather's gift to Lexton, around 1154, and married Beatrix – and had issue –
> 1. Ralf of whom presently.
> 2. John of Torleston.
> 3. Robert, m. and had issue –
> 1. Ralf de Boys, perhaps the Ralf de Boys who held Stanton Chase, Bucks, in 1235...

And so it went on. De Boys came from one of the great families of England. Ancestors had been in action against Richard I in the twelfth century; squabbled over land; acquired abbeys and priories; had been active in France during the Hundred Years War; seized monasteries under Henry VIII, and supported Elizabeth throughout her reign.

Wolf de Boys' father, Ralph de Boys, was a High Sheriff; patron of the living of Delmar in Notts; director of most of the large insurance companies, as well as a couple of the banks. He lived at Otters Grange in Chester – hence, thought Tom, the name of the company Otter Securities – and Wolf was the third son. The two elder boys were respectively in the Treasury and the Foreign Office.

Tom felt an uneasy shiver pass over him. Did a man on probation pursue this story, if he wanted to survive?

As he turned to the cuttings, the cab stopped. Tom had reached the Confederation of British Industry headquarters.

He tumbled out, paid off the cab and passed through reception after the inevitable frisking. He was escorted through a long dusty hall into a dull-looking dining room, set for about one hundred people. The room had the tired appearance of the routine official function.

Tom was welcomed by the PR man who thanked him for coming and shoved a drink into his hand. Tom watched the other guests, all industrialists in their too smart suits, or journalists looking shabby, arrive. Then they all sat down.

The menu was standard. Prawn cocktail, beef with two vegetables, red wine, peaches and cream, and coffee to accompany the speeches.

There were two speakers, the outgoing Director-General of the CBI and the new incumbent. Tom listened for a time and stealthily opened the file on de Boys.

He returned to the beginning of the deal and to the very start of the de Boys story, which began with the Cons Games deal, the section he had started reading when the mysterious voice first broke the story on him.

A week after the Cons Games deal, the cuttings showed that Otter Securities had formed, Investment Advisors Limited, to take in de Boys' personal investment advisory business.

'This has been trading only for a short time, and it is difficult for the directors to give a reliable estimate of profits in the current year. Mr de Boys puts the figure at about £75,000 before tax. About £850,000 has just been borrowed from the Prudential, and a further £250,000 from other sources. About half this amount has been invested in special situations and the balance in general quoted equities.'

A fortnight afterwards came, the cryptic announcement:

'Sweeping vigorously, Mr Wolf de Boys, new Chairman of Otter Securities, formerly Cons Games, has disposed of the group's main property, the head lease of Strone House, London E1.

'The buyers are S&K, who are already in the building. The selling price is £1,850,000, a big increase over the book value of £1,350,000. The deal will probably involve repayment of the £850,000 loan from the Prudential Assurance.'

Those first tentative steps were followed by a dizzy series of deals, which always netted a well-documented profit, plus a confident statement from de Boys that fresh fields to conquer lay before him, like his ancestors at Hastings, Crécy and Agincourt.

The cuttings showed a curious graft of the ancient, the military, and the chivalric on to the modern, hustling City. It was underpinned, so Tom felt, by a strain of neurosis, a kind of compulsive searching for recognition, approbation and applause. There was always a distance, too, between that severe countenance, which hinted at restraint and cruelty, and the more arrogant and wilder statements which issued from de Boys' lips.

After a year or so, the senior journalists got to him and the headlines got more flowery – 'De Boys and the Norman Conquest', 'Man with the Golden Touch', 'Why de Boys is hooked on drugs' (after he acquired a pharmaceutical company), 'One per cent of £3 million is worth a day or two of Wolf de Boys' time', 'The Norman with £200 million on his mind.'

Tom found a superb piece on de Boys by one of the 'pop' newspapers, which read:

'"No problem in being rich," says the laughing tycoon. In the City, where they're used to millionaires, the talk for the last three days has been about Old Etonian Wolf de Boys. He's thirty-one years old, and a millionaire maybe many times over – not bad even for someone whose family came over with the Conqueror.

'Since his company Otter Securities completed its latest takeover – for £6¼ million – which puts it right in the forefront as one of Britain's fastest growing companies, rival financiers have been asking: "How the devil does he do it?"

'And while they were wondering, Wolf de Boys was kicking his heels in Rome, pottering about the ruins, eating a few good meals, meeting old friends, and generally concerning himself with what he calls the good things of life – which he stresses are not free.

'Last night, three days after the £6 million deal went through, de Boys came home looking as fresh as a daisy and wondering what all the fuss was about.

'The fact that he is being hailed as a whiz-kid bothers him not a jot. After all, his family slugged it out on the battlefield at Hastings with William the Conqueror to gain a slice of English land. They're used to drama at Otter Grange, home of the de Boys family for nearly a thousand years.

'When I met de Boys at his beautiful oak-panelled office in Pall Mall, yesterday, he was lounging in an armchair, dressed in tweed jacket polo-necked sweater, casual trousers and boots.

'"You don't look like a financier to me," I said.

'He stretched back in the chair and laughed. It was like sunshine after rain, as that powerful face, with its hooked nose suddenly broke into smiles.

'"People have some very funny ideas about businessmen. Somehow they've got to be fat and podgy before they're believed. I had the same trouble convincing the family I was serious. After all, I'm the first businessman they've ever had in the family. But I won through with them, and I'll do the same with the City. The whole idea of making a success of life – which in my case is making a lot of money – is that you should be able to do the things you want.

'"When I signed that deal, I went to a big function at a London hotel, decided a break would do me good, and booked the flight to Rome.

'"You know something? I've never taken a sleeping pill in my life. But the day I have to, I'll pack it all in and stop work for ever. I'd rather lose a million than lose a finger."'

Tom leafed through more sober facts, like the advertisement panel for Otter's latest results. Record half year figures, it trumpeted, profits increase of sixty-three per cent.

De Boys' statement, as Chairman, read: 'Your directors have declared an interim dividend of 15 per cent, a 20 per cent increase over that of the previous year, and intend to recommend a final dividend of not less than 35 per cent, making a total of not less than 50 per cent – a 40 per cent rise on the previous year.'

The last cutting showed de Boys branching out into new fields, accompanied, typically, by a paean of fulsome praise from the journalist:

'SOLD – to the City gent who overtook the house bidders.

'Applying his City takeover tactics, Wolf de Boys, 32-year old millionaire boss of Otter Securities, has shown the house-auction world the importance of timing a bid before the opposition realises what has hit them.

'Auction bidding for ex-Grenadiers officer Captain Simon's estate – The Old House – had neared £200,000, when bustling Old Etonian de Boys made his entrance.

'Snapped de Boys: "The doorman didn't want to let me in because the place was full. Anyway, I offered them £220,000 straight off – I couldn't bear to hear them mucking about the way they were.

'"There was a great deal of head swivelling, then a stunned silence, and finally the gavel came down. But I'd bought it cheaper than I'd assumed possible. I was prepared to go up to £500,000.

'"Now, I'll let you into a secret. The Old House belonged to my family centuries ago, and I was determined to buy it back for them."

'Then off he rushed to clinch yet another deal in the City.'

As Tom came to the end of the file, he noticed Damian's name attached to one of the stories. Ah, I can pump Damian then on de Boys. They probably went to the same school. All these buggers know each other.

He was aware dimly, as he closed the folder, of clapping noises round him. The other journalists were writing hastily and looking worried.

12

The next day was the worst ever in Tom's life. He nearly went under.

Tom knew it was going to be tough from the moment he woke up. As he stirred from beneath the bedclothes, he saw all the morning papers under his nose on the floor.

Each one carried, on the front page, the story that the CBI had called for Britain to hold a referendum on trades union reform, urging its importance because of the critical state of the economy. Many led on the tale. Each paper, that is, except for the *Daily Standard*, which had no reference to the story. It led on mountaineers stranded in the Himalayas, a much less interesting piece.

Tom realised he had committed just about every cardinal sin that was possible on a newspaper. And he realised why Vaughan had been so attentive the previous evening, asking him how he'd got on at the CBI, before finally turning away, with a resigned air, from Tom's repeated denial of any story at the lunch.

Tom's mind raced through the possibilities of evasion through lying, as his stomach began to crash through his guts and his throat simultaneously.

Dully, he realised there was no escape. They had him wriggling on a pin. And Jimmy would have returned from his toothache. And Vaughan's opinion would be confirmed. And the office would shun him. And Pedro would get the job.

And he was finished. Finished before he even started, finished before he even really started out on his probation.

Tom turned over in the bed, no longer warm now, and thought of the other jobs he might do, now that he was leaving newspapers. Banking? Insurance? Stockbroking?

He felt his brain struggling for oxygen, as it tracked back over the CBI lunch, trying to establish why he had locked himself into oblivion when it had been so clearly pointed out to him that there was a story afoot. It was like adding up two and two and always getting five; the sums wouldn't add up. He couldn't understand why he'd been so stupid. But then, he rationalised, how can I be intelligent enough to understand my own stupidity – it doesn't work out. I'm just not up to the job.

But then there was a story, the de Boys story. Surely that proved something, that was why he'd got promotion. He thought again and wondered if indeed he did have a story at all on de Boys. We haven't run it once, he thought, maybe there's nothing to run. Is it all a put-up job? Have I just been set up by some bastard who'd know I'd get absorbed in the cuttings and then fluff the CBI assignment?

He dismissed that possibility as too fantastic. If, then, that was untrue, there was a story in de Boys, something worth following. He opened the paper, only to see a full-size mugshot of the man, boasting about the latest exploits of his company.

Tom felt rage at the man beginning to rise within him. So far, he thought, you've really fucked me around, haven't you, you little Etonian twerp. You've had me running round the City chasing a spurious rumour about you; you've had me transferred from an area where I was happy to one where I'm getting screwed every day. Now, maybe I don't even have a job because of you, you smirking, upper class, know-nothing unpleasant swine. So if I don't have a job, that'll make it a full house for you, won't it. You fucked me in the provinces, along with all my mates, and now you're going to fuck me again in the City, just to show who's boss. Instead of your minions running around waving cheques, you might throw me a bone in the gutter as you sweep by in the Rolls to your next deal. You and your Norman background, and your pontificating and your money. I'll show you! I'm going to nail you. I'm going to screw you, whether I'm on this paper or another, or even if I haven't got a job at all.

He jumped out of bed and took a great kick at the papers on the floor. They flew up into the air and scattered in all directions across the bedroom.

Dressing quickly, he went into the kitchen, where Ursula was sitting tranquilly drinking tea. She murmured good morning, to which he answered civilly. She then began to talk about the progress of yet another account she'd been given, because the Gunther account had gone so well.

Tom suddenly saw in his mind's eye Gunther and de Boys meeting together on the slopes of some Alpine ski resort, laughing together and pummelling each other in the sheer exhilaration of being rich and alive, and he coupled the two together and blamed his bad fortune on them both.

'Stuff Gunther,' he snapped. 'I don't care whether he lives or dies. For God's sake, stop rabbiting on about him, you're getting boring.'

Perhaps it was the sheer unfairness of the attack, because Ursula had barely mentioned Gunther (and anyway, it was a taboo subject now), perhaps it was because she wasn't used to such tones of command from Tom, but she hardly reacted. Only a look of surprise showed on her face. Then she went back to her tea.

Tom travelled into the office as quickly as possible. As he sat in the Tube, he could see the events of the immediate future just waiting for him, with the characters lining up to deliver the *coup de grâce*. It was all so predictable. Jimmy would scream; Gloria would shrink away; and Vaughan would probably sack him.

But then another thought stole across his mind, and Tom felt himself straying down fresh avenues of experience. If it was all so predictable, then it was only thus because of the nature of the product, that is, the newspaper. Could it be then that newspapers were utterly predictable, and that all his ideas about how to behave, and how to earn a living on them, were so much starry-eyed nonsense?

He turned the idea over in his mind, and parts of it seemed to make sense. The day was fairly structured, the work was pretty mechanical, if what Sidney said about producing was true; the level of commitment was pretty low. Maybe it's just like a factory, he thought, where all the stories are really just so many nuts and bolts which need to be produced to a certain specification, on time, and in a certain quantity to fill the requisition, which is the size of the page.

The more he thought about his inspiration, the more he liked it, particularly because it explained Vaughan and his harsh commitment to production. Vaughan's really just a works manager, he thought – and then realised again that he'd been fooled.

All that crap about Prime Minister's lunches and meeting glamorous people, it's all baloney so far as we're concerned. All we have to do is to produce the nuts and the bolts. It's up to other people how they interpret them. They see the show business, we see the split in the chorus girl's tights.

He felt a mounting excitement at the perception of his job which the idea presented to him. He felt, too, an additional reason for surviving the day which dawned before him with its grim pogroms. And he felt impatient to get it over, as if his development had now taken him beyond the punishment which his mistakes had provoked.

That is all in the past, he thought. Let's get on with it. And let's screw de Boys right into the ground.

All his assumptions about the day were correct. He was badly mauled. But he kept his mouth tight shut, and his hands by his sides as the screaming mounted, concentrating on de Boys' face, his hatred of the man and trying to remember the outlines of his idea, hoping that he would have a chance of putting it into practice.

The office was quiet when he arrived, with Gloria withdrawn. They all knew about his gaffe already. They were waiting for the explosion. Nobody could concentrate on work until it was over. They waited for the ritual killing.

Sidney hurried by with a 'good morning', while Damian was offhand and vague. Pedro, whom he hadn't seen for a few days and who used to be a good friend, was too preoccupied with pasting his latest scoop into the cuttings book to acknowledge him. But Tom noticed that Pedro seemed flushed about the cheeks, even though it was still only eleven fifteen.

Curiously, Mr Black seemed unaware of the situation. He was working away at Tom's desk when Tom arrived, and Tom realised that Black had a strangely lucid way of comporting himself before a typewriter. Most people surrounded themselves with loads of bumph, as if to take refuge in detail. But Black had nothing beside him except some government report. It was as if he was imposing his mind on the data, and hence the civil servant who wrote it, and the Government who might implement it, rather than the other way round, as it was with Tom, who had to report solely what had been published.

But Black, who was still in a bad mood, also had a jovial twinkle in his eye, as if he'd dished someone on a stupendously high level by some catty reference in his story.

Black turned to Tom, highly apologetic that he had

usurped his desk (which Tom thought ironic in view of the storms to come), and barked: 'The jabberwock is a fearsome beast, isn't it?' And Tom, who had been introduced to Lewis Carroll by Ursula, was able to agree without hesitation. Black nodded his thanks and returned to his typewriter.

Then Jimmy stormed into the room. His toothache had clearly done his humour no good. There was a kind of loose-limbed savagery about him and a wild look in his eye, the kind of molten cruelty and lust for battle which the clans must have shown centuries ago when they sprang from their plaids in the hills and rushed down to the battle, waving their claymores, shrieking their hatred, with the bagpipes droning mysteriously in the rear. Jimmy's hand was twitching.

But as he sprang towards Tom, he suddenly noticed Black sitting beside him. Jimmy executed a kind of half-balletic step in mid air, changing from ambushing primitive to fawning courtier in the space of half a stride and half a second. An insanely evil smile flashed across his face, although it took longer for the bloodlust to fade from his eyes.

'Oh, Mr Black, I didn't see you there. It's a difficult time you must be having now with the decorators in. If there's anything I can do to help, just let me know,' he said, and then, turning to Tom, cooed at him that his presence was required in the news room. Black said nothing as Tom followed Jimmy out of the room.

Since Black was in the Editorial news room all day, moving around to different desks, Jimmy found another way of driving Tom to the brink that day.

He'd give him a story to write, which Tom would do, and deliver it. Jimmy would then scream at him in front of all the subs, call him all the names under the sun – and then map out the way the story should be written, but very quietly, to Tom alone.

Tom would then go back and rewrite the story according to Jimmy's instructions. But Jimmy would then countermand his previous instructions, and insist the story was written in yet a third way. More screaming, more shouting, more abuse. All the time Vaughan sat impassively, watching the punishment.

Every story which Tom attempted had to be rewritten, each one had to be double-checked for alternative angles, each essay at journalism was accompanied by the hoarse rasp of Jimmy's voice.

Tom took it all quietly, his mind purposely fixed on de Boys. Other things happened to him as well, however, during the day. His idea about factories and nuts and bolts kept coming back to him, the more so, curiously, while Jimmy was shouting, since the very act of turning the stories round and round for different angles kept giving him insights into the process of composition.

By the end of the day he was tired, demoralised, and aching to crawl away and weep to himself. But they were also tears of chagrin he planned to shed, since he could see a little more now just why he had made such mistakes in the past. He craved a second chance.

Eventually, Jimmy had had his fill. Vaughan rose to his feet, still wearing the same faded blue cords. 'There must be a reason,' he said, 'why you lost the story. What was it?'

Tom felt a mixture of emotions, rage at the screaming, but gratitude to this man for his perception and hint of forbearance. Tom dug in his pocket, and he could feel the tears start to well up behind his eyes. He squeezed his thigh savagely as he felt for the contract note. He gave it to Vaughan, who glanced at it, and nodded.

'I had something to give you,' said Vaughan. 'Your cards. But now I'm keeping them. Goodnight.'

*

Tom discovered more on the way home that night. He was reading one of the evening papers which had also covered one of the stories he had written so laboriously that day. But Tom felt a thrill of pride when he saw that a quote which he had laboured to chisel out of Whitehall, and which gave the story far more punch, failed to appear in their version.

'Just shows, they can't compete with a real newshound,' he muttered to himself, facetiously.

Then he spied a story in the day's edition of *The Times*, which was atrociously badly written. The meat of the story was hidden away in the sixth paragraph, thought Tom, who then set about working out ways in which he would have treated the idea.

Gradually, he grew so engrossed in the possibilities offered by the story that he pulled out his notebook and began scribbling away at alternatives. Then he grew dissatisfied at the final version, as he realised that another phone call would be needed to stack the tale up as it really should be written.

By this time, he'd gone four stops further down the Tube, beyond his destination.

13

Life simmered down considerably for Tom in the weeks following the great CBI fiasco. It was clear he had escaped terminal disaster by a hair's-breadth. Equally, however, it was true that Vaughan's opinion of him had somehow risen, either because he stood up to the battering after missing the story, or because he had managed to land some kind of a lead on the de Boys story he'd been following.

Tom was also learning to cope with life in the news room. Every day, there was the same flow of banality, apportioned into data gobbets, but he learned the rhythm of production.

He developed the ability, essential in a news writer, to carry a completely open mind on everything without actually finishing up as a cretinous moron, or someone utterly ill-informed. He no longer read the papers for opinion, or even for facts. He read them for stories, little items which the other dailies had missed in their great hoovering up of the news, which could be taken up and expanded into fillers.

One day, for example, he found a small reference in the *Daily Mail* at the bottom of page nine about the imports of robots into the UK. He called the paper, posed as a reader, was given a contact reference, the importing association, and finished up with what Jimmy called a 'wee scoopicule' – a ten paragraph story, with a leading industrialist's quote on the need for more robots.

He learned how to read reports – from the end; how to

gut speeches, looking for the abrasive quote taken out of context; how to write a photo-caption; how to deal with pressure groups, like ramblers, or railway enthusiasts, who sent miserable scribbled manifestos to the paper.

As he settled into the work, he came to love the fixed dimensions of his world: the typewriter; the steel desk with its black top; the empty drawers in the desk (no need to carry files, or any surplus data, except on one story, de Boys); the chair with the nail; his pen, a battered old steel job he'd picked up from an antique dealer; and his three reference books which Vaughan had recommended, all of which gradually acquired the loving feel of familiarity, failing open, like reliable friends, at the vital page, when he searched for a word, or inspiration over a quote.

Across the room, he could see Gloria, and behind her the window. Reaching to his left, he banged his fist against a solid wall, while to his right were the filing cabinets and in-tray which made access to his desk so difficult. He had no hassles over expenses, because he rarely drew them. Jimmy gradually left him alone as Tom mastered the production flow, so that with the others flying in and out, Tom had the odd moment to chat to Gloria or to Black, who still popped in from time to time.

Gloria turned out to be far more complicated than he had thought. True, all the poise was always there, along with the boyfriends, smart merchant bankers to a man. But she loved someone who had left the country and had no plans to return, a Frenchman now living in Algeria. Tom found her weeping one morning, quietly doing her work, with the tears streaming down her face.

She had spoken to the Frenchman that morning, who said how much he missed her, but how impossible it was for him to return. 'Oh Tom, he sounded so close. I could hear the street sounds outside his office as he talked. He said how hot it was, and how he was going down to the beach that afternoon for a swim. In February, would you believe,' she sighed.

But then she did as they all seemed to do in the office, she picked herself up and carried on working, and gradually became the delicate, graceful urchin figure she was normally. Tom suddenly realised how much that grace owed to the fact that she seemed so isolated and alone.

She agreed, saying it was sad how such a glamour job as being a secretary on a newspaper set you apart from the other girls, just because they expected you to lead such a posh life. In reality, you had to do far more nose-wiping and hand-holding than would be tolerated elsewhere, as the shades of the paper gradually descended on you.

They both worried increasingly about Pedro. He was beginning to hit the bottle in a big way. The early promise of reform had faded under the pressure of the daily battering. His face was now permanently flushed. He wore the same clothes too long each week, suggesting that he was too preoccupied by drinking to change. He grew slower and less reliable on stories. Jimmy began to sniff round him, scenting a victim.

There were two doors to the office, one close to Gloria's desk, and Pedro developed the hair-raising trick of walking into the office through one, sitting at his desk for a few moments, and then walking out of the office through the other door. He seemed to grow so nervous that he couldn't sit still, he always had to be on the move, either shifting his files around, or picking up his phone and then replacing it, or simply wandering round the building at lunchtime, when Vaughan and Jimmy were eating. He seemed lost, pathetic, a shuffling victim of the mighty mother, the newspaper, and suddenly aged before his time.

There were money troubles too, times when Pedro plainly couldn't afford to buy lunch, and then Tom or Gloria would try to ensure that he had something to eat without robbing him of the tattered shreds of dignity which still clung to him. Tom contrasted him with the joyful extrovert he had known on the City desk, and shuddered at the change.

Then, he thought, a million years ago, when the world was young, I thought Pedro was my friend. I liked him because he seemed so carefree, so young and fresh.

But now he seemed like a mangy old dog, just hanging around waiting to be shooed off and knowing that it's about to be shooed off. Tom was appalled at Pedro's loss of confidence. He would not now attempt a story, or crash through the files, or ring up the chairman or the government department and give them hell. Rather, he concentrated on typing out the handout, and then fleeing the room.

As this process gathered pace, Pedro stopped speaking to his colleagues, and his colleagues, distrustful, suspicious and superstitious, as all people are who work under pressure, began to shun him. Pedro began to sight the ultimate and most tragic end which can befall a journalist in an office – alone, silent and ignored amid the words.

Tom was never certain whether Black registered what was going on. The decorators were taking an unconscionable time over his office, so that he kept popping in to use a desk. Tom found himself speaking more to Black, despite the great gulf between their positions, and even sharing a common attitude with him.

It was, Tom agreed with himself, an unlikely combination. The senior writer was an Oxford man, who took the usual first in Greats at a young age, went into newspapers because an arthritic knee made it difficult for him to do much else, and who had guided the paper through countless storms. Black knew everybody. Tom overheard him snap one day at someone who had invited him to lunch at the Reform Club, 'No thank you, I'll meet too many people there that I know.'

Another time, just before Christmas, writing on one of the nationalised industries, Tom rolled around with laughter when Black advised application for an Arts Council grant, because of the evident creativity in their accounts.

Possibly it was his other crack just before Christmas which finally led to their starting to talk together more or less each day. Told that the price of gold was shooting ahead, Black countered immediately by saying 'What about frankincense and myrrh?'

Possibly it was just such an enormous disparity between the professional intellectual and the apprentice writer from the northern background which cemented an alliance. But Tom was disinclined to analyse the reasons too closely. So far as he was concerned, he might be dead in three months' time, or he might live. But in the meantime he was going to do his best and make the most of it.

He invited Black out for a drink, and to his very great surprise, Black accepted the invitation, adding, as if Tom should be treated with all the deference normally due to close friends, that he would have to cry off for a week or so. But after that, he could manage a drink any evening.

Tom also struck up a slight acquaintance with Damian, over de Boys. He was still working on the story early in the morning, before the daily run started at eleven and had so far organised his notebooks together and consolidated his information on the topic, and clarified the situation in his own mind.

There was plenty of circumstantial evidence to suggest that de Boys was in trouble. His balance sheet looked nasty, although profits were still moving well, and people were talking about possible trouble, even if the shares were still holding up well. But what was also evident was the reluctance of the press, that is, the boys at the heavy end, to write anything detrimental about de Boys. It almost looked like a conspiracy of silence, although Tom was learning to mistrust such terms increasingly. All this was without touching on the phone calls he had received, or the contract note he had been sent. The whole situation stank.

Tom mentioned to Damian that he'd written on de Boys at some point in the past, and Damian, as Damian did when on secure ground, agreed immediately, with a smile.

'I was told to do it because I'd been at Eton with him,' said Damian. 'He was a year or so ahead of me, but we'd fenced together, so there was a sort of relationship. He was famous at school for dressing well, and for torturing young animals. God knows how he got into the City. We all thought he should be in a zoo. But he's done very well, hasn't he, even though he's probably cut a thousand throats to get there.'

Tom was so staggered that anyone like Damian should address a remotely friendly word to him, let alone credit him with any independence of identity, that he was silent.

Damian went on: 'Yes, I've been watching you. It's rather impressive. I thought you stood up to Jimmy very well that day. Even if you don't make it on this paper, there are plenty of others you can try.'

Tom thanked him gruffly for his advice and carried on working. By now he had worked out a plan of campaign over de Boys. He would call the de Boys public relations people, fix up an interview with de Boys himself, and see what information he could chisel out of the great man. But he would do it in consultation with Vaughan, since Vaughan knew about it anyway. If his direct approach failed, he would then go on to the Bank of England and see what advice they could give him on the subject.

He was preparing to put the plan into operation one morning when Vaughan walked into the news room, closely followed by Jimmy, a strange occurrence since the two were rarely seen together, except on the newsdesk itself.

Vaughan, wearing his faded blue cords, leaned on one of the desks and spoke, watched by Jimmy.

'You've all seen the story this morning about the *Hellespont* threatening to run aground off Dover. Well, we've just heard that the situation has deteriorated. The tanker should hit the rocks some time today and start breaking up. We're covering the story in depth. More oil is going to hit the Channel and the ports and the beaches than they used in the Second World War or something. It's a major disaster. That's why we're covering it in full. I've just been speaking to the Editor, who's given us practically the whole paper. We've got all the outside space, plus most of Page Two, for maps and diagrams and all that crap, plus a centre page feature, plus the top leader. So it's going to be the *Daily Standard* blitzkrieg report on the story of the day. We want to go all out to screw everyone else on this, and that means angles. Spend the whole day thinking about angles. All the other papers are covering like us. But our beat is going to be the surprising angle.'

He detailed the assignments. With typical Vaughan thoroughness, he'd worked out the jobs in terms of people's ability to cover a particular area, not in any special order of seniority.

'Sidney, I want you to cover the ship itself. We've a helicopter waiting to fly you down there immediately. If you look out of the window, you can see it on the other side of the Thames. I want you to get onto the boat itself, provided that you can do so without getting shot by the Navy or harpooned.'

'What if it blows up?' queried Sidney.

'What if it doesn't,' said Vaughan coolly. Sidney, thrilled at the assignment, started muttering about clean white shirts, the old Beaverbrook ploy when sending a man out quickly, as a sign, that he had the whole organisation behind him.

'Pedro, I want you to fly down with Sidney and do the shore angles, you know, locals, frothing over their beer, local clearing-up problems, sea bird pollution, and all that rubbish.

'Damian, you take the Commons beat and liaise with Tom over Whitehall. Talk to Ministers, Damian, get a feel over the party reactions, because it's quite a big test of nerve for the Government. You could finish up with the most surprising angle. Don't forget the French or Common Market side, either. Always a chance of trade-offs with the EEC Regional Funds over this.

'Tom, we want you to stay in the office as anchor man, firefighter and City contact rolled into one, but covering the Whitehall side too. Come on to the newsdesk with Jimmy and me, that'll keep you fully informed, particularly over the tapes.

'Before we break, a couple of final things. Stay in contact all the time. Jimmy and I think this story could change direction all day, so we want to know exactly what's happening to you. Second, we're running the story through editions in principle, so don't worry if you can't file for the first, in detail. Just send what you've got and keep working on it. Finally, it's the killer angle we're after. Last time, it was sea birds, this time it'll be something else. As you're covering the routine stuff, keep thinking of that sixty-four point head across five over the splash and what it could be saying.'

Vaughan smiled, added to Sidney that a photographer would be on the helicopter, and then said simply, 'Off we go. See you all later some time.'

Tom was reminded of the great commander, addressing his troops before a major battle. He had no doubt that similar scenes were taking place on the other rival papers. It was rare that newspapers committed themselves to such a major exercise, throwing all their resources into one big story, but when they did, the overwhelming priority was to show results. No good finishing up with a good lead for the second or slip edition, when you'd cribbed that off the *Express* or *Mail*. Reputations were made or broken on the strength of the front page lead in the first edition. After that, it was really follow-my-leader stuff.

But the great commander look was true of Vaughan, and, as Tom recalled, he too must be under some strain, since he too was on probation. But no stress showed on his face. He looked composed, even a little bored.

The military metaphor seemed even more appropriate when Tom sat down beside Jimmy on the newsdesk, after lugging his typewriter from his own desk. The two were poring over the make-up sheets, like generals before a battle, discussing what stories might go where, how the pictures would fit, whether the lead should be hard on the tanker, and soft on the human interest side, what Sidney, the front-runner in the whole operation, would produce.

The two worked together like piano players on a duet, with maximum economy of effort, each one fitting into the other's thoughts and actions, like hands into gloves. That harsh roughness of Jimmy's had disappeared, now that he was with Vaughan, and his manner was softer, almost feminine, and slightly beseeching, as if he just wanted the whole operation to succeed splendidly. Vaughan paced about slightly. Tom thought of Napoleon, but dismissed the comparison: Vaughan wasn't showy enough, although he had the common touch with the rest of the journalists. Too English possibly.

The tapes were starting to pile up on the desk, and Jimmy starting to riffle through and taste them for news, looking again for the surprising twist or detail which could be worked into the lead story. The evenings were flowing in now too, but at this point were largely ignored. The evenings had taken their stories off agency tape because their own reporters were still flying down to the disaster.

Tom began phoning the different departments in Whitehall, which were involved in the disaster. Environment were mainly concerned, but there were tie-ups with the Ministry of Defence, the Home Office, Customs and Excise, and the Ministry of Agriculture – over the fishing aspect.

Each department had its story ready and its briefing line well worked out, as if disasters were almost welcomed since they demonstrated just how versatile government Public Relations could be.

'At this stage,' said Environment, 'we see it as a medium-scale disaster, but we're watching the outcome closely. We're probably in the dark as much as you, but the Minister's keeping a very close eye on it.'

'Does he plan to fly down and inspect the damage?'

'All I can say at this stage is that you shouldn't rule it out. But I believe there's a Private Question down in the House this afternoon, so we may get some kind of steer later on over his movements.'

'So no story as yet?'

'Not for the moment. But we'll keep you briefed.'

Tom had a mental picture of the government PR putting down the phone after the usual misleading nonsense and half-truths, with a smile on his face. He'd fobbed off yet another inquisitive journalist. The next stage was the half leak to a favoured one, which had all the press heading after the angle, normally in the wrong direction.

The agency tape covering the Whitehall end was flowing on to Tom's desk, but it all told roughly the same story, with no strong leads. Evidently, the wire boys were having the same trouble over Whitehall. But it was only a matter of time before some hare escaped from behind the cloak of silence and secrecy.

Tom kept a note of the calls he made, and the times he

made them, so that if challenged he could refer instantly to his notebook. Vaughan saw this and nodded approvingly.

The phone calls were starting to come in now. Sidney had reached the tanker and called from the helicopter that he was preparing to try a landing. His voice crackled over the phone via the radio. He sounded scared yet exhilarated, the prospect of an exclusive interview driving him on, oblivious of the danger.

'We're in luck,' he shouted across the miles and the waves down the radio to Vaughan at his desk. 'No other bugger's got a helicopter. All they've got are planes, which means that all they can do is fly round, take pictures, and try and get the captain by the radio. So it should be to us, if we're lucky. I can see the captain now, he's on the bridge and he's waving. From what I can gather, he's telling me to fuck off, but I'm going to climb down the ladder and chance it. Ta-ta.'

Vaughan and Jimmy looked pleased, and Vaughan turned to Tom, indicating Jimmy with his thumb. 'He's not as dumb as he looks, you know. That was his idea to get a helicopter. Apparently he got the only one, right at this moment, in London.'

They all smiled at the prospect of landing the big story ahead of the other papers, although Vaughan cautioned that it all hinged on what helicopter availability there was at Dover.

'Probably just army stuff. At least, I hope so,' said Jimmy.

Pedro called a second later and said he'd got a line from the local pub about some old crone who'd predicted such a disaster last year, after the poor harvest, and this generated more excitement. If Pedro could stack it up, that was a candidate for the second lead, with or without a photograph.

Then Damian rang in from the House, saying they'd had

a Lobby briefing which suggested that the Government was a lot more concerned about the situation than it appeared. Apparently, the tanker was drifting on to some oyster beds, or something, which lay near the beach of one of the marginal constituencies. Full-scale destruction of the oyster beds could mean the loss of that seat for the Government, unless it paid out heavily in compensation at a time when it was trying to cut back on public spending.

'How strong's the story?' asked Vaughan. 'Can you build it up, or is that about it?'

'I'll try, but I don't hold out much hope,' replied Damian. 'It's all very tight-lipped down here, and they're just clamming up.'

'Why not file now, and then keep working on it?'

'That sounds a good idea. Put me over to copy. I've got about two hundred and fifty words worth here, and more later if I can get it,' said Damian.

The pace of the day was starting to hot up. The subs were in, and the background bits to the story, such as maps from the Graphics Department, were beginning to shuffle backwards from the newsdesk to the subs.

Two more journalists strolled across to the newsdesk. Black, who was now writing the leader on the tanker disaster, and another willowy character, whom Tom took to be the feature writer. They chatted casually to Vaughan, who detailed how far they'd all got with the story.

'The spending side is good. I'll pursue that,' said Black, and disappeared, while the feature writer lingered around the desk, riffling through the tape. The key and lamp phone unit on the newsdesk was now flashing continuously, with Vaughan and Jimmy reaching from one call to another, guiding, suggesting, coaxing, wheedling, occasionally shouting – and then, after every call, referring back to the subs and poring yet again over the make-up sheets to check on the flow of stories on to the page itself, frequently changing stories from column to column, and from page to page. Vaughan and Jimmy were also by now in touch with stringers overseas in France and Brussels, trying to grab stories on the international angle, and offering double or even triple lineage to get the copy.

Tom plodded on diligently with his task, phoning the different government departments and hearing the polite disclaimers hourly. But ideas were starting to move through his mind as he adjusted to the magnitude of the story and the contact he was having with Jimmy and Vaughan. On an impulse, he picked up the phone and called the Press Office at Lloyd's.

The results were electric. 'We wondered whether anyone would call, but so far no one has bothered. You're the first. Well done,' said a smooth, plummy voice at the other end.

They had a briefing ready, which was hardly surprising since it turned out that the tanker's hull was not properly insured. It was quite clear, according to Lloyd's, that nobody knew who would pick up the tab over the accident, if, indeed, accident it was.

Tom could feel the hair on the nape of his neck rise and a cold chill run through him as he heard this. He jotted it all down and shoved it across to Vaughan, who was looking out of the window and paring his nails. It was the one time that Vaughan's poise deserted him during the whole day. He reacted as if 500,000 volts had suddenly been passed though him. One hand reached for the phone, the other beckoned to Jimmy, and he shouted for the sub simultaneously.

Within seconds, he had Damian on the line from the House, and ordered him to chase the insurance angle, preferably through the Treasury. Black was told immediately, and the feature writer, and suddenly the whole context of the story swung round, away from politics and human interest, and into finance.

Vaughan congratulated him, while Jimmy slapped him on the back with a great grin. 'That must be the lead,' shouted Jimmy, exulting. 'We'll screw them all.' And he raised his clenched fist to the ceiling.

'Wait,' said Vaughan urgently. 'It's too good to go unnoticed. Watch the tapes.'

Pedro called in at that point, saying he'd found the old woman who agreed she'd predicted the disaster. Now she was afraid for her life, because the locals accused her of praying for the tanker to crash.

'Picture?' said Jimmy.

'Can't promise anything. I'm trying with the local press boys. But they're scared stiff of her,' Pedro replied.

'Do your best. Give us about fifteen to twenty paras on her. Go strong on the witch angle – they're all weirdos down there. But get her point in as well, so there's a follow-up if the locals really do beat her up. Buy her lots to drink, that'll keep her happy.'

A groan went up behind Jimmy and Tom. It was Vaughan watching the tape. Sure enough, there it surfaced, as the busy little cursor tapped out the letters. 'Hull not properly insured. Probe likely. Lloyd's chairman speaks...'

'You know what they did?' said Vaughan. 'As soon as you went on to them, Tom, they called up the wire boys and told them, the bastards.'

Sidney called in again, this time sounding less scared. He'd got on to the boat with a photographer. He'd got the pictures and the story about how they'd gone off course, and he was now preparing to come back. What were the instructions, since it was getting dark?

Vaughan said he didn't know. Tom wondered if he was cracking, but realised that, far from that, he was feeling his way through the story, like a blindfolded tightrope walker, trying to keep the whole concept afloat until it finally and inevitably crystallised into first, second, third lead story, and all the rest of the back-up.

'How much fuel you got left?' he asked.

'Just enough to get to London if we leave now. But enough to keep aloft and land at Dover, if we hang around. I can always phone the story through, refuel, and then fly back if you want me to. We can wire the pics from Dover,' he shouted. Tom could hear the helicopter engine roaring in the background as Sidney spoke.

Vaughan then produced a holding decision, one based exclusively on feel, hunch, instinct, and nothing else.

'Stay where you are for about ten minutes,' he ordered Sidney, 'and let's keep this line open. We may have something for you to follow up. How dark is it?'

'Getting that way.'

'Well, be careful. You may have to go back on to that boat.'

Turning to Tom, Vaughan then said, 'Get back to Lloyd's. Get on to whoever you spoke to and ask them about the captain of the boat. I smell something.'

Tom called Lloyd's again and asked for the Press Office. There was a delay this time before he got through. He felt the suspense mounting, as if now and only now was the dénouement of the day about to be revealed, as the definitive angle for the story.

'Do we know anything about the captain of the tanker?' he asked, and felt the question sinking home like the shaft of a lance. Then the press officer parried him.

'I'll put you on to the head of the syndicate. He should know,' he answered, and Tom could hear clicks and buzzes as he was transferred. He gestured to Vaughan that something was going on, and Vaughan spoke to Sidney, hanging in mid-air in the Channel over the Dover coast, telling him not to move. Sidney said he had no choice.

'James here,' came a crisp, decisive City voice, and Tom started to grill him over the captain.

It was the story, as Vaughan had surmised. The hull was badly insured, because the captain had been involved in something similar off the South American coast. He shouldn't have been in charge either, but someone had gone down sick. There were all kinds of complications.

Vaughan relayed them over to Sidney, who sighed down the line, cut the call and prepared to descend once again to the boat.

After that, the story burst wide open, with government departments snarling at Lloyd's; no one was sure who would foot the bill; local authorities were up in arms; and the Treasury was helpfully producing estimates of the total damage.

Sidney and Tom shared the by-line for the lead story, although Jimmy wrote most of Tom's part of the story. 'Don't want you to ruin such a good day, now do we,' he muttered as he chopped away at Tom's notes, slicing them into the house style.

Tom looked up from his work with Jimmy, to see the Editor in shirt sleeves tapping Vaughan on the shoulder and congratulating him for his skilful organisation and use of the journalists, while the sandwiches and beer arrived from the canteen.

Then the first editions came up from the other papers, and Tom felt a great gush of pleasure as he saw the rival leads. No one had come within spitting distance of the *Standard*'s angle. They'd all gone on the pollution story.

Tom looked at Vaughan as he tidied up his desk. 'Well done,' said Vaughan. 'I'll see you tomorrow at eleven.' Then he left the newsdesk, looking tired. Tom trudged home, fatigue washing over him.

14

Splitting the by-line that day with Sidney had a curious effect on Tom's relationship with Ursula. In the past, she had really run the relationship. She knew what was good to read, what plays they ought to go and see, how to dress for dinner, what wines went with what dishes.

Tom, as the grasping man on the make from the back streets, had been happy to learn all this from her, but he had at the same time been dazzled. Her way of flouncing in and out of a situation or a decision, with a twirl of her elegant hips and a flash of her long legs, exercised a hypnosis on Tom's more savage and basic instincts. Rather than just exploiting her and then moving on, as had been his original intention, he had in reality fallen victim to her charms, her caprices, her tastes, her habits. They were known as a partnership by their friends, and no one was under any illusions about who made most of the decisions.

Charlotte summed it up in her savage accurate way when she sneered that it was the perfect blend between high brows and low loins.

So they had gone to the theatre together, dined out with friends together, raved over music and opera together – but with different ends in view. Ursula was on the run from home and her parents. Little by little, however, she seemed booked to return to that milieu. She was playing a waiting game, enjoying a little freedom and a dash of independence before slumping back into the predestined mould. A wild man on her arm, particularly one whom she could partly control, was ideal in the role she had taken for herself; it added spice to the small risk she was taking. And if it worked out badly, she always had Charlotte and Theo and her parents to hand.

Tom, however, was developing differently. His stock of culture had always been fairly limited; he preferred the cinema to reading. But he had enjoyed the introduction to a new world, after scraping a living, coping with drunks, winoes, down-and-outs. For a time, he had admired the ability Ursula's friends had with thoughts, language and experience to reduce sensation to a flip remark, and then pass. He had been touched and scarred early on by certain events. He appreciated people who never let experience come too close.

But, almost despite himself, he found himself voicing doubts about Ursula and her pack as time went on. He worked harder, so that when he went back to Ursula's at night, he checked his work thoroughly, then searched for new stories he could write the next day. He took the newspapers every day, and picked out his favourite writers, on whom he might model his style, and he sweated over changing their stories round, to see if they could be improved. Before his mind's eye, he kept the image of Vaughan at the end of that great day reporting on the tanker, slouching from the office dog-tired, but still professional enough to remind him to be in next day at eleven as usual.

Tom found his sentences growing shorter as the scriptural economy he practised during the day took permanent root in his mind. By contrast, he now found that many of Ursula's sentences were too long, too indirect, and lacked impact.

It was a constant source of irritation to Ursula that she would find him staring at some hoarding, or a notice in a pub, moving his lips like an idiot (as she put it), as he mentally rewrote the caption and cut it into fewer words.

'Stop it! You've become a miser over words,' she would shout at him, as he explained that the statement could be made with far more bite in eighteen words than with the thirty-four used originally.

They had terrible skirmishes over Samuel Hector. All Ursula's set adored Hector. They said he was witty, brilliant, wrote well, and touched on all the topics they liked. Like a heretic, Tom said he couldn't stand reading Hector because his copy rambled around and was too personal. Tom maintained that Hector wrote to please himself, and only indirectly for his audience. Whereas the true hack professional, as on the *Daily Mirror*, reversed those priorities; the hack couldn't afford such indulgences. But of course, Tom was laughed to scorn.

Even greater storms blew up over Ursula's letter to Maureen, another old school friend now married to an engineer in the USA.

Tom had come back exhausted one night and found the letter lying half-written on the kitchen table. Unconsciously he had glanced at it (because he and Ursula still lived in conditions of relative frankness), been struck by the lumbering length of some of the sentences (as Ursula herself admitted, getting on with people, not writing to them, was her strong point), and started rewriting the letter.

He was about halfway through the first page when Ursula returned. Her opening sentence: 'It's been such a long time since you wrote to me that you must have nearly despaired of ever receiving an answer, but life has been just so busy here in London that I haven't had a single moment to pick up a pen and write to you. So, many apologies' had been reduced to: 'Life and tough times in London have stayed my pen too long. A thousand apologies'. And Tom was busy dealing with the second paragraph, on a second sheet of paper, quite oblivious of time or his surroundings, when Ursula snatched the letter from him and screamed at him about ruining all her old friendships. And in a twisted way, her logic was correct, because Tom was beginning to affect her old group of chums, the people she'd grown up with. They wondered what she was aiming for in such a relationship. They worried for her.

A major complicating factor was Ursula's job, working quite successfully for a very successful PR firm. In the beginning it had been simply a good job, and fully commensurate with Ursula's talents. She had handled her accounts well; she had worked busily; and the bright lights of the West End, where she went after work, were in keeping with such a life.

But her job now, as well as bringing her into contact with such superstars as Gunther, also involved meeting the press. Mainly, she dealt with the trade press, whom she could easily despise – as indeed everyone does, excluding the trade journalists who make a fat living on such contempt. She described them as a rabble; a scruffy, unreliable lot. Tom found it interesting that beneath the gay casual social attitudes lurked hard core authoritarianism.

When it came to the national press, with whom she had dealings only occasionally, she used the traditional grouse of PRs – they don't know how to handle a story and they're just plain rude. You have to spoon-feed them stories before they take any notice, and that makes for just *so* much aggro with the client. (She had a way of using the back street expressions as if they were her own – a form of appropriation which Tom thought typical of her set's grab-all mentality.)

But gradually, Tom was acquiring an identity on Fleet Street. His name was getting known, as a solid, hard-working journalist. Not one who was especially bright, but one who could be relied on to chase a story and handle it fairly well. 'Dogged' was the term normally used to describe him.

If Ursula was aware of these changes, she chose not to comment on them. But she couldn't ignore the implications of his half-writing the splash story for the *Daily Standard* after such a big disaster. She congratulated him. But the praise was slightly muted. She was cautious, guarded and slightly withdrawn in her congratulations. She couldn't market him as a crash news writer for the *Standard*, because he wasn't; he was still on probation. But she couldn't write him off as an ignoramus who ought to be put down by friends and neighbours for holding unpopular views on Samuel Hector and reading the *Daily Mirror*. She was unclear what he was, and so too was Tom, because he didn't yet know whether he would survive the probation.

Tom fixed up his interview with Wolf de Boys. True to his strategy, he had rung up de Boys' PR department and revealed, truthfully enough, that he wanted to prepare a feature on Otter Securities and de Boys, in the light of the banking crisis. Could they fix an interview?

The girl who handled the account responded immediately at the mention of Tom's name, much to his surprise. 'Mr Stone,' she said, 'we'd be delighted to help in any way we can. I'll come right back to you.'

She was back within an hour with a time for the interview – early afternoon in a week's time – and Tom, used to hearing groans about the press/PR relationships from both sides of the fence, but rarely experiencing the pleasant side of their dealings, invited the girl for a drink. She assented, and they had a pleasant meeting during which he was plied with flattery and free drink, because it counted as press entertainment. And he left a happier though more puzzled man.

Two days later, however, Ursula got wind of what had happened through the PR grapevine, and flew into a terrible tantrum, accusing him of disloyalty and every other sort of crime. But the tenor of her remarks had changed. In the past, he had always let her down; now he was deserting her. There was a subtle difference. She was jealous. Tom also calculated that it was coming home to her in professional terms what sort of changes had happened to him. How long would it be before that really hit home at her too?

At this moment Mrs Parker chose to make another dramatic entry.

Deep in the provinces, concentrating on her daughter's prospect, worried about Ursula's 'entanglement with that yobbo', as she later described it, Mrs Parker paid a lightning visit to the flat.

This did not come altogether as a surprise. Tom knew, and Ursula frequently reminded him, that Mrs Parker disapproved of him. After the dinner, there had been many secret telephone conversations which Tom kept surprising as they concluded, with Ursula looking flushed and bewildered. Tom had initially supposed she was communicating with the unspeakable Gunther – about work, of course. But that seemed to have died a natural death after a few weeks, with Gunther presumably deciding that the Fräuleins of his own country were less of a handful than flighty, expensive girls from London.

Tom only got on to the right track when he returned one day to find Ursula standing, white with rage, beside the phone, saying she would buy the lease for herself and damn them all. She was old enough to make up her own mind.

Tom realised that a discreet piece of middle-class blackmailing was taking place. The Parkers had grubstaked Ursula when she first came down to London, to the extent of buying her a long lease on a flat. It hadn't cost a great deal (because London had been cheap then) – say £10,000 – and property values had subsequently soared. But the lease was in the Parkers' name rather than Ursula's, which allowed them to apply considerable pressure.

Ursula couldn't repay the loan, because there was no loan. The lease was a present. Nor could Ursula purchase the lease from her parents. It would cost her too much, and besides, she had other things on which to spend her money. On the other hand, the Parkers could hardly throw their daughter out from the flat. But they could make their displeasure felt, and threaten and bluster until their daughter saw reason (as they would have put it) and returned to the fold. Ursula could resist for a certain time, they calculated, but they also reckoned, as Ursula knew, that eventually the threatened loss of standing in the family circle could have only one of two outcomes. Either she left the family and cut herself off, or she agreed to what they wanted, turned Tom out, and returned to being Mr and Mrs Parker's favourite daughter, albeit slightly shop-soiled. 'She got mixed up with someone unpleasant in London, and lost her head. She's far better off back home,' was how the locals in her village used to describe such grief-stricken returns to base.

*

Mrs Parker decided to pay a call to speed up the process. She arrived one afternoon, unannounced. Tom was at home to greet her. It was pure coincidence. He had taken an afternoon off, after working a Sunday duty, and was relaxing in the sitting room, which looked over the Hampstead fields, when he heard the bell ring.

He padded to the door in slippers and jeans, to find himself confronting a chic and sharp-looking Mrs Parker, wearing powder blue and gleaming bright black shoes, every inch a lady dressed to kill.

For a second, she seemed surprised to find him there. She rang purely as a formality, because she had a key to the flat. But, recovering herself, she allowed Tom to motion her into the flat, keeping a tight little smile round her mouth.

She glanced round the sitting room, inspecting it for dust, riots, orgies drugs and hippies – all the things she knew went on in London, when daughters left home. She found nothing. Tom had just finished hoovering the room, because he hated living in a pigsty.

Tom offered her a cup of tea, which she accepted, her smile now spreading a fraction. She still wore her hat, her coat, and clutched her handbag. Then, taking as it were a sudden decision, and with her mouth now cracking into a smile, she said, 'No, why don't I make the tea for you, so that we can have a little chat, and get to know each other better.'

She swept off her outer clothes and moved into the kitchen, clattering the kettle and the cups to feel at home, and to make her presence felt. Tom realised that she'd won the first round, merely by taking charge of the tea, because, in that way, she assumed control of the flat, almost as if she owned it – which, of course she did, ultimately.

He shuffled after her, asking about her trip to London. All her answers came out pat and well-rehearsed. She'd come to buy some things from Harrods, but they didn't have her size. She'd have to come back some other time; she didn't want to shop elsewhere. Buying at Harrods was her special treat to herself, and in the main, she shopped in her village.

The talk rambled on desultorily, as she slammed the tea into the pot, crashed the cups and saucers together on the tray and poured the boiling water with gusto onto the tea leaves.

They sat down opposite each other, in the sitting room, and she helped him to tea and then to some cakes, which she'd located after rummaging around in the cupboard. Tom thought she looked as if a good square meal of human offal might do her a power of good. But he said nothing.

'This is a wonderful opportunity to talk to you. Mr Parker and I have been looking out for your name, which we see every now and then. It's so thrilling to know a journalist. Mr Parker doesn't normally take the *Standard* – he prefers *The Times* – but he ordered it for Saturdays, just to get a chance of reading your stories. But they don't seem to appear all that often on Saturdays.'

'We carry very little on a Saturday. It's mainly colour stuff. But I write news. Normally on a Friday, I'm writing overnighters – Sunday for Monday.'

'It must be such an exciting world you live in, Tom. I think I may have spoken hastily when we had that memorable dinner together. You see, we know so little about what you do. We are simple people living in the country. Even some of your phrases are strange to me. What is colour? What are overnighters?'

She got her timing dead right on that one, thought Tom, as she uttered the dreaded Fleet Street jargon phrases, with the cup midway between table and lip, held with a finger delicately crooked, and then drank, as if absorbing serum to cancel any contagion from the words.

'"Colour" is how we describe copy that isn't news, more background pieces, like a feature or a personality story. Colour isn't hard, like news; the readers like it more than news, but it's tougher to write. You can make a fool of yourself more easily. "Overnighters" are just pieces for the following day, for the early editions.'

Tom felt a sort of betrayal talking about the beloved details of his job in front of someone who plainly hated the whole idea of newspapers. He differed markedly now from the Tom Stone who glibly used to invent pastiche jargon for outsiders. It was like revealing passwords. He wondered how Vaughan would cope with Mrs Parker – probably by reducing her to jelly just by looking at her.

'I see,' she snapped, not to be decoyed. 'Let me tell you more about ourselves. We live – that is, my husband and I, all the children have grown up now – in a small cottage in a small village. It is very peaceful. We know everybody, everybody knows us, there is none of this big-city bustle. Life is calm.'

Tom realised that she was growing impatient, unused as she was for her control of a situation to escape for more than ten minutes at the most.

'That is where Ursula grew up. She was always a beautiful girl. We all loved her. She had her friends there, from childhood. Charlotte, whom you know, is someone she met at university and brought home to us. We like Charlotte. She is respectable, well-behaved, and charming. She fitted in. We have always urged Ursula to bring as many of her friends down as possible, thinking the rest of them would be like Charlotte.

'Now, Tom, we are broad-minded people. We have mainly voted Liberal, because we believe in what the Liberal Party stands for, we believe in freedom, in people making up their own minds. But – Mr Parker agrees with me – how can we invite you to come down and stay with us?

'It's not that we have anything against journalism. Newspapers are precious in a democracy. But we don't know what your standing is. We don't know what your prospects are. We can't place you. We know you come from the north, but from where in the north, we don't know. What do your parents do? What do you want to do? You can't stay in this grubby little job, writing grubby little sex scandals for ever. You have to set out, make a career for yourself, in a bank or the Civil Service, or something else which is worthwhile and respectable.

'And Ursula,' Mrs Parker continued. 'Where does she fit in? We can't invite you down without knowing some more of the facts. How can we introduce you to some of our friends – friends, Tom, who could be very influential in your career – unless you are more open with us. I can't see you, even with the best will in the world, getting on with our circle, unless you clear everything up a lot more.'

She leant back with a confident smile, and Tom realised that this was only the first salvo. She had far heavier artillery to bring up, and she was going to use all of it.

Tom explained that he'd never known his father – he'd been killed in the war. His mother remarried, but he didn't like his stepfather. He'd run away to an aunt's, where his mother had largely abandoned him. The aunt had brought him up, or rather, allowed him to live there. She was hard up, with little time or money to spare for errant children.

It was a story Tom hated telling, because it left him exposed to such conflicting reactions. Either people decided that he was a poor, hard-done-by orphan, or they reckoned his background wasn't up to the mark, and ignored him. In Tom's view, the past was the past and unchangeable. Only the future contained possibilities.

Mrs Parker listened on, without a word.

Tom explained that he'd left school at fifteen, bummed around for a few years, and then landed a tiny job on a newspaper. He had only taken the job because of the free issue of cigarettes which went with the wages. Then, to his amazement – and to everyone else's – he discovered he could write. Not that this appeared in his conversation. Normally, he passed for the same illiterate slob of old. But, in front of a sheet of paper, with a pencil, strange things happened.

'It's hard to describe, Mrs Parker, but I have this talent. I look at the paper, and instead of white lines I see words, shapes, characters, and conversation. They flit across the sheet, and it's my pleasure to try and catch them as they move and clothe them in words. It's an uncanny feeling. I don't like talking about it.'

Tom always felt unease when discussing his writing. What he had said to Mrs Parker was true, but there was more to his involvement than he was revealing. What he had given her was the standard line he had used years ago to entice girls into bed with him. Sometimes it worked, sometimes it failed. It was even money.

But he had always been deeply aware of technical deficiencies, hence his perseverance as a journalist; hence, too, the punishment he had absorbed from Jimmy and Vaughan early on in the news room. It had been worth it to reach a new point of progress. But these were not ideas which Mrs Parker should hear.

She reacted as Tom had expected. She was intrigued. Immediately, she wanted to buy him, or buy his presence, as a real writer, something she could show off. She unbent slightly, as if something had been loosened, like a spring in her back. As she did so, Tom became aware that she was still well preserved for her age. Her bosom resembled Ursula's.

But then, just as quickly, she snapped back, although in a more contrite way. Almost, she was asking Tom to take her off the hook and provide her with a way out of the dilemma.

She was circling round him again, as in the restaurant, looking for a way in, deciding in that obscure, inscrutable way they had at that time in England, whether Tom would fit. Whether by any stretch of the imagination he could be bundled into the local circle to pass muster.

As they spoke, Tom could imagine the possibilities going through her mind. Promising writer? Hapless orphan? Hidden talent? Social victim? Up-and-coming journalist? As she came to the final tag, Tom could feel the shutters going down on the conversation. To fit in, he would have to quit the paper, and that he wouldn't do, not even if he were booted out later on. But that was the price she would demand for leaving him and Ursula alone, whether or not there was anything contractual like a marriage or an arrangement between them. Journalism didn't fit. It had the wrong image.

She knew it too, as she resumed the conversation. The hardness crept back into her voice, and with it the gusto and lust to reach a decision. Anything so long as it's a decision. They must have been like this in the Empire, thought Tom.

'I don't think you're one of us, Tom, even though I regret your unhappy background,' she began. Tom felt his flesh starting to creep.

'...And I'm sure that you realise that you are probably not one of us either. We are simpler, quieter folk than your turbulent past suggests,' she went on. Tom nearly burst out in laughter at the pontifical tone.

'But as a man of honour, I'm sure you appreciate the dilemma we're in. I don't think you'd want to feel responsible for losing Ursula her reputation at home, even if you never visited us. And I don't think you'd want to feel in the future that Ursula ever regretted one moment she'd spent with you,' she said. She was warming to her theme.

'We can't force you to go. We own the lease on this flat, and most of this furniture in it. But we'd never force you to go. We just ask you, as one civilised human being to another – and surely it's not an unreasonable request – to look for somewhere else to live. We'll give you plenty of time, say six months, and you can always see Ursula after that, if you want to. But if you moved out, it would make it so much easier for us. Of course, if you don't go, we could always apply for you to be evicted through the courts, and that might harm your job prospects, but I'm certain we wouldn't need to go that far. Besides, one can never tell with the courts, and they do cost money and take such an appallingly long time to come to a decision.'

So that was it. Tom sat back as Mrs Parker gazed at him,

with resolute determination in her eyes. He played for time.

'I'll have to think this over…' he began, when she interrupted him. She wanted to clinch this deal fast, and report back triumphantly to her husband that the yobbo was going.

She spoke to him now with that complicity housewives adopt with the butcher when trying to wheedle a cheaper, better steak out of him.

'We're willing to pay some money for you to find somewhere else. How does that seem to you? You wouldn't be on the streets. What if we gave you £500 now, by cheque. That would solve everything, wouldn't it? You'd have the money, you'd agree to move out in six months' time, and everyone would be happy.'

She fumbled in her bag, and produced a cheque book, and a long envelope, which Tom assumed was the agreement he would have to sign as well.

Then the door opened, and Ursula walked in. She saw Tom, and her face brightened. She saw another head, a female head, and she frowned, muttering something about 'I'm sorry if I'm disturbing you.' But then she recognised her mother, and smiled again, before seeing the cheque book. Then, realising what was afoot, she began to shout.

The moment was over. Mrs Parker lost her temper. She told Ursula she was to think of returning home to her parents; she must. Ursula flew into a mighty storm.

Tom left them to it and strolled down to the pub, reflecting that he'd defer any decision until he knew about his probation. But how like her mother Ursula was getting!

15

Pedro went rapidly downhill after Vaughan's great war operation over the wrecked tanker. Tom and Gloria watched him deteriorate almost visibly day by day, but felt powerless to intervene. To do so would have breached some hidden Fleet Street code. This states roughly that everyone is their own master, within the limits set by the newsdesk or other authorities. Everyone does their own thing; battles, struggles, kicks and gouges alone, to enjoy the reward alone. If it doesn't work out, too bad, you die alone.

Pedro would shuffle in sadly each morning, his breath by now ablaze even at eleven o'clock. Gloria maintained you could light a cigarette on the fumes after midday. Weekends were worse, and so were holidays. Without the slight curb presented by the office, it was clear that Master Pedro enjoyed the solitary company of a friendly bottle and a silent wall during his absences from the paper. His clothes, always the same clothes, hung to his frame as if glued, although he was now looking thinner and shabbier, so that paradoxically he also looked as if he could almost step out of his faded hush puppies, his russet sports jacket and green shirt, with brown cardigan, like an athlete changing out of a track suit. His face gradually disintegrated. The nose reddened, with blue streaks spreading down the greasy and pock-marked sides, while the skin began to peel and blister, presumably from malnutrition and dehydration.

His hands shook as he typed out the agency tape, word

for word, as his copy, and there were times when he had difficulty sliding paper into the machine, his fingers were so weak and jittery. His voice was becoming softer, more blurred, as the booze started to get to his brain, so that most of the time he spoke in a slurred burr. Until, that is, something happened which touched his dignity nerve, at which he would draw himself up and play the offended duchess, to the seething chagrin of those trying to winkle cooperation or work from his shattered teetering brain.

His only remaining mark of self-respect was his hair, still luxurious and bushy and even now only slightly greying. He kept it thick and slicked down in an immaculate quiff. Tom and Gloria reckoned the day his hair went out of kilter, that would be the end.

Eventually Tom could stand the situation no longer and he invited Pedro out to lunch. The spectacle of the ageing journalist now slipping in and out of the office for his bottle hidden round the building, while the other writers dashed here and there on their stories, always busy, always lunching out, always pushing for more space, called, thought Tom, for an act of charity, even though he knew he was stepping out of line. Perhaps he was trying to placate the furies unleashed by Mrs Parker's diatribe the previous week.

They met at the City Golf Club, off the bottom end of Fleet Street. The club had once boasted a driving range for keen golfers to practise on at midday. But so great was the thirst of the hacks that the driving range was torn down to build a bigger bar, at which point the PRs started to move in, to catch the journalists relaxing. This heralded an exodus by the hacks, so that the club was by now mainly inhabited by glib-tongued chaps drinking Camparis and soda. Tom chose the dive because it was shadowy, thus reducing the risk of observation.

They arranged to meet at one. Tom was there on the dot

and to his great pleasure saw Pedro already there, although he was even now shifting restlessly about in the gloom, and fretting.

They ordered food from the waitress, and Tom noticed again with gratification that Pedro asked for a sizeable meal – a rump steak, chips and mushrooms. Diplomatically, Tom called for a pint of coke. Pedro did the same, and launched into conversation philosophically.

'My boy,' he started off, 'today is a most auspicious day for me. It is my forty-fifth birthday. Much has happened to me in the near half-century I've been on this planet. Allow me on this memorable occasion – our first real meeting, I think, since we were both transferred from the City desk – to give you some of the fruits of my experience. You are not brilliant, Tom, not like those clever Oxbridge chaps. But you are dogged. You will go far, if you can only control your temper.'

'Temper?' said Tom in surprise. 'I don't have a bad temper.'

'But my boy, your stand-up row with Acres over that de Boys story nearly cost you your job. You must learn to simmer down.'

Tom was silent, biting his lip, hoping for no repetition of Pedro's prancing duchess act.

'Let's see now, you were in the provinces, were you not? On what paper, may I ask? There are some fine men in the provinces, men who could devour some of the young cubs in Fleet Street over breakfast – and for half the pay and half the expenses.'

Tom wondered whether Pedro was deliberately needling him, he decided not. He was feeling his way into the conversation, with the grace of a super-tanker berthing at a country port. Tom let him ramble, suspecting that some other chagrin was possibly working away inside him.

By now Pedro was on to the great men he'd worked for

in the provinces, those lean and hungry writers whose sole aim was to make Fleet Street and show the world. Tom was tempted to call for drink to shut him up. Then lucidity and real feeling crept into Pedro's voice. He changed in a split second, and Tom could see what he must have been like years before, an eager, driving, bright-eyed young man.

'I used to work with Patrick Sergeant, you know, on the *News Chronicle*. Those were great days. Pat was a wonderful man to work for, we all had such fun together. He had such magnificent style. You could tell he would make it, right from the word go. He was so slick and deft with his words. He beat us all off the field.'

Pedro leaned back in his chair, grinned like a small boy, and swallowed a piece of steak, nearly choking on it at first.

'There is a Patrick story, about the butler. At one point, Patrick hired a butler, so that when the newsdesk rang late at night to query a story, the butler would say in the most pompous way, "Mr Sergeant is not to be disturbed." That was that. There was no way they could get through the butler.

'Oh, and then, there was the story about the Latin headline. I must tell you that one. Patrick set a whole headline once in Latin – some rubbish to go with a piece about the Chancellor, I think – and started the story like this: "I would have set it in Greek, only my compositors told me my readers would not understand it." Great days, great days.'

'Why did you leave Patrick?'

'One has to leave the people one likes in Fleet Street. The closer you get to people in this business, the more dangerous it becomes. If he'd been a pig and I'd hated him, I'd possibly have stayed on the *Chronicle*. It was a fine paper. But I loved him dearly. So I had to leave.'

Pedro fell silent, thinking about the old days, and his food grew cold, untouched. He sat there with his hands clasped over his scrawny belly, staring at his shoes. Then he muttered to Tom, 'Today's another anniversary, you know. It's five years to the day that my wife left me. She walked out on me on my fortieth birthday, and took the kids with her. I've never been the same since then. She took all the sunshine away, all the joy I had in writing. Get me a drink, will you? Let's end the pretence. I know I'm just a drunk now. I might as well behave like one.'

A Scotch was placed before him, and he stared at it, fascinated, hypnotised, by the dull brown liquid in the glass which now spelled release and happiness for him.

'I hate the stuff, really hate it. I vowed I wouldn't drink today over our lunch. But now I've broken my vow. So I'll probably drink a lot now. Here's hoping.'

He threw the whole drink down his throat in one gulp and called for another Scotch. A fiery look was beginning to lick round his eyes. It came out in his speech too.

'When I left, Patrick stayed at my leaving party for three drinks. That was a record. That showed how much he thought of me.

'You know why you start drinking? It's the tension. You want to do well, to write so much the most fabulous story that you feel your insides beginning to burst with the excitement as you work at the piece. So you take just a little one to cool you down. And it works. You feel calmer. You carry on writing, you're more relaxed, and you say, Bingo! I've found the secret of good writing – a little touch of dope before the deadline.

'But you haven't at all. What you have done is to make a connection in your mind between effort and reward, between the pain of composition and the pleasure of oblivion, with just the faintest nuance that if you get the oblivion first, the writing comes later.

'It's fatal. Before you know where you are, you're drinking first, before you write, and the whole arrangement goes haywire. You miss stories; they shout; you get upset; you drink. You want to write; you drink. You've finished writing; you drink. Just one, then another, then another, and another, and another, and another...'

His voice tailed off. 'I remember breaking the Cunard story, but that was a long time ago. They wouldn't even remember it now on the newsdesk, they're all so young, especially that bastard Vaughan.

'We all get good stories, don't we? You've probably got one that you're nursing. But where does it get us? Nowhere. It's a terrible business. At twenty-five, you've got everything. Lots of money, lots of expenses, good clothes, pretty girls, and all the doors open to you. You're lunching at the Savoy; it's tea at the Ritz; the Cabinet Ministers hang on every word. You're courted and flattered, and it goes to your head. It's bound to. You wouldn't be a journalist if you weren't fairly sensitive to situations, and that in turn means that it goes to your head.

'But little by little, the booze and old age creeps up on you. By thirty-five you're on the scrap heap, knifed a thousand times in the back by the young men coming through, to whom you're a stale old has-been. And then they go through it themselves, punished by the people after them. It's a cruel, vicious, trade, Tom. The longer you stay in it, the more vulnerable you become. They won't take you in a bank or a broker's office or a government department after a time. They know you're used to rolling in at midday, then slouching out to the pub for a quick one before covering a press conference, late, and racing back to meet your chums in the local just before closing time at three. You're good for nothing, with expensive tastes and no money and no prospects. I've never met a rich journalist yet. How can you eat baked beans in the evening after caviare at midday? It's a mug's game, and we all know it.'

Tom sat there petrified, thinking of Mrs Parker's words,

and regretting the Pandora's box he'd opened by such an ill-judged gesture of charity. Why didn't I just let him collapse, he thought, why did I get involved with this old hack?

But then, if I stay in this trade much longer, I'll be the same, grasping at straws, at young cubs to talk to, just for the chance to break the silence of my own thoughts. What a come-down, what a degradation! Fancy finishing up grateful to someone for inviting you out to lunch just so you can have a drink and a chat in peace.

Through the gloom, he could see Pedro starting to scratch his face. He was running his nails down the side of his cheek, and this was tearing off the particles of blistered dried skin. Sooner or later he would draw blood. Tom could feel the man wracked by inner tensions, and realised he should have left him alone. Talking just made it worse.

Pedro started again: 'I'll tell you the best and worst experience I ever had now, and then I'll go. The best was with Patrick Sergeant, when he had his office in Finsbury Circus, overlooking the square. We used to have a paper-dart gliding competition every summer, in the evening. Patrick turned a blind eye; he was always very discreet; always good at managing people, to get the best out of them. The old men would be playing bowls in the middle of the Circus on the green. The air would be flat and quiet and still and hot in the summer eve, and we'd send the darts floating out from the office window.

'We were all so young then, so excited, so fresh and keen, we could all write like angels, we all wanted to write the splash. We'd watch with eager faces and bright eyes; as the darts flew slowly across the Circus, and we'd bet ferociously – but only a few pence really – on the winner. Sometimes, a dart would swerve and dip, and curl round the legs of the bowls players, and they'd always look up with a blink of surprise as, in the middle of their needle game, a paper dart suddenly cruised into view from nowhere across the turf.'

Tom looked again, and he saw two large tears rolling slowly down Pedro's cheeks in the darkness. 'I can't bear it any more,' said Pedro. 'I can't tell you the other half. I must go.'

He rose to his feet, looking thin and bony now beneath his jacket, and stumbled off, leaving Tom, stupefied and more worried than ever, to pay the bill.

That afternoon, Pedro went downhill all the way. When Tom returned to the office to tell Gloria the glum outcome to the lunch, there was no sign of Pedro, despite the pile of stories in his in-tray.

His desk remained empty, as the minutes ticked by to four o'clock. By now, Jimmy had got wind that something was amiss and was prowling around, asking for Pedro, shouting, 'Where the fuck is that bastard?'

He surfaced around ten past four. Tom was typing away, humming to himself, when suddenly he was aware of a dead silence throughout the office. He felt Gloria's eyes bore into him and he looked up, but she said nothing, merely motioning with her eyes down to the floor.

Tom looked, and froze. It was horrible. On all fours, a sepulchral, conspiratorial grin on his flushed features, as if somehow he was back in childhood and this was all some great game of hide-and-seek, crawled Pedro, in silence, back to his chair.

It was macabre as he padded like an animal across the floor, oblivious of the stares from his colleagues, deep in his fantasy. 'It's so easy, so easy,' he seemed to be saying as he approached his desk.

Tom looked at his eyes, which told a different story. They were red-rimmed, half-closed as if in pain; and the tears still cascaded down his cheeks. He was sobbing silently to himself, so as not to draw attention.

The pain of the tension was getting right into him,

burning its inevitable way through his brain, his character, his personality, his self-respect – breaking him slowly on Fleet Street's mighty wheel.

Worse was to come. Reaching his desk, still on his hands and knees, he turned left and headed towards the door. The office still froze. At any moment, Jimmy would come bounding in, fling the door open with a crash and send him flying, probably with a shattered skull. After all, you don't normally expect to find news writers crawling about on all fours, not even in jest.

Still to dead silence, Pedro reached the wall beside the door and started feeling for the door itself. Tom realised he was so drunk now that he was actually temporarily blind; he had to proceed by stealth and touch, like a bear. His fingers scuttered along the plaster, and instead of turning right to the door, he turned left towards a filing cabinet. His fingers then met the rim of the steel stationery cupboard, which he mistook for the door. He rose slowly to his feet, like a man in a trance, began trying to walk through the cupboard, his fingers fumbling blindly for the door handle and failing to locate it.

Gloria, with all heads turned at Pedro and agape, slipped silently across the room, took Pedro by the hand and gently led him to his desk. He responded as if an act of old world courtesy had been paid to him. 'Thank you, ma'am,' he said graciously to Gloria, failing to recognise her, with a queer inverted smile playing round his mouth.

A whoosh of breath came from the assembled journalists, as Pedro sat down. He sat down gingerly in the chair, as if testing it for weight and strength. Mechanically, with the experience of years working through him, he stretched out his left hand for the typewriter, while his right groped in the in-tray for the stories.

He drew the typewriter towards him, and Tom could see that his eyes were still closed, that he was at the extreme perimeter between fantasy and consciousness. He wanted to be somewhere else, on the quiet side of the moon where the sleepers lie and the light is soft. But the training of years still shackled him like a bridle and bit, still drove him to put words on paper, to worry about their accuracy, and wait for the next day's storm on publication.

The training lost. The bridle and bit dropped away. Pedro reached the promised land. His hand trailed away from the typewriter, failing over the side of the desk. He nestled closer into the chair and his head went down on to his chest like a weary elephant opting for the Valley of Bones.

Jimmy entered. 'What's this, you bastard?' he screamed at Pedro. 'You pissed on the job, you swine? I'll have you for this. I've been watching you for months now. I've got you now.'

He strode over, his hands outstretched to shake Pedro and tumble him to the floor. Tom thought, appalled, That's my friend there and he's going to die somehow if we don't reach him. How can they treat him like that, how can we allow that Scotch swine to manhandle him? He clenched his fists and stood up, ready for action.

'You...' he opened his mouth to shout, when he felt a pain suddenly lance into his back across his shoulder blades, and sear down his spine. Dimly he heard the crack which accompanied the blow. Tears in his eyes, he turned round, his back now smarting with shooting pain, and saw Black glaring at him, his stick raised in his hand, ready for a second blow.

'I wanted to remind you, Tom, about our drink tonight,' he snarled. Tom sat down. Jimmy called for the nurse, and they carted Pedro out together.

As all three shuffled through the door, Jimmy turned and shouted to Tom, 'We've got a man lined up. He would have taken your place, but he can take Pedro's instead now.'

Tom met Black (or 'the Sage', as he had privately nicknamed him, because of the grey beard and stick) in a small pub off Ludgate Circus later that evening. He expected an apology for the vicious blow from Black's stick, which had left a red weal across his shoulder blades. Not a bit of it. Black said immediately that Tom had to learn to take watching people collapse in the office; it was part of the job. Learning to cope with the replacement the next day, who was apparently fairly nervous about joining, was just as important as getting over Pedro's departure.

Tom looked startled at such brutally direct advice. Black went on:

'If I hadn't struck you when I did, you would have thrown away the endeavour of nearly six months. You're in a great deal of trouble as it is. If you go hitting senior people on the newsdesk, no matter what the provocation – and I mean that when I say no matter what – you'll be sacked. When is your probation period up?'

'In a few weeks, more or less. It depends whether holidays count or not.'

'Well, they're sure to question Jimmy about your progress. Imagine what his comments would be if he was nursing a broken jaw.'

Tom weighed what Black had said, and felt bound to agree with him. He asked what his chances were of surviving the probation. Black pondered the question for a moment.

'Officially, probably zero. Jimmy says your work is patchy but improving. But Vaughan is undecided. He doesn't want to make any mistakes over his first appointments. He says he'd rather pass you up and train someone younger, and more receptive, than go through the problems of complete indoctrination. And his views carry a lot of weight after the tanker incident.'

'But I half-wrote the splash on that. Doesn't that count

at all?'

'You also missed the CBI story completely. They still argue that they can't wholly rely on a man who's subject to intermittent brainstorms. But I said the *official* view is zero. Off the record, the tanker helped you a great deal. You may still be in with a chance. You never know.'

Tom felt his heart sink to his boots. It was what Pedro had said at lunchtime, it was what Mrs Parker had argued the previous week. Even he was now exposed to the threat of the younger man. But how much work had they wanted? How much effort? He'd been into the office punctually, day in day out, for months. He'd strived and struggled and worked away at home. He had taken it all so seriously. It still wasn't good enough. He couldn't believe the standards were that high.

On the other hand, it might be the best thing which had ever happened if they sacked him. Better to know sooner than too late. Mrs Parker hadn't slammed the door on him when she made her offer. She would be willing to take him in, plus Ursula, and show him off in the local circle, as the promising writer who'd come into the country to find peace and quiet for writing. A life in tweeds among the leaves? He could get used to that. It was possible to live for decades on the reputation of having been a Fleet Street writer.

Black was watching him closely. Black spoke again: 'It would help if you landed the story on de Boys. How far have you got with it?'

Without pausing to reflect that Black was highly informed about his progress, Tom took the bull by the horns and plunged into de Boys, Mrs Parker, and Ursula; his confusion about newspapers; the lure of the countryside; and asked in the end what Black thought he now should do.

Black asked him when his meeting with de Boys was going to take place.

'Tomorrow,' said Tom, 'after I've seen the Treasury over

some Loan Fund scandal.' Black winced at such a cavalier term for dismissing the Treasury and wanted to know whether Vaughan knew about the interview.

'Not to my knowledge,' said Tom.

'What if you get an enormous scoop from the interview?' Black pursued relentlessly. Tom agreed he should have informed Vaughan and asked for guidance.

'I have an idea,' said Black. 'First, you must call Vaughan, tell him your movements tomorrow. Then I will call my wife and tell her where I am. Then we can visit an old friend of mine. He may be able to help you. Have you got Vaughan's home number?'

Black sighed at Tom's ignorance – though he added later that it was understandable – and fished in his pocket for the number. Tom rang Vaughan at home. The phone rang once. Vaughan answered. He sounded alone. Music could be heard in the background.

'Tom Stone here. I'm sorry to call you at home…'

'Yes, Tom. How can I help?'

'I should have mentioned to you that I'm meeting de Boys tomorrow in the afternoon, after the Treasury. I've managed to fix up an interview on the pretext that I want to know more about his overseas plans. I'm hoping to get something out of him, at least.'

It sounded very lame to Tom. However, it might help to cement relations a little before the fatal decision was made about his future. But Vaughan seemed pleased to be kept informed.

'So you'll be in later on in the afternoon? Fine. Call me after the Treasury, just in case, and we'll chat about that first. Good luck with de Boys. Take it slowly. And don't worry if nothing comes of it. It's good background, worth trying and all you can do at this stage. Thanks for calling.'

After Black had made his call, Tom apologised for appearing to be so stupid and thanked Black for his help and interest. Black looked at him keenly.

'For Christ's sake, stop apologising. It makes me feel queasy. Let's go,' he said.

They left the pub and marched towards Smithfield, along Farringdon. They made a curious couple, thought Tom; Black with his stumpy gait, his fury when checked, his sudden charm and humour, and his evident concern not only for one person but for the paper as a whole. And Tom – awkward, uncertain, ignorant, under pressure from all sides, bereft of philosophy, but trying and hoping to make the grade.

As they wound round the lorries and warehouses silhouetted against the night sky in Smithfield, and stomped on (with Tom judging it wiser to say nothing), Black chatted about the day and his leader, and the problems he'd had getting through to the Chancellor, and Tom realised that a special sort of intelligence was being fed to him. An intelligence which escaped rank on the paper and which involved solely the ability to grasp ideas. He found it stimulating. He wanted to know more. He could see opportunities to develop further.

They reached a darkened square, with the lights of a pub at one end and a muted glow from what looked like a downstairs window at the other. Black seized his arm imperiously and dragged him into the pub, into the saloon, from where they could observe the square through the window.

'We're going to visit a restaurant, called simply Charlie's. During the day, it's a very expensive place where you can see half the paper lunching with crooks. But at night, it's very different. Charlie keeps it open for a few friends, plus his two assistants, and he cooks a meal for them if he feels like it. He's a remarkable person, mid-European, I guess, but spent most of his life probably travelling. Detached, urbane, and sceptical; a fatalist. Talk to him. Talk to his barman, too. You'll find him extraordinary. You may not have a chance to chat to the others, unless you play poker. Do you play poker?'

Tom denied he played poker.

'That's good. I didn't think you did. I – and a few others – play with a remarkable girl called Kate. Nobody knows where she came from either. She probably stopped by for some cigarettes, and stayed. But she has one of the best poker minds I've ever met. Sometimes I win, but most times I lose to her. So after we get in, you're on your own. Don't forget that if Charlie doesn't like you, he'll throw you out, and there's nothing I can do about that. But if he's interested, he'll talk to you. So enjoy yourself.'

They left the pub and hurried across the square.

'So, Black, you have come to learn a little more about economics!' hit the pair from the bar as they entered the restaurant. Glancing round, Tom saw a small softly-lit room, with tables to his right and a table under an archway to his left, where a slim blonde was sitting dealing cards to four City types. There was a bar dead ahead, with two people behind it.

Black snorted at the comment and made his way towards the cards. But he was not to escape so easily. The speaker, a short, plump man, with excited hands, gold rimless glasses and a small black pencil moustache over thick red upturned lips, hurried from behind the bar to cut him off. He was wearing an apron.

'It has been a bad day then, has it, for Great Britain Ltd?' he went on. Tom noted his exaggerated rolling of the rrs, as if he had learned to speak English one letter after another.

As Black headed past him, Charlie, as it turned out to be, shouted across to the blonde, 'Kate, you had better be careful this evening. Black looks as if he is in a very determined mood. He could well win a great deal of money, in which case I will charge him heavily for his meal. Of course, he might always lose a great deal of money, just because he is so determined, in which case I would take a rain check on my dinner.'

Then Charlie spied Tom. Black introduced Tom perfunctorily. Tom eyed Charlie. He was reminded of one of those German impresarios, the kind he had seen in *Cabaret* and which Ursula had raved over, saying it was a reincarnation of Weimar Republic Berlin. He had the same sarcastic, snarling, driving, brawling; knowing manner. But Charlie had more to him than just the smoothness of the *Cabaret* reincarnation, although the soft-light setting heightened the impression.

Tom thought he could smell, too, the sawdust of the circus, hear the big band beginning to play, see the horses and the nimble girls in tights slipping from steed to steed, glimpse the elephants and giraffes and leopards and tigers starting to prowl; he could laugh at the clowns. Charlie was no one single incarnation of these characters, he was all of them. He was the ring-master; he ran the show. When he joked, you laughed. When he sobbed, you wept. It wasn't that he wanted to take you over, he would always leave you plenty of freedom. But against that mocking, cynical, but also concerned and caring attitude which had floated from the wreckage of middle Europe and heaven knows what personal traumas, you had to be a brave and wise man to ignore what Charlie said.

'You look down in the mouth, my friend,' said Charlie after the introductions were over, and leading him to the bar.

'Have some retsina. Tonight, I am cooking my favourite Greek meal. You cannot stay for it, because I have only cooked for six. But you can have little taste of it. A moment.'

He raced back to the stove to the left of the bar, and started stirring a huge bubbling pot. 'It is casserole of oxtail, my favourite. Here, taste some.'

He held out the spoon to Tom, who sipped at it, tasting the onions and tomatoes, as they steamed from the spoon, with the meat.

'Hey, Gus!' shouted Charlie. 'For Christ's sake, stop reading those damned figures and come here and give Black's guest a retsina. You're getting boring these days, with your nose buried in those bloody statistics.'

A tough-looking slim young man with close-cropped hair and tight eyes, wearing jeans, swung off a stool at the end of the bar, put aside his paper, slopped retsina into a glass, crashed it down without a word in front of Tom, and went back to his deliberations.

'You see, my friend,' said Charlie, still stirring. 'Black is very good at writing about the economy and he is very good at talking to the right people and getting all the correct views. What he writes, we love to read. But he is an academic. Gus here is no academic. He learned his economics in Dartmoor, when he was doing a stretch for some crime or other. But he understands the gilt market. He gambles in it. And he makes money from it. That's what he's doing now – worrying about the market tomorrow. So while Black is writing, we are wheeling and dealing, and making plentee dough.'

He paused for a moment and moved to the other end of the bar, and fiddled with the radio, the calm tones of a Radio Three announcer suddenly filled the room. It was a concert – Wagner, Beethoven, Schubert.

Charlie added, 'They played Wagner in the camps you know, twenty-four hours a day, top volume. Imagine going to your grave to *Götterdämmerung*! In Russia today, they probably play the collected speeches of Lenin. Which would you rather die to, eh, that's the question. For choice, I would have Wagner, if you really twist my arms, as the Nazis used to say. What would you prefer, Gus?' he shouted at Gus, who was still poring over his tables.

'You've gotta take the risk, man. That's all I'm saying at this stage. You can't hold me. I demand the right to phone my lawyer,' said Gus mechanically, with a small smile, as if the phrases were a ritual incantation, uttered now without thought.

'Even the camps, though, couldn't destroy Wagner. Those sounds, I still love them after all these years of listening. Magical.' He started to hum in a deep bass an entrancing snatch, which he later informed Tom was the Spring Song from *Die Walküre*. He was still tasting the food, and he muttered, 'The only time to serve it is when the oxtail is poised – yeah – poised to fall off the bone. And that will not be for a good few minutes yet.'

To accompany the meat, Charlie had saffron rice, cooked with sultanas and peppers, a large salad tossed in olive oil, and plenty of fresh Greek bread, all of which was to be served on huge earthenware plates.

Tom couldn't help contrasting the gay, carefree atmosphere, as if they had all lived through their packet of human cares, with the tension of his dinner with Ursula and the Parkers, in all their finery.

'Hey, Kate, how's Black playing? Is he making money tonight?'

From over beneath the archway, where the blonde sat with the men, came: 'I can't hold him, Charlie. He's got all the aces tonight. He's reading the odds just so.'

From Charlie: 'That's not too good, Black. You wanna bankrupt me?' Then suddenly, as if a fresh thought had occurred to him, 'Hey, Black, I got some news for you. Tell you later over dinner. But I hear of a nasty little currency scandal brewing in the City. Big, big names, you know. Seems Old Lady's been caught with her little panties well down. Lots of people been making lots of money. Except for me, that is.'

And Charlie laid his hand virtuously on his heart and sighed melodramatically, rolling his eyes heavenwards. Then, noticing Tom's continuing silence (which was not the result of the day – Tom was speechless at the new world he'd penetrated), he addressed him again:

'Still down in the mouth? No girl? Too many girls possibly? I know, you've got mother-in-law problems. You have tangled – hey, Black, are you listening to this, I coined a good phrase here – with one of those strong-minded, misguided, hopelessly cack-handed creatures from Basingstoke or some other place teeming with those lunatics.'

'I lost a friend today,' said Tom, determined to give no quarter. He noticed that Charlie's brain seemed to streak ahead, always anticipating what he was about to say and preempting his thought. It was a different mental process from, say, Black's. It was the sharpness of survival which comes from living after dying.

Charlie's next words confirmed what Tom had surmised. From laughter he swooped into seriousness, without breaking stride.

'I had a friend once. He was shot before my eyes. That what happened to your friend today? I can still hear the bullets. Some hit the wall, some went through him. One moment he was my close friend; the next moment I had to leave him dying in the road. You know the only connection between the human being and the semi-corpse slumped there in the moonlight? He groaned. He was in pain, and I couldn't help him.'

Charlie went back to testing the oxtail, murmuring little incantations over the pot, as he sipped.

'Friends are a big risk,' he said. 'Don't get too close to losers, or to the fragile. The memories outlast the friends – and that hurts.'

Something cleared in Tom's mind. All these comments about risk? Wasn't that the answer he was looking for? That was the big factor Mrs Parker had never mentioned. That explained Pedro – he'd gambled and lost. It told him why he was still pursuing de Boys instead of opting for the cushy number. Maybe Charlie did have something to tell him.

'What do you mean – risk?' he asked Charlie.

Anticipating him, Charlie had his answer ready. He asked for confirmation that Tom was a journalist like Black. Tom agreed.

'Easy job to do badly,' said Charlie with a faraway look. 'But I don't know how they can call themselves journalists in this country. That's what I always attack Black for. They've never done anything for themselves, never struck out on their own, never tried to learn something and felt the pain of getting it wrong, and being forced to retrace their steps. I tell you, where I came from, a journalist was a big man, you understand, an important voice in society, people listened to him, what he said made an impact. But here, you see those blond-haired nobodies, full of Daddy's money and Mummy's caresses (English mothers like their sons too much), slipping into cafés, enjoying the big lunches, claiming the big expenses, and being spoon-fed the party line from whoever is in authority. No thought for themselves; they take it as gospel, provided the source went to the same school as they did, because they're snobs. Newspapers in this country read like Burke's Peerage. You want to check that? Read the by-lines. Gus does, and sniggers when he sees all the sons and daughters of famous men getting on so easily. What's the justice in that? Gus only committed a little crime, and he has had to learn in Dartmoor what they learn in a warm office.

'As for the others, the ones who didn't go to Oxford, well, they're just the cannon fodder. Sure, they're willing to take risks. But they don't know enough to work out the odds on a big story. They just get killed and replaced. They don't count. They never get close enough to live long enough to learn, work it out and make a contribution which would really change things.'

Tom thought of Pedro that afternoon and was forced to agree with the justice of some of Charlie's remarks.

'All your upper-class twit journalist wants is what his peer in the Treasury or the FO wants: the thatched cottage, you know, the smoke rising from the chimney as he turns the corner of the drive and his kiddies running to meet him, as the wife dries her hands on her apron and prepares to kiss him. Well, my friend, that may be good enough for civil servants – and look at the mess they've got us into – but it doesn't fit the journalist, now does it?'

Tom thought he saw a little of what Charlie was driving at. Charlie snorted. He had clearly made the speech before. Neither Gus, Black nor the blonde was listening. Maybe it was some kind of initiation ceremony. Tom stuck it out. It was all helping. He didn't want to be told to go.

'You find this a little strong, my friend? Okay, I make it easier for you. Imagine, twenty, thirty – it doesn't matter how many years ago – I was given up for dead okay, you got that? They wrote me off, kaput, finished, finito, right? Nothing much, just a little piece of investigation work that went wrong, they thought. Another number on the list, they thought, step forward number 21334567, because number 21334566 has bought it, gloriously. Only I wasn't dead. I was on the wrong page of the dossier; not the dead bit, but the living part. I got back, and I saw the hut where they all were, and I thought Ho-Ho, I'm going to give them all a big surprise, and a big joke, because you always got to have jokes. So I just tapped on the window. Someone came; they saw me. You know, they thought I was a ghost? They didn't believe it. And then they did, and we all clapped each other on the back, because we were all just so glad to be alive after we'd thought, me included, that I was dead. We cried so much we couldn't drink, and I couldn't smoke, I kept coughing over my cigarette.

'Now, after you've been through such things, you are entitled to worry about life. But not until then. Just let yourself go. Do your best. It may work out, it may not, but who are you to know. The gods decide, as they do each day in the gilt market, eh Gus? All you can do is try, and also to keep your head cool, so that the knocks don't throw you off balance.

'I give you another story, before I kick you out. This is stronger. But try to think how you – and you're no different in lots of ways from the young people we see trooping through here at lunchtimes – how you would write your stories if you'd been through this. Hey, Gus, give this man more retsina. He'll need it after I give the Charlie stomping bit.'

Same performance; silent drink crashed down in front of Tom, who took a long swig; immediate refill; no talk of payment; Gus returned to his seat.

'You are standing outside a building, right? It is late, say nine in the evening, when everyone is supposed to be at home, because there is a curfew. Right, got it? You have to get into the building. Not only that, but once you're in, you have to steal, thieve, snitch, nick, however you say it (and the way you say it in this country matters) documents. Then you have to get away alive, and get back. Got it? What happens?'

He stared at Tom, waiting for an answer.

'I shit,' said Tom dully.

'Of course, you shit, my friend (and even that is one of the better answers I have heard, because it is realistic), but your excrement is not enough. You have to go on and complete the assignment. Anyway, you do. You knife one guard, you decoy another. You get in (and you're trembling, make no mistake), you find the safe, you hear them coming and at that moment…' – here Charlie paused dramatically and held his wooden, dripping spoon at Tom – '…you can see the butcher's hooks, and the Alsatians, and the powdered glass. All the other unspeakable things the Nazis did just waiting for you. But you get out; you run, Christ, do you run; round the corner, down the darkened street. You hear them pounding after you; you're hit in the leg. Then you see an open door – someone going shopping – you dart in, close the door as quietly as you can, with your wound, your pounding heart; and then you turn, and you see an old couple staring paralysed at you. What do you do?'

Tom started. 'Well, you motion them to keep quiet, and…'

'No, my friend, you are wrong, and now you are a dead man. I'm sorry, but you must be a dead man. But I am alive. And why? Because I killed them, killed them both with a knife. Simple as that. Either they lived or I did.

'That is where risk leads you. But if you want to live at all and do your job in this world, you have to accept those things. Otherwise, what are you – Mother's Darling?'

Charlie left the question unanswered and instead switched his attention to the food, which he now decided was ready. Imperiously he called the rest of them to dinner, saying: 'There is sweet, too, for the greedy ones. It's a goat's cheese with sugar and fruit juice.'

Turning to Tom, he added, 'You must go now, but you can come again in the evening. But not too soon. Wait until you've worked out whether you stand alone with the dice in your hand, or not.'

Black nodded to Tom as he came to the bar, and Tom departed. Black looked as if he'd been winning.

16

Next morning, Tom sat alone in the office, preparing for his two interviews that day, with the Treasury and de Boys.

The office was clean and quiet and cool. All the telephones sat quietly in their cradles.

His discussions the previous evening had given him a fresh insight into the possibilities on newspapers, and a potential antidote to the Parker manifesto. 'You gotta take the risk, man,' kept booming through his brain. He knew that both interviews could go either way, producing either copy or disappointment. But he could contemplate such moveable possibilities. He fingered through the files.

★

The Treasury encounter was a fiasco. Tom was happy to have the crutch of his new philosophy. They sat, ten of them, in a grubby office, deep in the Treasury mausoleum, and watched and listened to a senior official play-act his way through an hour of gobbledegook. No story.

The Treasury man, tall, with a thin bloodless face and large white hands like fans, crouched behind his four telephones, or draped himself – like a weary giant bat – on the radiator behind him. It was like a byzantine ritual, empty of meaning, devoid of sense, when the magic has departed but the high-flown rhetoric lingers on.

Was the point at issue public expenditure, or wasn't it? That was the vital question, and it all depended on the angle of approach. To the extent that the Treasury advanced certain sums, and to the extent that these were spent, then it was public expenditure, was subject to cash limits. But to the extent that the cash was spent in lieu of goods and services received...

A colleague from another paper whispered to Tom as the Grand Vizier swayed on through his incantations, that anyone submitting copy on this would be out of a job.

The Vizier had a way of joining his forefingers together and then squinting down them as he made a point, which infuriated Tom. So too did the Vizier's mincing and exaggerated attention to the woman journalist there. He congratulated her for asking such clever questions, and answered in riddles.

But the inhospitableness of the institution was emphasised by the dirt beneath the edge of Tom's chair. He ran his finger beneath the chair as he fidgeted, and it came up black.

The epitome of the mandarin high-flyer, thought Tom, cocooned from the cradle onwards in a tissue of approbation, from ticks and 'Good Point' in the margin at school, through alpha minuses at Oxford, then on to the Civil Service, to be dubbed 'brilliant' – that weasel word in England which connotes chronic instability.

The encounter with the Parliamentary Select Committee, which wanted to spend the money that the Treasury was withholding, went equally badly. The news was drowned by the smooth young men who rose from the back of the hall to smother the committee in congratulations.

All the journalists winced, apart from the *Guardian* man, wearing a muffler, who sat tranquilly eating sandwiches, after missing his breakfast.

17

Tom found that his hate for de Boys, sustained over many months, had given way to a more dispassionate feeling, as he waited to be shown into de Boys' office.

He no longer saw the chase for the story as a personal quest. Rather, it was just another job he was doing for the paper. He couldn't muster that amount of personal aggression which he had evoked the morning he kicked the papers flying. The situation was more like a sentence; he was the subject, and de Boys the object which would yield beneath his pressure and deliver information.

But Tom also accepted that the interview might go badly and yield nothing. Nothing was certain.

He was shown into de Boys' office. This was the vital encounter, he thought, this is the end of the trail, one way or another. But he recalled all their shock on the Lancashire paper when they learned the editor was dead. He saw again the swarthy young men with the cheques buying up the machinery.

He was struck by the stark white of the walls, the sun streaming through the windows, the broad expanse of carpet, the heavy brown desk positioned beside the window and guarding the entrance.

De Boys came to meet him. He was in white shirt-sleeves. He moved quickly. He was shorter than his pictures suggested, bulkier and more swarthy. Three warts fell in a single line down one cheek. But the nose was hooked and fierce, while the eyes were tight, hard, mobile. If de Boys was a playboy he kept it to himself, no matter what people might say.

De Boys shook hands with him. It was two thirty exactly. They sat down at a table between the window and the door. The sun played on the polished surface. The chairs were hard.

De Boys had a breathless way of speaking, and the words came with a gush from puffed cheeks, as if too many thoughts were trying to escape at once.

Tom thought of a Norman count out hunting, followed by his men, in the clear air of an autumn afternoon in Sussex, with a hooded falcon on his wrist, the combination of grace and savagery. De Boys had a chunky, roly-poly look, but with strong hands and deep shoulders – a strong man who punished his body to keep it fit. Probably a killer.

De Boys looked at his watch, as Tom fumbled for his notebook, and smiled: 'Let's start, shall we?' he said.

'At Otter Securities, we are very interested in expanding overseas. We see this as imperative, if the Group is to expand, because the UK has such a slow growth rate. But we are held back by two factors. One is Exchange Controls, which prevent us exporting capital as we want to. The second is management. I'll deal with the second point. We all know about the first.'

The words came tumbling out, and Tom struggled to keep up and to keep his mind on the trick questions he wanted to ask.

'We don't have enough good managers. They're hard to find, harder to train, impossible to keep. We can't get abroad on the scale we want to until we have strength in depth there.'

'What about finance?' asked Tom. 'Isn't that a problem? There have been rumours in the City about cash problems.'

'I never comment on City rumours, unless they help me,' snapped de Boys, and then grinned. A happy, schoolboy's grin, with an axeman's look behind it.

'According to your balance sheet, a lot of cash falls due for repayment shortly. How will you finance the business if the cash is withdrawn?'

'Mr Stone, is this interview about Otter overseas, or about Otter's balance sheet? If the latter, I'll cancel the meeting now and ring your Editor in your presence to complain about your interviewing techniques. What's the answer?'

How the hell did this tough cunt get a reputation as a playboy? thought Tom. He's like a scorpion.

Tom trod water, explaining that he thought Otter's expansion overseas could be hindered by cash problems. De Boys looked at him hard.

'I'll give you a piece of news, Mr Stone. You may print it or not as you choose. Yesterday, Otter signed a long-term financing agreement in France – you know I have Norman connections – which ties up the left-hand side of the balance sheet for five years.'

Tom's heart sank. De Boys went on relentlessly.

Was there a flicker in his voice as he said that? Tom asked himself. Possibly, but who could tell? He might have a cold coming on, or a bad tooth. Tom couldn't read anything into it.

By now de Boys was well launched into his favourite themes. The thumb flicked noisily against the table lip as he emphasised his points: poor management; parochial outlook; need to expand; growth areas; taking it slowly; recruiting correctly.

He's cantering down the track now, thought Tom, looking for the prey in the sky, lord of all he can see, with his men far behind. Just his killing tool on his arm – a fitting combination.

Tom found himself slowly agreeing with de Boys about business. The man's charm was insidious. His ideas were sound. Tom felt baffled. How could the stories be right about his collapse? Had the voice been that of a lunatic?

He manoeuvred de Boys on to his wealth. De Boys was happy, perhaps too happy, to discuss the topic. Tom asked him if he'd been adding to his share stake. De Boys replied that unfortunately not. He'd been forced to sell a block of shares recently, for tax reasons. He hoped to buy more, though.

Tom found another avenue blocked, another hope dashed. The discussion turned again, with Tom now feeling himself sucked increasingly into de Boys' orbit. He questioned de Boys, despairingly, about the accounting dodges which the voice had mentioned.

'As you know, Mr Stone, we stayed out of property during the boom. That allowed us to survive, albeit with a slightly reduced growth rate. But we now have no assets which are failing to earn their keep. Does that convince you too that Otter is still viable?'

Tom assented, with visions of torn-up notebooks in his mind.

'Now the deals we are looking at mainly are in the US. We may get our capital from Europe, but the opportunities are in America. That's where we aim to be over the late seventies and eighties. It is possible we may apply for a quotation on the New York Stock Exchange.'

Tom scribbled down another little bit of market trivia, fed him by de Boys as he might have nourished his falcon.

'We also want more women in business management, Mr Stone. They have a cool head for business. They are good at taking decisions. We must find more of them.'

Tom listened hard to the clichés gushing from de Boys, trying to hear a chink in the argument, a gap in the logic. What was that about Exchange Controls?

'You say Exchange Controls are a problem. How do you get around them?'

'We can't get round them, Mr Stone. Nobody can get round them. It takes time to get the Bank of England to make up its mind. That kind of delay can make or break a deal.'

De Boys paused. Yes, he agreed there had been some jiggery-pokery with the accounts. But that was all over now. They had enough cash to survive and to expand.

'Mr Stone,' de Boys galloped on, 'you have got a long way into my company and my accounts. Congratulations. I don't think much of City journalists. Too venal, too stupid, too vain. They can be bought and sold just like that, or twisted round your little finger – like that.'

De Boys twisted his two forefingers together, and a flash of manic savagery crashed through his eyes. He'd stop at nothing, thought Tom. No wonder he cultivated the playboy touch. The real thing was venom.

Tom contrasted de Boys' forefinger play with that of the mandarin earlier in the day. Two different worlds.

'If you ever thought of leaving journalism, Mr Stone, give me a ring. You got further with my balance sheet than anyone – I don't see why you shouldn't do the same with my organisation. Usual deal. Small company to start with; share stake; salary at least £20,000, plus incentives. Until then, however, let's concentrate on the feature. Now take this down about the USA.'

Tom wrote down what he said. It was going to be a very interesting feature. Mrs Parker would be pleased.

18

With no stories at all from the day's effort, Tom returned to the office in despair. It was like losing an arm. He had lived with the de Boys story for so long – at times eaten and drunk and slept the idea of his scoop. But now, it had gone like sand through his fingers in a few brief minutes of discussion – there was nothing left.

The voice on the phone? Some hoaxer had been playing tricks on him, some malcontent sacked from Otter Securities possibly. He'd turned the City office upside down over the story, and rowed with his boss. All for nothing. He'd been put on probation – quite rightly, it now seemed – and the net yield of his striving for the story and the job would be zero.

Reality kept breaking in as he trudged down Fleet Street. Time seemed to slow down. He felt like a man falling through the clouds after losing his wings. He could linger now for the afternoon coffee in the coffee shop, anywhere in London. All over.

This issue of his probation was sealed. Black had made it clear – and he wasn't someone to spin a yarn – that Vaughan was undecided, but that a de Boys scoop would help. Having no scoop must tip the scales against him. He must now be out of a job. He regretted his enthusiasm for the story which led him to step out of line. It hadn't been worth it.

He reckoned he'd be seeing a great deal more of Mrs Parker. The beckoning woodland track suddenly seemed far more enticing, like the smoke rising from the chimney at the bend as the children rushed to meet him. I come from the provinces, I return to them, it is logical, he thought.

I'm willing to kiss hands, he decided. I'll go quietly. It's all very well for these toughies from mid-Europe to preach the philosophy of risk-taking. They're used to winning, or surviving, or getting away with something. I'm just a poor stupid hack, who put too much hope into a story. It's Goodbyesville.

His resolve to quit was strengthened by the day's changes in the office. The replacement for Pedro had arrived. It was a girl.

She wasn't striking like Ursula, or slender and delicate like Gloria. She had a kind of smudged look, as if the dirt still lingered beneath the make-up. She wore an outfit of brown and black with no shape, contour or line to it, into which simply merged her face, black hair, and hands.

His desk had also been changed, he learned with dismay. He had been rooted out from the corner, where he had hammered out stories happily for the last five months or so, and the filing cabinet had been removed.

His desk had been moved up against the newcomer's, so that they shared a common in-tray. Plainly, they were meant to do the same work from the same basket. She looked a competitive girl.

He no longer had Gloria in his line of vision. He could only see her by turning his head. One potential source of beauty, consolation and inspiration had been removed.

He introduced himself to the newcomer, conscious that Gloria was also upset at the arrival of another girl. He felt self-conscious and let-down.

She answered brightly, with no nonsense in her voice, marked by the strong vowel sounds of Yorkshire.

'I'm Brenda Steel,' she said. 'Great to meet you.'

Then she dropped her head and carried on working.

Brenda had a disconcerting way of working. She smoked incessantly, blowing the smoke straight over the prow of her machine into Tom's eyes. She had dispensed with ashtrays. Instead, the ash went where it fell. She sat glued to the typewriter, transfixed by the blank page in the platen for what seemed like hours, as the ash grew steadily at a crazy angle on the cigarette, either dropping onto the desk, the floor, her dress, or anywhere, if she whirled round in her chair in creative frenzy.

Then the long pause was followed by a whirr of activity, as, having worked the story out to the last comma and semicolon, she burst into action. Her fingers whizzed over the keys in a blur of speed. It was frightening.

Tom trundled into action at his normal pace, which, he found swiftly, was less effective than Stop-Go opposite. Then, as he reached into the in-tray for what looked like an interesting story, he encountered fingers also scrabbling for the same handout, and heard the chilling words: 'I think that's *mine*' from La Steel as she whipped it out of the basket.

Vaughan appeared and briefly introduced the two to each other, looking relaxed. Tom explained that nothing had come of his de Boys interview, apart from a few snippets. Vaughan hardly seemed surprised. He seemed happy, as if now confirmed in his appointment. He told Tom to put the details of the interview on file rather than write a story on it. It looked like the end to Tom.

19

He left the office early that night, nearly broken-hearted, feeling that the whole world was moving ahead without him. He was meeting Ursula. They were going to Covent Garden to see *The Magic Flute*.

The opera had been chosen by Ursula with care. Tom had never seen a Mozart opera, and she recommended the *Flute* as an acceptable introduction. She had asked him carefully whether he would like to see the opera, and he, just as gingerly, had answered that he would. They were going under their own steam, as Tom put it. No free tickets from the PR firm, courtesy of some client. Ursula had paid for the tickets – good seats in the stalls – and Tom was to pay for the meal afterwards. Ursula had booked the table, because she knew that Tom would be too busy to think about it.

They met in one of the new wine bars beside the opera house. Tom had never been so keen, nor so pleased to see her. She was the reassurance he craved at that moment. She was delighted to see him. She lit up as he approached. Instead of discussing her accounts they talked about the opera. She wore a short white dress with sheer, classically simple lines.

As the curtain went up, and the darkness lightened slightly and the orchestra struck up the overture, and the audience in its splendour sighed with pleasure at the familiar bars, Tom felt himself relaxing. This is where I belong, he thought to himself. She's not a bad girl; she'll improve as she matures: I haven't done too badly after all, with something like that on my arm. And, eventually, you have to compromise.

He adored the music and the spectacle in the opera, Papageno and his mate Papagena made him feel nostalgic and sentimental. Ursula felt the same way. She squeezed his arm, and he smiled at her in the semi-darkness. 'It's such a good choice. I can see my education is in good hands,' he whispered, and she felt for his hand.

During the interval, they made their way to the Crush Bar, and he retailed his impressions of the first part. As they approached the bar, Tom saw a huddle of men dressed in dinner jackets and black ties, gathered together in a small circle. They looked as if they had come as part of some company facility, perhaps a permanent box, since their relief at release from the opera was clear. Temporarily allowed to escape from the culture, they were all halfway down the first cigarette, or puffing strongly on cigars, and showing that special sort of abandon which businessmen exude when talking shop in alien territory. They brandished their cigars, stuck out their posteriors and laid into the gossip with gusto, forgetting all restraint but not raising their voices overmuch.

As Tom passed by, en route for the bar, he heard one, a wizened white-haired man with a well cared for look, say to his cronies:

'De Boys is in it up to his neck, so they say.'

Tom froze, and as he did so, he felt their eyes light upon him. He turned to Ursula, who smiled her soft smile at him, and whispered, 'Darling, I love you.'

He opened his arms. She fell into them. He felt her warm body crush against his and he could feel her heart beating quickly on his chest. Her hair rustled in his mouth as he nibbled her ear.

Undisturbed, the businessmen carried on, as Tom kissed

Ursula slowly, drinking in every word, memorising as much as he could.

'It's a really big dollar premium fiddle... So many accounts you couldn't work it out... Fraud Squad's on to it now... Bank of England petrified... about £12 million he made out of it... kept his company going... did it through the Mexico Stock Exchange... bent solicitor in Harrogate... amazing swindle... would have been bust months ago otherwise... such a smart boy... but he's bent... like a clockwork orange... and we know what they're like.'

Tom felt gingerly in his pocket, as Ursula murmured in his ear, and the press in the bar grew worse. All the odd details were now slotting into place. He knew how he'd been fooled, he knew what the story was. But he had to have a pencil. Christ! I must have a pencil and write it all down, he thought.

He had no pencil. Nothing at all to write with. He'd left everything behind at the office in his chagrin.

He prised himself away from Ursula, who gazed at him with warm tenderness. He held her close to his mouth, and muttered, 'Give me your eyebrow pencil.'

She looked at him as if he'd gone mad. The soft look faded slowly and reluctantly from her eyes, and a dull glare sprang up instead. The businessmen had moved away to the Scotches in the corner, out of earshot. It was imperative that he had something to write with.

'Give me your eyebrow pencil, or I'll strangle you on the spot.'

She didn't understand. The fine glow was vanishing from her cheeks. But she obeyed him, presumably attributing the warmth of the evening until a few seconds ago to the same madness which had prompted the outburst. She looked disappointed.

She fumbled in her handbag and produced a pencil. He whirled away from her through the drinkers, as the bells warning the end of the interval started to go, and found the Gents. He raced into a cubicle, ripped the toilet paper from the roll and scribbled down furiously what he had heard.

When he returned to the corridors of the opera house, thy were empty. Ursula must have returned to her seat. Fuck the silly bitch, he thought, forgetting his previous tenderness, I'm calling Vaughan.

He called Vaughan at home – no reply. He called him at the office and was put through to the stone. Vaughan was checking a story for the second edition.

Vaughan didn't sound awfully surprised, and then Tom recalled Charlie's comment in the bar about a big currency scandal brewing and big names involved. Black must have tipped Vaughan off, with or without knowing the names. Now he'd stumbled on the name. Was it too late to swing the balance with Vaughan?

Vaughan gave no clue in his final comment to Tom: 'Be in early tomorrow. It'll be a tough day.'

Tom was in the office by ten. Vaughan was there already, looking resolute. 'Call the Bank of England. Speak to the Press Office. Tell them what you told me,' he said. He sounded as if he'd been up half the night working on the story.

Tom rang the Bank, one of the easiest numbers in the City to call – 601/4444. His finger stayed in the '4' slot on the dial as he thought of the long trail he'd been following with de Boys. Is it the break, or is it just another blank wall? he wondered. He felt resentment at the seclusion created by the story and the investigative impulses working inside him.

He was put through to the Press Office, and a cool voice spoke. Tom recalled from his days on the City Desk, what Acres always said: 'Bank of England press officers are amateurs, because they're professional bankers – it's just a career posting for them. But they aim to run the financial press – as they run everything else in the Square Mile –

gently but firmly. Whoever called it the Old Lady got the sex right and the age wrong.'

Tom introduced himself, mentioned that his news editor had instructed him to call, then detailed his story. No interruptions as he went through the tale. It sounded thin to Tom as he spoke. Silence when he finished.

The voice spoke: 'I've heard nothing at all about this, Mr Stone, and you must admit it sounds slightly out of the ordinary. But of course I'll check it out. I'll come back to you.'

Tom thought he heard a laughing sneer in the voice, but put it down to nerves. At least the man was professional enough to look into the tale. And what had Charlie said that night in the restaurant – big currency scandal brewing? A pity it was too soon to return to Charlie's.

He was calling Vaughan on the internal when his phone went again.

'Bank of England here. We'd like to see you at eleven thirty. Can you manage that? Right. See you then, at the New Change entrance. Ask for the Press Officer.'

Tom changed what he'd been about to say to Vaughan, who told him to get some breakfast and not to be late.

A flunky in a pink eighteenth-century frockcoat showed Tom into an office the size of a football pitch, which was dominated through the window by St Paul's opposite. Tom realised from the size of the office that he was dealing with the Bank's tip-top elite. He licked his lips and continued rehearsing his speech.

Four men with grave faces filed in. They introduced themselves as Exchange Control experts. They sat down. Tom felt that he was being judged rather than checking out a story. They sat in silence, evidently waiting for the chief to arrive.

Tom eyed them. They had the serious mien of sober bankers, but other elements glittered underneath, close to the surface. Their eyes moved quickly. They looked alert, like long-distance poker players, the ones who play all night and spent their days working on the odds. It was a curious combination of the raffish and the responsible.

The door opened, and the atmosphere changed. In came a short, sturdy man, built like a heavy cavalry officer used to charging the guns, one of those men of sensibility who is at the same time outrageously and foolishly brave. He strode across the room, slightly awkwardly, as if trailing a sabre, and sat down at the head of the table, tilting himself back immediately in the chair.

The chief's name was Crosz. He took charge of the interview straight away, in the same way as de Boys had done. Tom felt slightly hallucinated, but oppressed by the mystery of the whole thing.

They pooh-poohed his idea. According to Crosz, who detailed his views as if about to lead a charge across an open plain, it was inconceivable that a fraud of such magnitude could be mounted. Thieves fell out among themselves, he said, such confederations don't last.

He attacked the men at Covent Garden as typical businessmen, balancing himself as he did so with care on his back-tilted chair so that his foot rested against the table on which Tom was trying to write; that made the table top rock and nearly prevented Tom from taking notes. He barked away in his curt, clipped, self-assured way, and the poker players who flanked him nodded approval.

Tom's heart sank as he felt official disapproval settling in on him. He apologised for disturbing the Bank with such gossip. They accepted his apologies with grace.

Bowed out by the flunky Tom left the Bank, deeply distressed, feeling on the one hand that something, somewhere, must be true, but conscious on the other that no way existed through the thickets of authority.

Why, why, why – oh *why*, though, had such prestigious men bothered to turn out for him if the story was rubbish?

20

More shocks awaited him in the office.

He trudged into the editorial news room, hoping to slide quietly into his desk, and found Ursula sitting there. She wore a cream silk blouse, a blue jacket and trousers. La Steel rasped on a cigarette opposite.

'Don't know where you've been, but I've done all this morning's stories. This bird's been waiting about half an hour for you,' said Steel with disapproval.

Ursula brightened as Tom came in, but underneath lurked pain from the previous night's fiasco. She spoke nervously, hesitantly, conscious that she was in enemy territory, and a hostage to fortune.

'I had a press release,' she began, 'and I thought I'd drop it in rather than send it round. I thought it might interest you.'

Steel snorted contemptuously and typed loudly.

'I wanted to remind you about this evening, Tom,' she went on. There was a note of supplication in her voice. 'My parents are coming round for dinner, d'you remember? No talk of cheques or anything else. They just want to talk to us.'

Tom felt the intimacy of his life with Ursula sliding into public view as she tore down the barriers separating the two.

'It would be helpful if you could get away early,' she finished.

Vaughan walked in. He ignored Ursula.

'What did the Bank say?' he queried.

'They rubbished it,' answered Tom, tearing his mind with difficulty from Ursula to Vaughan.

'Who's this?' Vaughan asked suddenly.

'This is Ursula. She dropped in with a possible story.'

'Handouts go through the desk.'

'You must be Vaughan,' Ursula interrupted unexpectedly. Tom gaped at her. She was transformed. The weary, suppliant air had gone. Her eyes glittered as she spoke to Vaughan, and her mouth had tightened to a trap. Vaughan nodded, preparing to move away.

'Don't go,' whispered Ursula. 'I just want to say a couple of things to you.' There was a sort of enticement in her voice, which made Vaughan pause and turn.

'Before you got your hands on Tom, he was a kind, affectionate soul. We lived together, we had a great time. But now that you've come along, you've destroyed him. All he can think about are his blasted stories and his blasted job. You've changed him, and you've destroyed him.'

Vaughan said nothing. Tom watched him growing whiter. He waited for Ursula to finish.

'You've ruined my life and my love. But you're going to sack him, too. So there's nothing left. You're a great puffed-up selfish bastard. I wish you were dead.'

By now, Ursula was standing up. It was unreal. Her voice pounded on in a strange whisper, as if she was asking for an exotic cocktail. Only Steel's horrified expression revealed the true impact of Ursula's outburst. It was happening so quickly that Tom felt miles distant from the events.

Vaughan stood still, his foot tapping the ground softly, as Ursula's words, conditioned by her money, her furs, her diamonds, her easy, rich, casual, comfortable life and her tight-knit circle of smart friends poured over him in a tidal wave of contempt.

'If this is yours, muzzle it,' he remarked almost confidingly to Tom, and jerking his thumb at Ursula. She took a step forward. Vaughan flung open the door.

'Get out. I hate your slime. It causes even more fucked-up journalists than booze. I can't control your activities outside the paper. But I won't have you infesting my office. Out.'

This time, he jerked his head. Tom thought she wouldn't go. She stopped. Then she left, ducking her head as she passed Vaughan, and the door slammed.

'Keep working on the story,' said Vaughan to Tom. 'We'll discuss the Bank of England later. Miss Steel, come with me. We have to agree on a correction for one of your stories yesterday.'

The smile vanished from Steel's face.

21

Mrs Parker had taken charge of events by the time Tom arrived home in Ursula's flat that night. She opened the door to him with a glowing smile, as if welcoming a timid lover, and poured him a drink. In the kitchen, she asked him about his day as Ursula and Mr Parker sat gossiping together in the lounge.

Tom realised that Mrs Parker had squashed whatever outcry Ursula had made over Vaughan's treatment that afternoon. 'Ursula,' Tom imagined her saying in her swift, slightly menacing way, 'when I was a girl, we didn't wander into people's offices and create a scene. That's not the way to get a man, still less the way to keep him. All you acquire that way is a reputation. I'm certain you don't want to add to the one you've built up for yourself already.'

It was called a cover-up in diplomatic circles, Tom judged. Mrs Parker had made her decision, she had passed her point of inertia. Tom was going to marry Ursula. Now, having made the decision, she, Mrs Parker, would put all her resources behind Tom to ensure that everything went off smoothly.

She reminded Tom less of a beast rampaging outside the stockade, but rather of a huge cat, when it has caught a bird, playing with the creature, never letting it out of paw's reach, although always seeking to give the impression the bird is free.

But it was a fairly painless experience. She had clearly been through the process before, either with her own family or with friends in the family circle.

Mrs Parker had also cooked the evening meal, although Ursula had selected the wine. Mrs Parker was a better cook than her daughter. She had prepared a Lancashire Hot Pot ('to make you feel at home,' she confided to Tom), which was incomparably superior to anything Ursula had ever produced. Normally, Ursula failed to buy a vital ingredient of the meal, which gave her the excuse to eat out. But Mrs Parker, from the country, worked in a different way.

They sat down to eat, with Mr Parker saying cheerily to Tom that his teeth were looking better, and Ursula, under the searching eye of her mother, blossoming into smiles and resembling increasingly a well-brought-up girl now planning to resume her rightful place in society.

Tom poured the wine. Mrs Parker asked Ursula rather sharply how she knew how to choose such a fine vintage. Mr Parker asked Tom what plans they'd made for holidays. Outside, the night was still.

The phone rang. Tom answered the call. It was Vaughan. 'Get down to Montpelier Square. We've had a tip about de Boys. He may be arrested tonight. Expect you in thirty minutes. Just walk round the square. Don't make a noise. And get a move on,' he snapped, and rang off.

Tom turned and looked at the scene. Ursula assumed it was a routine call and ate on oblivious; likewise Mr Parker. But Mrs Parker knew. She stared at Tom without a sound.

Her moment was passing, but she fought on. Tom glimpsed through her gaze the easy life with Ursula, the assured position, everything he would always aim for. He saw, too, the futility of rushing down to Montpelier Square – he, a man half out of a job, lurching out of time, rhythm, society, for a story which would never stand up, which could never be written, a story indeed about a man who epitomised the very life he was hoping to lead. Why go? Why not ditch Vaughan where he was?

Mrs Parker knew. She stared on. Tom hesitated. But then he stirred, as he had stirred when the words refused to come and the brain to function and the fingers to write in the news room.

He left the flat, tearing on his coat suddenly terrified he might be late and miss the arrest. He caught Mrs Parker's eye as he went, screwed up in chagrin. But he thought he glimpsed a flash of envy in her eyes, as he bundled through the door. It was all over now. No going back to the tweeds. He had the sun, the wind and the rain on his back. He was out on the heath and away from the shelter.

22

Montpelier Square is one of the best residential areas in London. It is a quiet square just north of Harrods in Knightsbridge, with trees in the middle, which hissed and rustled in the night breeze as Tom arrived. Georgian houses slumbered on all sides. The air was full of money.

Tom walked slowly round the square and found nobody. Then he stopped, wondering if he was mad. A figure stepped quietly from the shadows. It was Vaughan.

'We're over here,' he whispered, and led Tom back through two sides of the quadrilateral to a sleek-looking Citroen DS 21. They both climbed in, Tom registering with some surprise the contrast between Vaughan's shabby appearance and the implied opulence of the car.

'It's the office's. It's very fast,' said Vaughan, reading Tom's thoughts correctly. Tom felt relieved, after recoiling from the obscenity of glimpsing aspects of Vaughan's private life.

'I'll brief you first, then we'll get down to details,' said Vaughan as they settled into the seats.

'Look straight ahead and you'll see at the angle to the square a house with a white-stepped approach on the corner. The house next to that is de Boys'. I'm told he may be arrested tonight, possibly in time for the final edition, or tomorrow. That's why you're here. I couldn't write the story myself, I don't understand it. As I told you over lunch, I know nothing about finance. Perhaps you could explain to me what's been going on, bearing in mind that you may have to phone the story through in about three hours' time. So get it right.

'One thing I can explain,' he went on, 'is the Bank of England. They bluffed you. You had the story, they hoped to clear it up their way, but it passed out of their hands. That's why you saw their top men and why they spun you a yarn. You were right, and they were right. That's the way they work, I'm told.'

Tom started to explain the solution which he had rehearsed in the taxi. The essence of the situation was that he'd been right, as he understood it all, from the word go, but that events themselves had changed. He pulled out his scrap of Covent Garden toilet paper and gave it to Vaughan, telling him he'd need that shortly when he came to the fine details.

As he spoke, Tom thrilled to the excitement of the scene, sitting at nine thirty at night in a fast black Citroen waiting to witness the arrest of a leading financier, with the prospect of a scoop in the morning papers. Glory might only be an hour or so away, so too might his job.

To understand the story, Tom explained, it was necessary to grasp how the dollar premium worked. It was a device set up before the Second World War to prevent capital being exported from the United Kingdom. Subsequently, it had been refined. But it was operated and monitored by the Bank of England.

In order to export capital from the UK, investors had to pay extra, as if they were paying a tax. They paid the extra by converting their pounds into what were called premium dollars, which could then be used to buy the assets the investors wanted.

Tom gave an example. To buy a house in, say, Arizona, which cost $100,000, he would have to pay £50,000 if the rate of exchange was two dollars to one pound sterling. But, buying such a house fell into the category of exporting capital. So the cost of the dollars was higher, because the investors had to pay the premium.

Tom explained to Vaughan, who listened intently, that the cost of the premium dollars varied enormously because of supply and demand. The premium cost of dollars could be as high as sixty per cent these days.

'That's all you have to remember for the time being; the figure nought to sixty per cent for the extra cost of buying your house in Arizona or wherever. It'll cost you that extra for the privilege of getting your money out of the country. There are other finer points, but that's the essence of it.

'Now, let's consider who looks at the scheme. It's administered by the Bank of England, but it's actually run by what they call Authorised Depositaries, who vary from being responsible professional people like bankers, accountants or solicitors, to just good chaps. They actually hold the titles to these foreign assets. So, it's not unusual to find, say, provincial solicitors holding deeds to foreign houses. In the case of the house in Arizona, the deeds would most probably be lodged with a solicitor. It makes it cheaper for the Bank of England. But it puts the professional man on his honour not to fiddle. Right?'

Vaughan nodded, looking slightly bewildered. Tom told him not to worry, marvelling at his own fleeting superiority.

'Now, let's consider what you can buy abroad. Houses, gold – everything, including shares. Let's assume you buy some foreign shares. Right; you pay the premium (which will restrict UK demand for overseas assets, of course) – at whatever level the premium stands – say, fifty per cent. After getting permission from the Bank of England, you lodge the shares with your solicitor. Everything is done according to the book.

'But now you want to sell. This is the interesting part, which is where de Boys comes in.'

Vaughan looked more interested.

'When you sell, you also sell your premium dollars, so the two sides of the deal match, buying and selling those investment dollars. Let's assume again for the sake of simplicity that the premium was still fifty per cent, so everything would balance out. Right?'

Vaughan nodded, as if he understood a little more.

'Let us assume you sell those dollars and just *say* they're premium dollars.'

Vaughan looked startled. For a moment, Tom thought he was about to exclaim that that was cheating. Such are the hard men of Fleet Street.

'Assume you hold ordinary dollars and you just affirm that they're premium dollars. Then, they're automatically worth fifty per cent more. All you need is a bent solicitor to say that they're the result of selling an overseas investment – then they're worth so much more when converted back into pounds. Once you get the ball rolling, there's no limit to the number of times you can recycle the cash. And, each time, it's worth more, because of the profit on the deal before.

'Now, look at this piece of paper. What it means is that de Boys or his confederates turned up at some bank, with shares they said they'd bought on the Mexico Stock Exchange. Hard to confirm one way or the other. But a solicitor – the bent one in Harrogate – says it's true, so it must be. Trust the system – the banks sell the shares, in come the swollen pounds, on you go to do the same thing a week later. They say de Boys made £12 million out of it. If he made that much, his boys must have made about £100 million between them.

'That was the way de Boys must have bailed out his company when the balance sheet went up the pictures. He's too tough to go down without a fight, and he hit on the scheme to keep his company's head above water. Doing a bit each week, no wonder his company survived. He must have been making about £100,000 out of it, every week, for himself, at the end – let alone what went into his business. But, of course, as time went on, and he'd rescued Otter, he probably got greedy, decided it was an easy way of making money. And that's when they tumbled to him. That's the currency scandal I've heard about – it must be.'

Vaughan stared at him in wonderment.

'You mean you worked all this out yourself?' he asked, incredulously. Then he frowned.

'But how the hell d'you turn it into a news story?'

23

'I've got it', exclaimed Vaughan, after a few seconds' silence. 'The premium turns into a handout, every swindler's dream. Get that down, Tom, that's the explanation. About the third or fourth para, I reckon. We can't have all this technical guff, it'd give a Disprin a headache.'

Vaughan mused on, 'You'd need accomplices in the bank and elsewhere, otherwise it wouldn't work. It's too simple. That's why I was told so many people would be picked up this evening, they'd need an army.'

He returned to his simplification exercise. 'We'll say something like this. De Boys arrested for currency swindling. Right? Get in something about the fact that the UK's very strict about this, which is true, though we don't know how strict precisely. Yes, and so after "currency swindling", say something like the Bank of England runs a complex system of currency controls – right? – based on taxing investors very highly if they wish to export their capital. Right? Then, let's say something like the tax falls into two parts, what you pay out and what you get back. By avoiding paying out the tax, but simply collecting the rebate, speculators can transform the tax into a handout. How's that? Does that sound right? Good, now we can concentrate on catching de Boys, now we've worked out our clichés.'

They sat in the car and watched the house. The minutes ticked by. The breezes rustled in the darkened square. There was no doubt in Tom's mind who was back in charge, running the show. He wondered how Mrs Parker had coped with the rest of the evening. He ruminated on the cost of bed-sitters in East London.

Around eleven, Vaughan looked at his watch. 'The final drops at three. That gives us about three hours, assuming half an hour to write the story and half an hour to set it. Possibly less, if it turns out just to be an insert in bold on the front page. Between three and three and a half hours. Long enough. I imagine the police are now trying to carve up the Bank to get clearance to make the arrest. And the Bank will argue that any such move will spark off panic in the exchanges, so they'll try and block it.'

Tom noticed how Vaughan's speech, with a strange combination of the vernacular and the slightly pompous, but always turned towards conversational directness, resembled a newspaper article itself. Each line was end-stopped and subbed for grammar and precision before it came out, as if through an automatic self-censoring machine.

Then a light flashed in the hall behind the front door of de Boys' house. Vaughan reached forward and checked the ignition. The door opened and laughter was heard as a merry crowd of perhaps four or five bright young things trooped out of the house. Orange light cascaded out from the house into the square. Tom recognised a stumpy figure silhouetted in the door. 'That's de Boys,' he whispered to Vaughan, who grunted.

The door closed. 'That was the cover. Now they're setting to work,' muttered Vaughan. A car glided up to the house a few minutes later. Vaughan peered as two men sauntered up to the door, rang and vanished inside.

'Wrong car,' said Vaughan. 'I was told a Ford. They're having difficulty making it stick.'

To relieve the tension and make the time pass, Tom told a story he'd heard recently on the Street, involving an assignment where every Fleet Street super-bitch had been sent down to get the story – at all costs.

'Apparently, some society moll had had some terrible misfortune, so they sent the lot down. But none of them could get in to interview the woman. So they camped out round the door and sharpened their nails on the woodwork. Then, one of the girls had a bright idea. She went back to her hotel, ordered some flowers, sent them off to the woman with a little note saying that if she wanted to hear a friendly voice, or wanted a little chat with someone who appreciated what she was going through, she should ring such and such a number – the girl's hotel number. The flowers were ferried in past the blockade. Within half an hour the phone rang in the hotel. Beautiful story, don't you think?'

Vaughan riposted with a tale about a man he'd worked for years before, who used to take off at weekends and tramp the country and stay at country inns. His favourite book was *The Oxford Book of English Verse*, and his clothes – foul trousers, grubby sweater, startling green and tan checked sports jacket – were the reverse of what his position implied.'

In one pub, this man fell into an argument about how hard journalists worked; he grew very excited. He was about to be thrown out bodily, when he called for the phone, called the pub's brewery, revealed his identity and had the landlord fawning on him all the way to the door after that, asking him to stay.

'He took advantage of the situation; he kicked the landlord very hard and painfully – though discreetly – on the shin as he went out. He was a toughie. I learned a lot from him.'

The words died on his lips. In one movement, looking straight ahead, Vaughan reached forward, turned on the ignition, and the engine sprang into life.

The door of de Boys' house had opened and two men

had exited, as a long car, probably a Bentley, had emerged from the shadows. It stopped to pick the two men up – one of whom was clearly de Boys. One man got out. Then the car moved off.

'That's the chauffeur getting ditched. It's for real,' muttered Vaughan as, with one movement apparently, he put the car into gear, turned the wheel and glided to the corner of the square.

De Boys' Bentley moved out of the square and finally into Old Brompton Road. Vaughan looked graven in stone as he manoeuvred the car into the traffic, keeping a couple of cars behind de Boys.

'He's making a break for it. He must have been tipped off. Or it's less fuss to get him out of the country,' said Vaughan from the corner of his mouth, still staring right ahead. 'We'll tail him as long as we can.'

Both cars swept on to the flyover by Hammersmith. The night was fine now, with bright stars out and a clear moon.

Tom saw that it was one fifteen. Still time to file the story. The tyres sang on the surface as the cars surged down the road, Vaughan keeping his distance from de Boys, staying in the slower lane, as de Boys cruised along, his Bentley looking the image of respectability and elegant speed.

They reached a set of lights. Red, red and amber, green; they moved off. Then de Boys stopped dead in the fast lane. Vaughan was carried past in the slower lane as the hooting built up in the fast lane.

'Fuck, they know they're being tailed now. Watch them go,' snarled Vaughan. True enough. The Bentley suddenly screeched into second, gathering speed the whole time, and then into top, as it stormed past Vaughan and Tom in the Citroen. Tom distinctly saw de Boys' harsh face with the hooked nose at the wheel, as the Bentley passed.

Vaughan accelerated, saying he had almost as much

speed as the Bentley. The two cars rocketed ahead, all pretence of secrecy now gone. Vaughan's hands were steady on the wheel as the speedometer needle crept up to the 100 mph mark. The car hardly seemed to be moving, he held the wheel so coolly.

Both cars approached another set of lights, which began to change from green to amber. Neither slowed down. A pedestrian began to take off from the pavement, walking directly into de Boys' path, as de Boys accelerated, blaring his horn.

For a moment it looked as if the car would crash directly into the jaywalker, as it bore down relentlessly, with Vaughan only a matter of feet behind. The lights turned.

At the last moment, the jaywalker realised the car wouldn't stop and sprang out of the Bentley's path, straight into Vaughan's way, who swerved sharply, then braked as he skidded across the road, then accelerated out of the path of the car waiting to cross from the other side, then braked again, then glanced off the crash barriers, then bounced, into the middle of the road again, to miss the sideways traffic, by a fraction.

Vaughan was riding the car as it swerved from side to side with deathly intentness, like a rodeo rider. But as he fought to control the car, de Boys accelerated smoothly and triumphantly into the night. Tom watched his red light dwindle into the darkness as Vaughan brought the car to a stop, surrounded by blaring horns and flashing lights. Vaughan slumped for a second over the wheel.

It began to pelt with rain. Huge drops hit the windscreen and slid down the pane as if on a toboggan ride. Vaughan looked suddenly very happy.

He started the car again, just as the police constable was marching over to the Citroen, and raced away. His face was taut in silhouette. Tom asked him what on earth he was doing.

'Don't you see?' said Vaughan. 'If it's raining, that may delay their take-off. We could still catch them. It's worth a try. We don't want those fuckers on the evenings to get our story.'

The car swished along. The rain by now was slashing down, so that it drummed on the bonnet and lashed against the window. Yellow light streamed from the oncoming traffic. But the sky was clearing. Vaughan kept his hands clasped to the wheel, as the speed built up. Soon they were hitting eighty again. But no sign of de Boys.

By Ealing, Vaughan suddenly wrenched on the wheel, so that they shot off to the right. Tom gasped in astonishment. He'd assumed they were heading for Heathrow.

'Just a hunch,' muttered Vaughan. 'If it's Heathrow, we'll never catch them. But my guess is that Heathrow's useless for a rapid getaway. Takes too long to get air clearance to take off. Too public, as well. My guess is that he is heading for Northolt. Makes far more sense. But we may be disappointed.'

They tore along, with Tom hunched in the side seat, and Vaughan lightly balanced behind the wheel.

'Keep a close look-out,' snapped Vaughan. 'I think we're getting close. I've been this way before to Northolt, but it was years ago.'

Suddenly, they were traversing a wide open space, bounded by a wall. Tom stared grimly, hoping for a sign. They flashed past an opening. Vaughan jammed on the brakes. They began to slide across the road. He swung the wheel and they headed towards the nearside verge again.

They ground to a halt. Vaughan slammed the car into reverse, and they shot backwards past the opening again, with Vaughan then abruptly changing gear again. They shot into the aerodrome and raced towards the control tower.

'Ah!' gasped Vaughan as the headlamps picked out a Bentley sitting motionless and empty, to the side of the main entrance. 'We bet right.'

He swung the wheel again, and they tore past the control tower and onto the tarmac itself. Far away in the distance, a light monoplane could be seen taxiing forward for take-off. It was still raining steadily.

'Right,' shouted Vaughan. 'Hang on to yourself, and make sure the seat belt's fastened. We're going in.'

He settled himself in the driving seat again, and the car zoomed forward across the runway, moving at an angle to the plane.

Then Vaughan changed direction once more. He was clearly hoping to head the plane off. Then the car hurtled onto the grass, bumping a little as it took the shock of the uneven surface. Tom glanced at the speedometer – 90 mph.

Vaughan had changed his tactics. He was not aiming for a spot a long way further down the runway, but bisecting the path of the plane's take-off. Unhurriedly, the tiny machine in the distance turned, then revved and began to move forwards. The Citroen whined across the turf.

'What the hell are you playing at?' shouted Tom, suddenly realising Vaughan's plan. 'You'll kill us both.'

'Fuck you,' shouted Vaughan. 'I'm going to ram the wheels. That'll scupper their little game.'

Flashes of light suddenly sprang from the plane as the Citroen drew closer. Then, here was a crash against the roof, as something ricocheted off and into the night.

'Christ, they're shooting at us,' screamed Tom.

'At least we know it's them,' snarled Vaughan, unperturbed.

The two objects began to converge, as if drawn by magnets. It was clear that Vaughan had gauged the distance precisely, since as plane and car accelerated towards each other, there looked to be an optimum point at which they had to collide.

Tom wondered how much attention the French paid to

building Citroen roofs, since a collision would bring the whole body of the plane tumbling down on top of the car. And if they crossed a fraction too soon, they'd run right into the propeller and get sliced to bits.

From the flight-path flares, Tom could see the spray scuttering from beneath the plane's tyres as it laboured to take off, whilst its body, hunched low down and poised, thrust its way down the runway.

Nearer and nearer they drove, and the shots still rang out from the plane. Just at the last moment, the pilot eased the plane into the air and the wheels scraped lightly against the roof of the car as it shot by underneath. It was the closest of close calls. A split second before, and they would have hit the plane broadside on.

Vaughan careered on to the other side of the runway, cursing as the plane climbed awkwardly into the sky, ferrying de Boys to safety.

Tom looked back at the control tower. He saw excited bustle and heard shouting as the authorities reacted to the invasion of their airfield. Now comes the reckoning, he thought.

All Vaughan could say was that he'd tried the same thing before and it had worked then. 'The bastards on the evenings will have it all to themselves,' he groaned.

24

Vaughan was right. The evenings had it from the first edition onwards. Tom saw the story as he rode into the office on the tube, after sleeping on the couch from two till seven. He'd had little to say to Ursula, and she'd had few words for him. Mr and Mrs Parker had departed.

'Millionaire Financier Flees Currency Swindle Rap' shouted the headlines, with Tom unable to read the story. He reached the office, to find Vaughan, still in his faded blue corduroys, ready for work.

'Seen the story?' he asked briefly. 'The Bank must have been feeding them too. It takes nine to get a story, they always say. Their clichés were worse than ours, though. According to their splash, de Boys has been "milking the country's assets in a sophisticated financial swindle". He could have been fiddling the social security, for all that means.'

Then he paused. 'The Editor wants to see you. Good luck.'

Then he left the office, leaving Tom and Miss Steel alone together. Miss Steel sniffed and carried on smoking.

Tom went fearfully to the Editor's office, knocked and was told to enter. The Editor waved him to a chair, then looked at his watch. He leaned across his desk.

'You have tried hard, but Mr Vaughan is still convinced that you are unsuited for news writing. I accept what he says. He is my new News Editor.'

Tom's heart sank. Vaughan had the job. But he'd contrived to lose everything – the story, Ursula, and his job in the news room. A full house. He waited for the blow to fall.

'Mr Vaughan, however, has advised me that you should be kept on for further training. I am seconding you to Mr Black, to learn to write in a different way. Let us hope for better results. In the meantime, I am increasing your salary by £500. Your expenses, however, in the new job will be minimal. Whoever heard, after all, of a trainee leader writer who claimed the earth from a paper. People lunch *him*.'

The Editor then asked what Vaughan had planned for the de Boys follow-up. Tom said he didn't know.

'You are writing the front page lead, and a feature, I understand. Good luck – although it is bad luck that de Boys is now probably in Argentina or somewhere.'

Tom twitched slightly, as the voice sounded familiar. If he closed his eyes and listened, he could have sworn that that was the voice he'd heard on the phone tipping him off about de Boys.

'One final point, Mr Stone. You have lost the story, but kept your job and won a promotion. That is unusual. I advise you to change your address. Luck has a habit of running out. Good afternoon.'

Tom returned to his office; he ignored the pile of stories gathering in the in-tray and sat down to write the splash. He left the smaller stories for Miss Steel.

25

Tom felt calmness descend on him as he punched out the lead story. Fatigue crawled through his body, but it was diluted by the exhilaration of landing the story, of being allowed to lead the whole paper, to mount upon a rostrum and crow to the world about his sleuthing. He felt good.

'Easy, Tom, easy boy,' he found himself muttering to himself, as he put the first paragraph together, then moved on to the second. 'Don't take any chances, just tell it straight, don't fuck about with it. You don't want any corrections – sorry, amplifications – tomorrow, do you?'

But it would have been hard to make a major error. The paper gave him the star treatment. As he wrote, the night subs surrounded him, removing the story in takes as it emerged from his typewriter, then scurrying back to the news room silently, but filled, as it were, by a hubbub of excitement. Tom felt almost that he was rejoining the paper, but on a different level, as if all the past mistakes and misconceptions were being swept away. Now, instead of personality clashes and aggravation, all that anyone wanted was to nail the story to the ground.

The chief sub came in to check a detail, found that Tom had run out of coffee and personally – he himself, a man who rarely spoke unless a curse would do – fetched Tom another refill. They chatted idly about how one paragraph might be recast as Tom staggered to the end of his allotted six hundred words – a bigger splash than normal.

But it was neat too, it all fitted, it all felt right. They set the headline in 72 point, nearly the biggest size they had, and then added a strapline in bold above so that the story really stood out. Then they completed the impact by inserting a jumbo-size photograph of de Boys across three columns, so that in the end the story dominated the whole page. They warned Tom that the layout might have to be changed after the first edition, and he nodded happily, too tired by now to care.

Then they showed him the size of his by-line, a great thick wodge of type which stretched halfway across the page. 'That'll look good in the cuttings book,' they laughed, after bringing up a page proof for him to check the final corrections. Tom felt himself reviving at the sight of his name in the page.

Vaughan clapped him on the back without saying a word, and then the Editor hurried by, pausing slightly to nod to Tom before making his goodnights to the rest of the staff.

Tom's thoughts turned slowly to Ursula. He thought first of how pleased he would be to show her the story with his name plastered all over the page, but then he realised that his thoughts probably belonged to the past tense. She wouldn't be there to meet him when he got back to the flat. No, she'd be out somewhere, smiling her eternal smile at someone and having a good time, all in the spirit of the game she always played.

But, thought Tom, that's not my game any longer. I can't accept that artificiality, that perpetual laughing and trivialising, and gaiety and carousing, and keeping up with the latest fashion and gossip, and knowing so much about someone and so much about someone else, and always the latest book or play or film or opera or exhibition.

I nearly killed myself just now over that story, and I did it because I belong here – he felt himself growing tearful at such definite thoughts – yes, here on the Street, with the ink and the dirt and the worry and all the hassle over stories, and collisions with people. I've worked for this story, and I've taken a lot of shit to get it. I'm not going back to her now, not unless she accepts that there's more to life – to *my* life – than bright lights and canapés.

He had stuffed a pull of the front page in his pocket to show her when he returned, but he'd no great hopes that she would be there to greet him. He telephoned her as he left the office, but there was no reply.

He let himself into an empty flat, where a cold wind blew through an open window and dishes lay on the dining room table. A note was sellotaped to the TV. It was from Mrs Parker. It had a tone of finality.

'Ursula has decide to spend some time at home with us and will probably only return to her flat when you have found somewhere else to live. We wish you the best of luck with your career in journalism.'

Every word a winner, thought Tom, as he crumpled up the note and threw it out of the window into the night. She should have been a journalist, she knows enough about spikes. Or maybe she's close to the Editor – after all, they're both telling me to move on.

But at least, he thought, I know what I have to do. No, I'm not going to smash the place up, I will find somewhere else. I think I'm well out of it.

But then he thought of the times he had had with Ursula, when she had introduced him to the theatre and books and new people, and he thought of her body beside him in bed, her groaning in ecstasy as they made love, and he felt sad. He took out the page pull of his front page story, crumpled it up as well, and threw it out of the window to follow the note.

I'm sorry you're not here to read it, dear Ursula, because you helped me to write it. But since you're not, you're not and there's an end to it. Again the new sense of independence, the feeling of belonging to something new, flamed through him, and he stood before the window and breathed in the night air.

He padded over to the broom cupboard, opened it, and fumbled about by the hoover. This was where Ursula kept her special brandy, the one she drank herself during periods. Tom reckoned she would have had no opportunity to transport it away with her mother, and he was right. He found the bottle nestling against the furniture spray. Tom had found the bottle a long time ago, unbeknown to Ursula, who subsequently used to complain about the uncertain quality of brandy on the market – not surprisingly, since Tom used to drink half her bottle and then dilute the remainder.

He poured out a drink, glanced at the clock and discovered to his surprise it was only just ten. The night was still young. It was time to celebrate, alone or in company.

A thought struck him, and he grinned in devilment.

I know who I'll call, he thought, I know just the person.

She can tell me to get stuffed, or not. But she's the only person in London I know who doesn't have to go to work tomorrow.'

He picked up the phone and called the number of the de Boys PR, the girl he'd had such a good lunch with when he was still trekking after the crook. She sounded tired, but not ill-humoured.

'Oh yes, it's you, is it? What do you want? More information? I haven't got any and I'm sick to death of talking to the fucking press. Just leave me alone.'

Tom thought she sounded just right. She struck an earthy note.

'I rang you up to apologise,' Tom lied. 'We had such a good lunch, and you were so kind to me that what's happened to de Boys now makes me feel very upset for you.'

The words just kept coming as he penetrated the new world of freedom. She responded well.

'That's very kind. I'm touched.'

Tom asked her if she would like a drink. At first she demurred, but then assented, adding that it would be ironic. She lived a cab ride away in Hornsey Lane. Tom said he'd be there in a flash. She giggled down the phone at him.

He called a cab, bought a litre of white plonk on the way, and within a quarter of an hour had arrived outside her front gate. It was an old house, set back from the road in a becoming sprawl and flanked by dark whispering trees. Tom spotted a phone booth beside the house, glowing in the dark. More devilment gripped him.

He rang the operator and put in a call to Ursula's home, but reversing the charges. The phone rang in Ursula's home, then Tom heard Mrs Parker answer. A confused shouting, half muffled by the operator's interception, followed the request to reverse the charges. Mrs Parker was not happy at the idea. Looking after the pennies was a favourite maxim of hers. But Tom was past caring about her precepts.

'Tom, it's you,' she said, with rage spitting out around her voice. 'What can I do for you?'

'I wondered if you'd heard from Ursula,' said Tom.

'What do you mean?' she fenced. 'Have you been back to the flat yet?'

'Not yet,' lied Tom. 'That why I'm calling from a phone box. I rang her from the office, but there was no reply, and I got so worried. I got my story, and it's leading the paper. You'll see my name all over the country tomorrow,' he finished. Inside he could hear himself chanting – Fuck you, fuck you. Stitch the fucking bitch, stitch the fucking bitch – but outwardly he was calm. Nothing mattered to him about that family.

But Mrs Parker drew her breath in sharply, and Tom

realised she was still unclear about her decision. She answered slowly, with the cooing tone returning to her voice, that he would find a note for him when he returned, that the note would explain a certain amount. But why didn't he call back when he'd read it, and Ursula could explain matters a little further?

Tom was too tired to work out whether he should register surprise or chagrin on the phone. Instead, he agreed to ring back shortly.

He walked up the drive to the PR girl's house, and pressed the bell. After a few seconds, a hazy shape shimmered behind the glass, and the de Boys girl opened the door. She was tall, with red hair, and she wore a kaftan.

Her eyes lit on the wine. 'That's good,' she said. 'I've run out, and I didn't plan to traipse to the off-licence. Come on in.'

Tom felt like a soldier returning from the front. Battle-weary, with filthy kit, carbine slung over his shoulder, ammunition pouches weighing him down, but triumphant; he knew that he could offer nothing more. But pleasure would be offered to him. He did not intend to turn it down.

Her flat was on the second floor. The front door was purple. Tom commented on the colour.

'Gerry did that,' she said. 'Gerry lives upstairs. He's very jealous. But he's away in Leeds. At least that's what he said a few minutes ago when he rang. You can never tell with him!'

Tom took more comfort at that, and still more from the accidental touch of their hands as she poured out the drinks. Instead of recoiling, she smiled at him and then tossed her hair back over her shoulder. They were very close. Tom sat down. He wanted to take his time.

Tom sprawled in the chair beside the fire and watched the TV which stood at the other end of the room, in front of the window which opened on to the blackness of a garden.

Warm and cosy. The gas fire blazed beside her. The girl stretched out on the sofa beside him. Her cat, a Persian, began to scramble over her, but she shooed it away. 'Piss off, Hercules,' she said. 'Can't you see I'm busy?'

It was so easy. Full of warmth and wine, Tom just stretched out a hand and stroked her hair. She purred.

'You've got nice eyes,' she murmured. 'That's why I invited you over.'

Then she sprang suddenly to her feet, fished in her purse and pulled out a handful of 10p pieces, and began feeding them into the meter beside the gas fire.

'What's that for?' asked Tom.

'You'll see,' she breathed, and pulled him towards her. He tasted her lips, as he lay on her, crushing her, while his hand groped for her breast beneath the kaftan.

'Go on, you silly bugger,' she said. 'Just unzip it.' He pulled the zip slowly downwards, and gradually the curve of her breasts slid into view, the smooth expanse of her stomach with its trim navel, and then the white frilly frontier of her briefs.

'What have you got those on for?' asked Tom.

'I've got to offer some resistance, haven't I,' she said, then stood up and slipped out of the kaftan.

Her legs seemed endless, long, slim and poised shafts of white flesh. She flexed her shoulders and her breasts shifted, as if even the kaftan had been an unnecessary encumbrance. She plainly enjoyed nudity and the freedom of being unclothed. Then she hooked her fingers inside the band of her briefs and, stooping, withdrew first one leg and then the other.

She finished off the wine in her glass and then, crouching down, began to refill her glass, all with a quiet smile of anticipation on her face.

'Not a bad line in plonk you bought,' she murmured. Tom eyed the neatly cut triangle of hair at the apex of her legs and felt happier.

He stood up and kissed her with feeling, and her back was cool to his touch. Then he removed his own clothes, taking off first the grubby shirt with the stained collar, then his sweaty, creaseless, trousers, his socks with holes, his ripped underpants.

Then they kissed again, and Tom standing with his legs to the fire, with a breeze blowing slowly through the window from the night, saw both their shadows on the wall opposite like sketches on a primitive painting.

'Why did you put all that money in the meter?' asked Tom, half-guessing the answer.

'Because I don't like screwing in the dark. I like to watch the shadows on the wall,' she answered.

Tom felt as if he had all the time in the world, such a contrast to the hectic rush and bustle of the day with its minute by minute emphasis on the clock.

'Will Gerry suddenly return?' he asked, as they slid down together onto the rug in front of the fire.

'I doubt it, and I don't really care now. He's probably doing the same thing in Leeds. Anyway, I've always defended the one night stand to the death,' she said firmly. 'But it has to be a one night stand,' she added. 'No hanky-panky tomorrow to ruin it. Okay?'

'I promise,' said Tom, but then, as her tongue was starting to explore his navel, he suddenly stiffened. 'I promised to ring someone,' he said lamely.

'There's a phone right beside you.' And her kisses continued to flutter over his flanks.

Tom had a moment to feel revulsion at the idea of such a betrayal. But, collecting himself, he realised that whatever he did wouldn't matter now. Besides, that was just how the geometry of time and place worked out. He had no control over it.

He called the number as slim fingers caressed him and

the warmth of the fire sank into his bones. He sipped more wine from the glass.

Ursula answered the phone. She answered his announcement with a curt: 'So it's you, then,' and there was a pause.

Tom felt his resentment, his frustration, his hatred for her rudeness, and his chagrin at writing such a great story when she'd skipped away home, all boil up inside him and crash through his head like a great wave. But he felt calm too, quite detached, as if in some way he was speaking through time, at someone he had known in the past.

'Why did you leave the dishes all unwashed, you bitch?' he cried. It was all he could say. The girl beside him laughed. Ursula clearly heard both Tom and the girl. Some nameless sound was wrenched from her, and then the phone crashed down.

'That's one way of doing it, I suppose,' said the girl.

But Tom was in a hurry now. He no longer wanted to delay. He rolled on top of her, and her legs opened, and her mouth was smooth and moist. She hooked her legs around his and Tom could glimpse their silhouettes on the wall as they moved.

Her hair grew more straggly, and perspiration stood out on her brow as Tom moved relentlessly inside her. But she smiled, at him. 'Quite a little soldier, aren't we,' she said.

Tom pounding on, deferring the flash of lightning which would spark upwards from his loins and engulf him. She writhed beneath him.

Her head went back and, gripping her hands round his buttocks, she pulled him further and further inside her. Her eyes were closed and her breath came in huge retching spasms. Tom felt his mouth hang open and sweat cascade down his back. A croaking cry came from her mouth.

It was over suddenly. The tautness in her body eased, and she slowed the rocking. Her arms wrapped round his neck, and she kissed him deeply, a smile crinkling round her eyes. Then she sighed profoundly and turned to the fire, leaning on her elbow.

Hercules appeared. 'Shoo him off, can you,' she asked Tom. 'I'm too fucked to move.' She took another sip of wine, then stood up unsteadily, pulling Tom to his feet in her wake. She led him to the bedroom.

'Climb in,' she ordered. 'Another five seconds and I'll be asleep. I'll turn everything off.'

Tom climbed between the sheets, she scrambled in after him, and Tom fell into a trance-like sleep, with her arm trailing across his chest.

He awoke to sunlight streaming across the room and registered the blue of the duvet and the discreet pattern on the curtains. She sat beside him on the bed, dressing. It was that moment of wakefulness for women, when their faces have not fully adjusted to the day, and lie suspended and almost lopsided between oblivion and self-awareness.

She kissed him, but more perfunctorily than the night before. She wanted him to go quickly, to avoid any problems with Gerry. He dressed, and she disappeared into the kitchen, returning a little later with a cup of tea, which she thrust into his hand as she began combing her hair.

'I'm lunching today with Gerry. I don't want to look half-shagged for him, do I,' she said, as she peered into the mirror, by now on to making up her face.

She was forgetting him, although he still stood beside her. But Tom was indifferent. He tip-toed down the stairs and out of her life. The sunlight stood in quiet ranks outside the house as he opened the front door. It was still early, not yet seven, and Tom felt the exhilaration of being alive and of having survived rush through him.

He walked slowly down the road, hoping for a bus and looking out for an early cab. Would Gerry guess at lunchtime what had happened the night before, Tom wondered as he stopped to buy a copy of the paper. It was a late edition, but the story was there on the front page, with de Boys' picture across three columns. Tom felt cheered, as the early sunlight hung bright and silent in the air.

He thought about the incongruity of his de Boys story appearing in the paper – thus saving his career on Fleet Street – and the de Boys PR the night before, who had eased his chagrin.

'Maybe I owe that man more than I realise,' he brooded as he plodded home to the flat.

26

It seemed natural at the end of the day for Tom to meet up with Black, and even more natural that they should rendezvous at Charlie's for a celebratory drink. Tom reflected that he didn't really have anywhere else to go. Doubtless when he returned to Ursula's flat, he would find the locks changed; the bird flown abroad on a sudden impulse holiday; and a cold, empty street to sleep in.

Black was subdued as Tom entered the restaurant. He sat at the bar and looked down his glass as Tom attempted to whip up some enthusiasm for his own survival. All Black would say was: 'We have various plans for you. There is scope for movement within a static situation.'

Tom had the impression that it had been a split editorial decision to keep him on, and that Black had argued strongly in his favour but was now counting the cost of winning the argument. Tom sensed that the next few months would be very tough.

But Charlie was exuberant. His lips were blood-red beneath the black moustache, and his eyes glistened behind the spectacles as he dashed about the restaurant.

'No meal tonight,' he yelled out. 'Nobody's here, I ain't got time, and we gotta celebrate. Not every day one of these English boys make it back from behind the lines. In Europe, of course, we know all about danger, we know how to cope with it. But here, in cosy old Angleterre oh dear no. It's a foreign idea, something imported every now and again. Rubbish!'

He shouted at Gus to bring the retsina, but then changed his mind.

'I tell you, I got something special. When I came back to the camp – you know, I told you that, and how I tapped on the window and they all thought I was dead; and then they called out "My God, he's still alive" – well, we had nothing to toast with except tea. But *this* time, we're gonna drink some of my special brandy. It don't come out often, but when it does it's unforgettable. You like brandy?' he asked Tom.

Tom said he drank it occasionally.

'So you don't like brandy. Well, you'll like this brandy.' He rummaged around at the back of the bar, opening cupboard doors that squeaked a little, and cursing because the light was so poor he couldn't see where he was fumbling. Evidently, such drinks came so rarely.

Finally he straightened up and emerged from round the side of the bar, puffing a little, and clutching a strange squat-looking black bottle with a long neck. He took five glasses – apart from Tom and Black, the only people in the restaurant were Charlie, Gus and Kate – and poured carefully. A thick, black, treacly liquid gurgled out. It was even dark against the light.

'Let me see that bottle,' said Black, reaching for the brandy. 'I thought the Nazis drank the last of that.'

But Charlie, evasive and ambiguous as ever, held the bottle to his chest and refused to let Black check the label. He winked at Tom, tapped the side of his nose at Black and replaced the bottle in its secret cache.

Black stared at the ceiling, calculating.

They raised their glasses in the air, and Charlie proposed the toast – to Tom, to Black, to all those English mothers' darlings, and to the man who first thought of the recipe for the brandy they were drinking.

Tom felt a strong, dark, warm sensation creep down his

throat and into his stomach as he drank the brandy. It was unlike anything he'd ever tasted before. He thought of little Alpine passes, and sheep, and sunlight in the meadow.

Charlie shouted at him again, 'You wanna believe that bit about the mommas' darlings. They're against you, but you're winning. You're better than they are. Keep on going.'

Then Charlie turned to Black and accused him of doing Tom down. 'Hey Black,' he said, 'you done him wrong. You said he wouldn't get through.'

Black smiled, ready for that one.

'No, I said that the odds were against him, but he had a chance.'

Charlie sniffed, then burst out again.

'You take good care of him, then. He's tough enough to keep going. We don't see many of them around. In fact the last one we saw was...'

His voice tailed off, and a mischievous look stole across his face. He changed the subject, with the subtlety of a rearing horse.

'You play cards, Tom?'

'Only brag,' said Tom, firmly.

'No bridge?' asked Black, a little resignedly.

'Definitely not bridge,' answered Tom, with the Alpine bells by now clanging in his head from the brandy. 'That's a game for old women in church halls, isn't it? No, brag's my game.'

'Maybe,' said Charlie, shooting a glance at Black. 'How much you got on you?' he asked Tom.

'Fifteen pounds.'

'That'll be enough. Play with Kate and Gus. You'll win from them. Hey, Kate! Shuffle Tom in too, he's joining the card school.'

Tom felt an infinite glow of pride spread across him. See, he thought, it really isn't that hard, all you need is perseverance.

Kate smiled at him and shuffled the cards with her long fingers, then dealt them out swiftly. Gus grunted.

Tom picked up his cards, looked at them, felt the nostalgia for the old all-night card school, and bet low.

Kate went £1 blind. Gus stacked. Tom bet on, and so did Kate. She bet steadily, almost encouraging Tom to carry on, so that he could win. He had the distinct feeling that she was helping him.

Eventually, Tom had staked all his money. It lay in the middle of the table, all of his £15. But Kate was still blind. Tom looked round wildly. He had never experienced this kind of gambling before.

'Anyone got any cash to stake me?' he cried.

Charlie came over to look. His face had changed a little. It was harder.

'That's rule one you have to learn,' he snapped. 'Don't tell people how much dough you got. Otherwise, they take you to the limit immediately. Don't they, Kate?'

Kate smiled sweetly and nodded, again the innocent smile of someone who is trying to help. Tom found himself again adrift in a sea of change he found it hard to understand. They were all so friendly. But they were all so tough.

'Take a look, Kate,' commanded Charlie.

She picked up the cards. Her face was expressionless as she read the hand.

'What you doing with it, Kate,' bellowed Charlie.

'I bet £100,' said Kate with a coy smile, as if looking for approval for her cautious plan.

'What?' said Tom. '£100?'

She nodded. Charlie grunted. Black, now standing behind Tom, asked him what he planned to do. Tom felt a fool. On the one hand, he'd given all his money away; he might just as well have burned it for all the hard gambling he'd done. On the other hand, he couldn't raise to £100, let alone to £200 to see her.

He sat there paralysed. Then Kate, again with her demure smile, laid the cards down one by one on the green baize, very deliberately. She looked at them, then looked at Tom, as she turned the first one over. It was a three of spades. She turned the second over, again very carefully and slowly, leaning now on one elbow to emphasise her nonchalance, and looking sideways at the cards.

It was also a three. Tom felt relief clutch at his heart. She must have a prial of threes, an unbeatable hand with no wild deuces, the best hand in the pack.

She stared at him and now the smile faded from her lips. She looked at him hard as, without glancing down, she turned over the third card. It was the Ace of Spades.

Tom had a pair of aces. He had a better hand. He could have won £200 plus, plus, plus, if he'd carried on betting. He felt sick at how stupid he'd been. And now he had no money, to make it worse.

Charlie interrupted as Kate scooped up his £15.

'Not this time, Kate. He's just a learner. Give it back.'

She shook her head. Charlie leaned over and repeated the order. She pouted, but then reluctantly handed the money to Charlie, who patted it lovingly and gave it to Tom. Kate looked disappointed.

'You've gotta take the risk, man,' said Tom mechanically wondering what all this would lead to.

'Something to learn and think about, Tom,' shouted Charlie. 'Those who didn't do time in the camps never know about the odds of betting on raindrops down the window panes. Think about it.'

Black interrupted. A quiet smile played round his mouth. 'Ever thought of learning bridge, Tom?' he asked again. But now Tom knew the answer.

'Never,' he answered. 'But I'm told it's a wonderful way of learning to work out odds. I'd love to learn.'

Black smiled again as Charlie clapped Tom on the back.

'See, he's no fool. You don't have to tell him the same thing over and over again. He won't make the same mistake more than three times.'

'Time to go,' said Black, and rose to his feet. Tom felt something unexplained tug at his mind.

'Who was that other toughie you were going to mention?' he asked Charlie.

'But you should know,' said Charlie slyly. 'You've just had a lot to do with him.'

'Vaughan,' exclaimed Tom.

'Oh dear no,' said Charlie, by now moving towards the bar, as if to turn out the light above it and start preparing for the next morning. 'Someone more important, and someone I've known for many years, and always tried to help, because he's clever and tough.'

A sudden storm and rushing wind broke in on Tom, and he whispered the only name he could think of.

'De Boys.'

Charlie turned out the light and left them all in darkness.